D1121867

Lot America.

GP 109

Castang's City

Books by
NICOLAS FREELING

FICTION

Love in Amsterdam

Because of the Cats

Gun Before Butter

Valparaíso

Double Barrel

Criminal Conversation

The King of the Rainy Country

The Dresden Green

Strike Out Where Not Applicable

This Is the Castle

Tsing-Boum

Over the High Side

A Long Silence

Dressing of Diamond

The Bugles Blowing

Lake Isle

Gadget

The Night Lords

The Widow

NONFICTION

Kitchen Book

Cook Book

Castang's City

NICOLAS FREELING

PANTHEON BOOKS NEW YORK

Copyright © 1980 by Nicolas Freeling

All rights reserved under International and Pan-American Copyright Conventions. Published in the United States by Pantheon
Books, a division of Random House, Inc., New York. Originally
published in Great Britain by William Heinemann Ltd., London.

LIBRARY OF CONGRESS CATALOGING IN PUBLICATION DATA

Freeling, Nicolas.
Castang's city.

Reprint of the ed. published by Heinemann, London.
I. Title.
PZ4.F854Cas   1980   [PR6056.R4]   823'.914   80-7699
ISBN 0-394-50895-5

Manufactured in the United States of America
FIRST AMERICAN EDITION

'Boots–boots–boots–boots–movin' up an' down again!
There's no discharge in the war!'

Rudyard Kipling

Foreword

'CASTANG'S CITY'

A reviewer once said that it just had to be Toulouse . . . It isn't, and nor is it Strasbourg.

Inevitably it has features of both: numerous French cities are ancient regional capitals; seats of powerful dukes, and even kings. With palaces, Gothic cathedrals, Renaissance and Classical buildings.

The mayors of many such cities are or have been eminent figures in national politics. This alone would prevent me following the precedent of Stendhal's 'Nancy'.

Castang's city is imaginary, and to make the point it is deemed to exist where no major city is to be found; at the geographic centre of France.

These disclaimers are needed. I live in Strasbourg: a real Commissaire Richard was named as chief of the Regional Service of Police Judiciaire in that city. He has now been promoted to Versailles . . . He laughed and forgave me. Neither in physique nor in mannerism does he remotely resemble my invention of Castang's urbane and wary superior. Nor has my 'Mayor' any base whatever in any gentleman prominent in the affairs of the Republic.

The city has thus no name; its every feature, and everyone in it, has been brought there by the four winds.

1. Major Strasser has been Shot

Commissaire Richard had seen *Casablanca* on late-night television and thought it funny, as one can at fifty-seven years old and having had, in the consecrated phrase, 'a good war': Richard as a young aspirant officer in La Rochelle had climbed aboard a fishing-boat and Joined The General in London.

He liked to quote bits from time to time. The most successful beyond doubt had been a moment when the mayor, much flown after a good lunch and happy to be gambling on a certainty, mayors do from time to time, clapped him jovially on the back (a thing Richard detested).

"Commissaire, I bet you – I bet you ten thousand francs . . ."

"Make it five: I'm only a poor corrupt police official."

The mayor, disconcerted at such bluntness, had been vexed and had to have the joke explained.

In the offices of the Police Judiciaire to say 'Round up the usual suspects' was a corny synonym for 'Do nothing at all' One had to be careful, for Richard had several ways of delivering the line: like Sloppy in Dickens he could 'do the police in different voices'.

He put the phone down and said it in an entirely new voice, so that even Lasserre knew better than to go ho-ho.

"You push your red button," Richard said to him. Lasserre was a Commissaire too, though a more junior kind. He was the sous-chef, the Chief of Staff, the Co-ordinator. The phrase meant a general alert, to the urban police as well as the PJ: to the gendarmerie who have authority outside city limits and come under the Defence not Interior Ministry. Even the C.R.S., the Auxiliaries. Their uniform is dark blue but to Richard they were known naughtily as 'The Black and Tans'. Road-blocks: check-

1

points: machine-guns: Would-you-please-open-your-lug-gage-compartment.

What the hell had happened? A terrorist attack?

"Castang, get two boys, my car, wait outside: I shan't be a minute." Lasserre was leaping for the levers of command, turning while you watched into the Foreign Legion Sergeant from Dayton, Ohio, about to snarl "Move your chicken ass".

The car was a big Citroën, the best they had. Orthez, the best driver they had, got into the front, Castang with young Lucciani in the back. Castang was a Divisional Inspector, a middle-rank officer, superior to the other two.

Richard came out tidy and unhurried. Blue and white checked shirt, dark red tie; his accustomed country-club look. "Cours La Reine," he said. "Opposite the Opera." Orthez made a spectacular U-turn. "Etienne Marcel," very deliberately, "has been shot. That is all I know at present." Well . . . Anybody less like Major Strasser – or come to that looking less like Conrad Veidt – was scarcely imaginable, but Castang knew what he meant. Marcel – always called Marcel, and by everyone who claimed to be friends with him which was almost everyone called Etienne – was a municipal councillor, an adjunct mayor and a great deal else. All that red-button stuff was now explained. Orthez turned the Priority signal on, Pim-pam, Pim-pam, and went majestically through a red light.

It was a day in early May. Everybody had been complaining as usual about the weather, which had been unusually cold and spilling rain. It was late afternoon: the sun was out between showers, beginning now to get some warmth in it. A French city of some three hundred thousand souls. Neither truly north nor of the south. An Atlantic climate when the west wind blows, which it does a lot; central-European in easterly weather: cold winters and hot summers.

Castang liked every sort of weather. He liked this; the young growth of trees, bushes fresh and moist, the whole town for once smelling wonderful. The planes were in leaf, the chestnuts in flower, so that what he would remember first would always be the myriads of sodden blossoms under foot, the white and pink turning to pale tobacco colour; and everywhere the powerful scent of rain and springtime. He was wearing an old camel pullover, but prudent man, he had his trench-coat in the car, and one of his mildly eccentric hats.

The Cours La Reine is a creation of eighteenth-century town-planning (the reine is Marie Leczinska, Louis Quinze's plain, patient, and pious Polish wife). Double avenue, with broad pedestrian alley down the middle: six rows in all of pruned trees and underfoot a vile gravel, muddy in wet weather, dusty the moment it was dry. Crammed with parked cars for a generation: the municipality, creakingly, moving towards banning them and planting grass and flowerbeds, thirty years late as usual.

The place was still full of cars claiming privilege: France has a terrible number of privileged persons. Regulations are for the poor. The end of the alley, with a nice formal garden in front, is the old Palace of the Dukes, now the Préfecture. Along the sides are big buildings – many beautiful, others merely pompous. The Banque de France and the Opera, the Seat of the Military Governor and museums where nobody ever goes.

Up at the other end the avenues degenerate into mere streets and here is the commercial centre of the town with banks, insurance companies and the palaces of industry.

Orthez had to push the car slowly through a mill of sightseers arriving faster than cops did, the bush telegraph functioning as usual better than electronics. Cops, growing irritable, had stopped saying 'Dégagez' and 'Circulez' and were beginning to link arms to heave back masses of morbid flesh anxious to see more morbid flesh: there was nothing much to see. Castang was aware that he had been brought to use his eyes. Richard would have, simply, too many distractions to be able to concentrate – and yes, there came the mayor with his television face on, saying "My poor Etienne – a friend for twenty years. Shocking, quite shocking." Yes, he meant it, it was all true, it was all sincere. But professional, inevitably. The press had arrived as soon as the police, plus a gaudily painted station-wagon from regional television: already one chap was flourishing a hand-held camera, and three more with microphones. And has there been such a crowd since the last State Visit? An acutely Public performance for a thoroughly public figure.

The very publicness of it all had created a small but distinct area of privacy within a nervous ring of exasperated constabulary quarrelling with some half-dozen persons who had cars parked on the alley and were complaining that Time was Money. "Everything is to stay as it is" repeated the police meaninglessly. Yes.

"Lucciani, get the number plates, names and addresses. Witnesses, Orthez, try to find who was first." Body. Let's get to this body.

The body lay between Marcel's car, a typically flamboyant Porsche, white with black this-and-that, and a humble pale-blue car belonging to the principal eyewitness, a young woman torn between shock and voluble self-importance, at present held in check by a young urban cop who had taken his képi off to mop the sweaty brow, terrified of doing something wrong. Castang looked at the car. There'd been a right fusillade, big holes in the bodywork. Identité Judiciaire would be here any moment, but that was big artillery, Blazing-Colts stuff, forty-four or -five calibre, eleven-sixty-threes if you count in millimetres. Maybe two guns, no considered kneecap work there but bang bang bang like Frankie and Johnny. Magazine emptied. The body had been covered with somebody's raincoat, legs sticking out. Castang peeled it off. Medical details were of no importance. Be hit at a closish range by three or four of those and it doesn't matter what they hit or where: massive shock and haemorrhage take you out of the vale of tears while you are still falling down.

A doctor had of course been summoned and there by God he was, telling Richard at the greatest possible length what Richard already knew.

The car keys were on the floor at no great distance, jerked out of his hand by the impact. One or more gunmen had waited by the car. As he bent over to unlock it he got mashed. Had he had his back turned? – the impact might have spun him round. Had the killer known him? – mean-

4

ing did you wait by the car to identify him? Or because the unlocking it immobilised him handily for long enough? The killer hadn't been a very good shot. Or with a gun of that calibre he hadn't cared. Or there were two guns and when I.J. got the bullets they would know.

Castang felt a presence behind him, unobtrusive but making itself felt, named the Divisional Commissaire and more of his kind. Fabre, the stout professorial Central Commissaire of the urban brigade; the mayor with a graveside look. The man's misfortune was that in a moment of genuine emotion he would always look insincere.

Castang got up off his knee and dusted it. The damp gravel clung. A gunman might well have left a recognisable footprint, but it would be long gone beneath the tramplings of populace.

"Orthez, get this ground completely free and sweep it. The cartridge cases and whatever you can find. Things get trodden in: get one of those treasure-hunting gadgets. The angle and the distance is going to be difficult, unless this lady of yours actually saw the gunman."

"I've told this gentleman –"

"I'm afraid you'll have to come back with us. You might have a lot more to tell than you realize."

"But the Banque de France . . . And my boss will be . . ."

"Monsieur Lucciani here will go with you and explain. We want that car, Orthez. Will it start? – here are the keys."

"Get all this mob off this ground," said Richard's voice.

"I've given the order."

"Well, see it's enforced. And see that photographer doesn't forget the angle of the sun this time – fellow to my mind had the light in his eyes."

Detail, a great deal of detail. The car wouldn't start either. As well as Etienne Marcel, a perfectly good Porsche had got itself assassinated. The technical squad went on working till well after six. Buses, when again able to make their way down the Cours La Reine, crawled at foot pace with everyone hanging out of the window. Till night fell a football-size crowd eddied and clung like bees swarming, changing and eventually moving, but constant in number.

5

The whole city wanted to see where Etienne Marcel got shot. Quite a lot of people brought flowers and cast them on the spot where all the blood in a robustly-built man had leaked out on to the gravel. The police were patient about this.

As night fell, it began spotting again with rain. Heavy clouds gathered blackly as though in civic mourning. The national television news at eight had a long section on this coldblooded and dastardly killing in our midst that must surely be the work of extremists. Whether extreme right-wing or extreme left was at present unclear but extreme, very. Castang saw small opportunity of getting home before late, and phoned to tell his wife.

2. A Servant of the State

Henri Castang. Quite a common French name. In the south generally spelt Castaing, pronounced with a flat American *a* and a nasal *n*. Etymology – vaguely, something to do with the Latin for chestnuts; up to modern times an important, even essential food-supply for the people in the poorer areas of central France. He was by birth a Parisian, which meant nothing. He didn't have any family history. More of a small bullet-headed Gaul than a bony long-headed Frank, which meant nothing either. Blood from anywhere in the Mediterranean basin and probably, he thought, Iberian. There wasn't anything especially Latin about him, certainly not in a conventional sense of excitable, volatile, explosive. Vera, his wife, who was Slav, said indeed that he was a northerner by nature, and called him The Aquitainian Bastard: when pressed to explain this talked vaguely about Normans. The fact is that France is a melting-pot. The French have nothing in common, said Castang gloomily, save vanity, avarice and the mania for centralisation. His detestation for the State grew year by year but he had not allowed it to become cynicism. The

6

State paid him; he was a servant. There was much he disliked about that, but one had to keep things simple. France is not Argentina. No, agreed Vera, and it's not Czechoslovakia either. Just that things do close in rather. But Vera, almost full-term pregnant with a first child at nearly thirty, while he was quite a long way over thirty, thought a lot about the future of the world.

He had stayed on the scene till six. This was one job that had better be well done. Make a mess of this, and you're the navigating officer that hit a rock in the Brest Estuary, and found himself commanding paper-clips at the Recruitment Depôt in Bourges.

He didn't do anything very spectacular. Found nine cartridge cases, and a good notion where seven bullets had gone: found an eighth in a tree, shortly before leaving. His mine-detector thing supplied by the fire-brigade had also turned up a lot of petty cash, several false teeth, assorted jewellery, a handsome nineteen-thirty model fountain-pen, and nineteenth-century antiquities of unguessable purpose and small aesthetic value. Nothing significant, though a lot of police time would get wasted on parking-tickets, shopping-lists and cashiers' receipts. The body had got taken to the mortuary, the car towed to the police parking-lot. Clothes, contents, and contents-of-car stowed away in plastic bags, but no clue that pointed to anything. No handy menacing letters, assignations or whatnot.

The best thing he had done was turn up two witnesses. One was a young man in the cashier's office at the opera. Monsieur Marcel had picked up two complimentary tickets for friends. But this young man had run out earlier, for a woman who had bought tickets, paid for them, and then left them absent-mindedly on the ledge: he'd pursued her, overtaken her as she drove off, and noticed a man leaning on a car, smoking. Woman had been profuse in talkative thanks and he hadn't really noticed the man. A man smoking . . . The other was a taxi-driver who'd been reading a comic while parked in the rank further along. He'd heard shots, jumped out, seen a man running. Man jumped into an already-moving car. He'd jumped back into his own car, laudably, to give chase. But the two avenues were one-way streets like an autoroute, and he was parked facing the wrong way. He'd reversed back down to the corner but the fellow was long gone: not a chance. Man seen running, tallish, brownish: well, not an Arab or anything. Hair short rather than long. Dark glasses. Short bloused jacket or might be a pullover, dark green, brownish or beige trousers. Wearing some kind of cap with a peak. Way he ran – youngish man; he'd say around twenty-five. Sorry, can't do better. Car – easy: this year's pale green Simca, Chrysler job. Clean, polished. Accelerates well, that thing; lost no time. Driver had been on his side but sorry, he'd not noticed the driver. Long hair but whether man or woman couldn't say. Fellow running had jumped into an already moving car and whizz, off he was. Apart from telling Lasserre to persecute anyone in a green Chrysler there was little Castang could do. It was easy enough to reconstruct. When the smoking man – same man, little doubt of that, brown with a green top – saw Marcel approaching, he'd given the signal to a confederate to start the motor and have the car moving slowly along the parking lot, as though looking for a gap.

He found Richard alone, thinking, which didn't mean sicklied over with a pale cast, but looking as he always did.

"Any use?" he asked.

"Evidence of planning," answered Richard. "Even if we'd got to your green Chrysler earlier it wouldn't have helped. Found empty on the Place de Lattre. Nothing in it of any interest. The plates hadn't been changed. A local car, which Fausta traced effortlessly. The registration office gave us the name and address, she looked in the phone book, the wife was on the line: all simple. The owner left this morning for Paris on the morning plane, will be back this evening, not best pleased.

"Very simple: they wanted a car for a few hours whose theft would be unnoticed. Go to the airport, watch fifty-odd men on to the plane, help yourself to any car you fancy. Is that professional? Anybody who has seen a few films can do as well."

"So all these road blocks . . ."

8

"Precisely, gave us four Arabs forbidden to be in the district. What could one go on? Anybody seeming flustered or incoherent or failing to give a reasonable account of themselves? What's the average none-too-bright cop looking for? Scowling Palestinians with grenades bulging their pockets out? Terrorist girls reaching nervously for their suspiciously large handbags? There are evidently quite a lot of men with greenish shirts and brownish pants, angry this evening at getting home an hour late. The one in question put a jacket on, took his cap off, went peaceably home to the suburbs; very likely never left the town at all. Roadblocks please Prefects, but never catch anyone save a couple of juvenile delinquents. Now how does this strike you?"

"Confirms. There's nothing professional save the gun. Colt .45 automatic. Our man with the sun in his eyes sprayed it round a good deal, but there's no other sign of haste or nervousness. Emptying the magazine like that could be to intimidate any eventual eyewitness, or a professional wanting to appear amateur, or a great accumulation of vengeful rancour – or simply that he did have the sun in his eyes, except that he had dark glasses. The ground was hopelessly scuffed and trodden. A lot of litter but no pointers. No further useful witnesses. You got the best."

"Worthy woman," said Richard. "Couldn't give a description, which shows at least she's telling the truth. The man called out 'Etienne' in a startling voice, described as a Nasty voice, and the cannonade began. Does it mean they knew each other?"

"A simple technique, I should think, to point a target towards you, making it bigger."

"And immobilize it, quite. The good woman stood there paralysed. As Etienne did. He stood there with his mouth open with no sign of recognition. If of course she was looking at him at all. If someone calls out in a sharp voice that's the person you look at, or am I abnormal?"

"You think she was there as a device to distract him or stop him if need be?"

"I think no such thing. I think she's a clueless biddy that wasn't looking at anything but says whatever she

9

imagines we might enjoy hearing. She can't give a description because she didn't really take anything in. She let out a monstrous howl and lots of people came running. She didn't recognize Marcel. You can see people in photographs or even on television a hundred times and still not know them in the flesh."

"This is the point, isn't it. Very well-known man."

"That's exactly right. Any thoughts about that?"

"That it makes for a very difficult enquiry. Unless his wife has a demented lover or something."

"Round up the usual suspects," said Richard pleasantly.

"There'll either be none, or far too many."

"Right. I don't know what you're going to find. So as well as being an honest, competent and persevering servant of the state, you will also be fairly bright. You are all these things, aren't you?"

"I might try reminding you that my wife's due to have a baby any moment."

"Yes I knew that, even without Fausta reminding me. You get your day off, and more days if you need them."

"What does the judge of instruction –?"

"Your old friend Madame Delavigne. Go and see her tomorrow morning. The Proc, Castang, doesn't like this any more than I do. I need hardly say that he's not keen on terrorists." No, the Procureur de la République, chief legal authority for the district, would not be pleased with anything much save perhaps a demented lover. "Terrorists however have one very attractive side: they provide an excellent excuse for telling the press to keep its mouth shut. That reminds me, it's nearly time for the local news: who's got a box around here? . . . I just love seeing myself on television," said Richard amiably.

The regional news naturally could speak of nothing else and one saw a lot of Richard – that, after all, he remarked, was what he was there for – and nothing, Castang was relieved to see, of Castang. The national news, twenty minutes later, delivered in hushed wise tones by the resident guru, invited France to meditate upon the dreadful consequences should the dread Italian-German disease of Terrorism attack this dear Motherland. A heavy responsibility weighed upon us all: he certainly looked as though it weighed heaviest upon himself, but his smile was kind, and very very brave. Chin up, he conveyed; with me beside you we will see this through together, and our President is also watching over us.

"I hope the President will ring him up," said Richard, "and ask his advice before doing anything Rash." The Minister of the Interior also had a few well-chosen words about the defenders of order.

"And I hope," said Castang, "that that oily bastard won't be coming down to pronounce a eulogy over my coffin. I don't want to meet him head first or feet first."

"Nor even dick first," agreed Richard. "And you refer the press to me. And who do you want to have assigned to work with you? I rather think not Orthez. We'll keep him in reserve for terrorists."

"On the understanding it's not terrorists, can I have Maryvonne?"

"You can," said Richard. "That's quite a good idea. Let's go home now . . . I'll be at home," he told the switchboard operator.

"And so will I," muttered Castang hopefully.

3. Domestic Habits of the Inspector

He went home by bicycle. He generally did; it wasn't any slower. It wasn't over fifteen minutes; he lived in the town, in a nice street of old houses facing a canalised piece of river, in itself boring but there were poplars along the disused towing-path. The rent was not very high; the charges, for heating, the lift and so forth, very high and getting all the while higher. Castang, who had never taken any bribes yet – well, hardly any – was faced with the unpleasant alternative of moving, which he didn't want, or rounding out his income, as it is generally known: not

11

keen on this either, but we're all getting hit by inflation these days.

He was delighted, if frightened, about the baby. Vera wanted one badly and had been tardy about producing one. Legs that didn't work for a long time (she'd fractured her spine); and doctors made faces about a pregnancy. For some years afterwards, while the legs became less helpless though still unforeseeably queer ('Motor Handicap' and a sticker on the car saying GIC which means Grande Invalide Civile) the harder she tried to become pregnant the less she did, a thing that often happens. Having succeeded she was very serene: Castang wasn't. She couldn't walk much, and how was one to make walks with the baby? The inspector of police, cloaked in anonymity, didn't mind pushing prams or washing nappies – often had his hands in much worse than babyshit – in his free time, but free time, for cops, is a rationed and irregular commodity. What is wanted – no, not wanted – is a Little House in a Garden Suburb, with a little back lawn to stand the pram on. Such things are beyond the income of all but senior police officers. Would one try to get promoted to being a junior commissaire (adjunct) and get posted to some hole of a little country town? He didn't like this notion at all, but would be forced to think about it. Pay a student to promenade the baby in the park? Vera wasn't keen on the idea, and he didn't blame her.

She was sitting round and ripe on the balcony, where she had geraniums and stuff in pots. Little bag all packed in the bedroom, because she was due any minute, unless that stupid gynaecologist had got his dates wrong. Some people said a first baby was always lazy. Room booked in a clinic and everything, just in case it was her pelvis that was lazy. The great beast had been quiescent lately, as though working up energy. Gathering for a spring. No relatives had gathered gluttonously round. He didn't have any, and hers were all in Czechoslovakia.

She didn't say anything about his being late: it was enough of a commonplace. Vera's supper was mostly soup in winter or salad in summer: both would keep an hour or two without spoiling. May mostly announced the salad season. Today there were potatoes with gherkins, raw carrots, olives, and something green. Tomatoes were still too dear, but chives grew on the balcony.

"Etienne Marcel got killed."

"Who's he?" Typically, Vera was profoundly ignorant about things or people that didn't interest her. Doubtless the only person in a city of three hundred thousand who didn't know, didn't care, and hadn't heard the news.

"Oh a sort of fat cat. No great loss. No, seriously: he was a bit of everything around here. Adjunct mayor. City councillor of course. Cultural affairs guy. Theatre, opera, anything. Pillar of the football club. Pillar of youth clubs, folklore, singing, dancing, any sort of sport. Gladhander and backslapper. Great one for local history, local customs, local anything. Always chatting in patois to grannies. Very popular guy."

Supper was on the table. "I've eaten already; the child got hungry," said Vera. "Tell me more."

"I hardly knew him except by sight. Why are you interested all of a sudden?"

"I suppose I'm allowed to be interested. Other thoughts pass through my head. It's not all just safety pins and navel bandages." Not nasty; just a bit prickly. Waiting for it isn't the easiest thing in the world.

"One of these stocky tough men with a lot of energy in the back of their neck. Big round head, a bit bald and strands of long hair arranged across. Skin that doesn't go brown, so his nose and forehead were always a bit reddened. Big booming jolly voice. Ready hand and ready smile. Started with a pub. Worked it up to a big café restaurant with music and a cabaret. Used to sing himself and play the guitar; nice light tenor voice." Castang put his elbow on the table, stopped his fork in mid air, waved it in circles, pointed it at her. "I think perhaps his secret was always to take an awful lot of trouble. He'd let himself be buttonholed and give you his total concentration, and always leave you with the impression that you were immensely important. Nothing was too much trouble. And always on the go. Very thick solid spinal column."

"Now I have a picture," satisfied.

"Well, somebody shot him to pieces this afternoon in front of the opera, with a big gangster pistol. Emptied the whole magazine, turned the car into a vegetable strainer. One would have been enough and he got hit by three."

"Somebody demented, with a grudge."

"On the face of it, certainly, but then there was another demented body waiting with a car, made a very smooth getaway. Car stolen that morning at the airport, so wouldn't be missed till tonight. Abandoned five minutes later in the suburbs, on the main road south, so all the roadblock stuff looks foolish. We don't even know whether they're in the town or out of it."

"So Red Brigade."

"Maybe. A big bourgeois all right, but worked up from proletariat origins, always making a great thing of being one of the boys and speaking patois. Not perhaps a typical target. Richard's content to advance Red Brigade as an official theory, until we learn more."

"Considered a traitor perhaps to the class. The man sounds a big hypocrite to me."

"Oh yes, could be a football player dropped from the team. Except that the season's over. It could be any damn thing. Castang takes his pointed stick and stirs about in the compost heap. Liable to create a massive stink."

"Business, thus, as usual." Her voice was unusually harsh, the tone particularly acrid. Jolted out of placidity, Castang looked up. Hadn't there been rather a lot of this, lately? He hadn't taken it too seriously. Pregnant women, he told himself with comfortable male vagueness, tend to have fantasies.

"Look, I know it's not much fun for you, having to hang about biting your nails. Chipping at me, though, isn't likely to help either of us much."

"Oh, you always say this," contemptuously. "You've had a hard day too, yes; and you're tired and worried as well, yes; so why don't I keep my mouth shut because what good will an argument do?"

"I can't help it if it's true. I mean what can I do about it?"

She was alone too much. He didn't have any handy

sister to come and stay. She didn't have her mother, or anybody. Other side of the curtain. Not so much iron as a silence curtain. She wrote, regularly, but she never got any answer much. Politics of course. Vera was a traitor. Stalinist lot, those Czechs. Leaving your motherland in the lurch is bad enough. Treachery to the gymnastics team which has educated you, made you a privileged person, taken you abroad and everything, enabled you to live in luxury . . . And brought your family honour and prestige too . . .

Personally they'd never understood either. Vera had always been a sensible girl. To run away like that; and with of all people a common or garden French police officer, a nobody. Young girls getting a passion for Rudolf Nureyev would be understandable. But just a vulgar cop . . .

"I don't mind. I've never complained." Quite true; she hadn't. "But when do I see you? Late at night. And then if I want to talk, you say oh, woman, stuff it, I've had a long day."

"It's this goddam waiting." It wasn't just professional patience. He felt extremely sorry for her. But what was he supposed to do? Life was like that.

"When will it ever be any different? Can't you see? – you're a lamp post: everyone can piss up against you. The slightest thing goes wrong and who will get the official blame? Castang will. Yes, so far so good, and isn't that exactly what the man said who jumped off the building as he passed the first floor."

"I'll make us both a tisane, shall I?"

"Herb tea! My kidneys are fucking well awash with it." Vera! who never swore. "I must have absorbed a kilo and more of sage. Makes labour easier, or that's what they always said in that backwoods village of mine."

"Listen. This is an awkward job, right. Local politician, sure, not exactly the number one choice for the subject of a police enquiry. It might get cleared up tomorrow and it might be an instruction that goes dragging on for a year. Sure. But get this straight, even if it gets to be a mess Richard's not the type to say oh well, that's due to a cock-up by the investigating officer."

15

"Stirring in the compost heap with your pointed stick!"
Yes, it hadn't been the most fortunate phrase. "It's
Richard's dungheap, and right on his front doorstep, and
if there's a bavure ..." Bavure! The consecrated word. A
blot, a splash. Every time the police make a balls of something the government talks about a bavure.

There've been a lot. A hell of a lot too much of a lot, if
you take my meaning.

He knew what she was on about. The latest and blackest
blot had been the three – drunk, off-duty – cops in Saint-
Denis who'd raped a fourteen-year-old Algerian girl. He'd
tried to explain. Look, girl, these are oafs, and the worst
sort, racist. An undisciplined rabble; good Jesus they throw
this lumpenpack into a uniform, give it a meagre six weeks
training, so-called, and call it police. We agree, this is an
appalling scandal. But far, far worse is the attitude of the
government, which has neither the courage to do some
radical surgery nor the competence to find an adequate
blanket. Halfhearted shushing and shuffling, a feeble-
minded attempt to stifle. And then when forced to take
action by the entire press of the country ringing with it, a
lot of hypocritical talk. As though the police hadn't a bad
enough name as it was. These miserable gun-happy little
cowboys who go about beating up Arabs – these aren't
police!

What was he to say? That the Police Judiciaire is very
tightly disciplined indeed? That Richard for all his languid
golf-club manner is a tiger? That there are, at a pinch, a
few ruffians – in the antigang brigade they can't, you know,
be choirboys – but that if one of them made a blot, to
admit this obscenely prudish word so typical of government spokesmen, Richard would peg him out in the blazing
sun until his eyeballs dropped out. He'd said all that, many
times.

"Look, I've said it often. You like the town; I like the
town. I can try for a promotion. It means that almost certainly we'd get sent to some backwoods place, and we
thought we wouldn't like that. But we can try. It would
mean a house – a garden! For the baby ..."

"Put me to bed," said Vera. "Hold me tightly. Just put

16

your arms round me and hold me, nothing else. I know I'm very large."

"Trust me," he said softly, stroking the fine hair behind her ears.

"Look after me," she whispered.

4. Instructions, from the Instructing Judge

Frenchwomen are rarely 'pretty' though when they are they can be breathtakingly beautiful. Striking-looking, handsome, attractive; this they frequently succeed in being. Good bones; faces full of drawing. Colette Delavigne was a good example. Fine forehead, fine eyes in beautifully modelled orbits; the usual sharp pointed nose: broad serene mouth, furiously kissable. Lower jaw too narrow, throat and ears magnificent. All in all a very French face: Castang had fancied it a good deal once upon a time: a bit too much. Nice speaking voice too, unshrill.

"Hallo, Henri. Haven't seen you in ages."

Perfectly true. The junior magistrate of instruction, and a woman at that . . . does not have a great deal to do with the Police Judiciaire, which by definition has to do with grave, complex, sophisticated and showy crimes. In a big city there is a Sûreté Urbaine, a criminal brigade attached to, and part of, the municipal force. The Regional Service of the PJ is spread over a large district; two, perhaps three 'departments'. Outside the towns there is the gendarmerie, French equivalent of the Sheriff's Office.

On the tribunal side, a judge judges . . . 'sits' according to his qualifications and seniority. Madame Delavigne had had a spell in the Juvenile Court, where only one judge sits: had 'filled in' from time to time in the Police Court. It was rare that Castang found himself in these. In the higher courts she might have found herself acting as assessor, sitting next to the President, but French law, which

17

provides for the elaborate and often lengthy system of 'Instruction' (in essence a thorough preliminary inquiry to determine whether in fact an accused person should be required to stand trial at all) forbids an instructing judge to take part in the same trial. She – many are women – or he sends the completed dossier to the Chamber of Accusations, and their rôle in the affair is complete. He'd lost sight of Colette for some time.

The judges of instruction, half a dozen at least in a city this size, have a row of offices called their 'cabinets' on the ground floor of the Palace of Justice. Outside in the wide corridor is a long row of benches, permanently occupied by the accused, some on bail, some from the local jail, with handcuffs on and attended by guardian cops; and by the endless procession of subpoenaed witnesses.

Colette was alone behind her desk. Her greffier or clerk, who is present at all the official business to make a record and legalize proceedings, hadn't arrived yet.

A lawyer in robes, some defending counsel or other, popped his head in.

"When can you fit us in, Madame?"

"A quarter of an hour, Maître."

"I have to plead around ten, in the Correctional."

"Well, we'll have to put it off then, won't we? Let me know when you are ready." People have to sit on those benches, blowing their nose and staring at the floor, for hours sometimes. One's counsellor must be present, at interrogations . . .

"How's Vera?" asked Colette, smiling. They hadn't many friends: a PJ cop isn't all that popular a neighbourhood character. Colette had been a close friend of Vera's. They'd drifted a bit apart, the way people did sometimes. Castang himself . . . well, Richard had thought it wasn't very clever, one of his close collaborators being quite so thick with a – female – young – pretty, all right, pretty – judge of instruction. Colette had had her daughter kidnapped by an oaf. Castang had been on that job. Fact was, they'd come close to what nasty-minded people would call . . . Least said soonest . . . Vera's friendship with

18

Colette, and Colette's friendship with Henri, got cooled off rather. Well, that was past history.

"Having a baby, more or less any moment." Grinning, proud pa.

"Oh, how lovely. Give her my love. And for goodness sake, keep me in touch. How was I to know? You want me to read these things in the paper? I must rush out and buy something extravagant."

"She'll love that. Nice of you."

"Well look, Henri, all these people battering at the door. Must get this business settled, and then when you come back next we'll have a drink, right? She's not started yet? What a moment! " the big mouth stretching into a grin, a bit rueful.

"Yes, idiotic business this."

"And could steer us both full tip into the shit. Which is why your great friend Commissaire Richard, not really one of mine, entrusts you with this delicate huh, inquiry. And why the Procureur de la République, bless his warm heart, finds that Madame Delavigne, still always known as Little Madame D., is just the right magistrate to examine and instruct, hm, this humhum."

"At least you haven't been posted to Béthune yet." It is the standard 'judge' joke; a sour one and not always a joke. Young, earnest and idealistic magistrates have quite frequently progressive liberal tendencies and left-wing sympathies. They have even – how dare they? – formed a splinter syndicate of judges who sometimes ask quite openly whether the separation of powers is all it might be, and whether the judicial branch doesn't get leaned on a bit too heavily and obviously by the executive.

Judges are independent, yes, of course. But they get promoted on their 'marks' awarded by their seniors. They can't be sacked. But they can be posted to a hell ship.

Junior judges, just out of school, get posted anyway to a hell ship unless they're somebody's cousin. The biggest and best-known punishment squad in France (the Bataillon d'Afrique, the army used to call it) is Béthune, that grim and forbidding mining city in the Pas de Calais near the Belgian border. Something like half the magistrates in

Béthune, and it is one of the largest busiest tribunals, are in the 'wrong' syndicate. They do naughty things, like ordering the owners of industrial empires to prison for persistent infraction of labour laws. The owners don't stay long in jug. The Court of Appeal in Douai lets them out within a week. Funnily, the C. of A. takes around three months to get to business as a rule.

The mention of Béthune is not always greeted with a grin by junior judges of instruction. Colette smiled, but without conviction.

"I wouldn't much care for it, Henri. A woman, you know; they've got you coming as well as going. Suppose I said yes, and we'll by God make Béthune the best judicial district in France, the example to all the others where people can by heaven see justice done – what would Bernard say?"

Bernard was her husband. Director in a small but dynamic concern making milk products, known as 'the yoghourt factory'. A nice man. And she was a loyal wife.

"It's what I tell Vera all the time. Life is splitting ideals into compromises. Supping with the devil, long spoon. All cliché, as she says. I've no particular wish myself to be Commissaire in a village of five thousand souls in the Massif Central. Where no human eye would ever again behold me. I like this town. Oddly, I like Richard. He's some six or seven years to go till his pension. He'll stay here – they don't want him in Paris. Suppose he made a bad blot, it'd be Nantes for him or Rennes: imagine his face! So he'll be mighty careful."

Colette was thinking: we've grown up all right; he and me both. What a long time ago it all seems.

"And how's Rachel?" he was asking. Rachel . . . When a child has been stolen, even though not in any real sense ill-treated, is it ever going to be quite the same again? Confidence . . .

"She's a big girl now . . . We're of one mind, Henri. None of us would want to see this thing get out of bounds."

That's right. There may be waves, the boat may rock a bit, but see that no water gets into it. Be sure you can count

20

upon the members of the crew. She's ambitious . . . and who blames her? For her a test. The Proc is wondering, now that she isn't really little-madame-D any longer, whether larger responsibilities could be entrusted . . . and her marks will depend on how well she handles this. Good – she'll trouble me less.

"What exactly is it you want done?"

"Want done! Come on Henri, you're the experienced man at the confidential enquiry. What is it that Richard 'wants done'? You have the usual powers. If you want any more you must come and ask me, and account rather closely for whatever you propose. It's obvious that under the cloak of this terrorist pretext you must make a discreet personal investigation, and keep it underground. Nothing to the press, that's flat. That the whole affair is confidential goes without saying. I'll phone Commissaire Richard. I imagine that the answer will be found in a vengeance drama, but the man was an adjunct to the mayor and he's precious touchy about the dignity of civic office, so you be mighty careful how you go about your winesses. Any sort of a lead, you'll communicate your findings to me without delay."

"Understood." You take that up with Richard, my girl.

"I'll have to ask you to excuse me now, Henri."

Decidedly, he thought, he preferred the Colette of – what was it, six years ago? But that was when we were both young and foolish. Bernard will be putting on weight now; he was always rather thick around the neck. You've kept your figure pretty youthful.

5. Well Said, Old Mole

The weather was important.

Summer – was this summer? The weather experts, most of whom keep pubs, were already announcing with perfect certainty that there hadn't been any spring, and there wouldn't be any summer either. No good asking the farmers: they grumbled whatever happened. Rain and sun, sun and rain, very hot and rather cool; everything green, at least, was growing like fury. All leaf, and no fruit? One didn't know what clothes to put on. Castang had a new summery thing, rather nice: sort of a zipper jacket, sort of gabardine, pale green, with white stripes. "Looks like a pistachio ice-cream," said Richard.

Richard had Massip with him, Massip-the-Fraud, the fiscal and financial expert, whose one virtue in Castang's eyes was that he made out all their tax declarations. A mole. There was nothing really wrong with Massip: a quiet man who said little. A financial face. One didn't particularly like him, but there was no earthly reason for disliking him.

"Now that you're here at last," said Richard.

"Little Madame Delavigne . . ."

"Yes I know. She's been on the phone. Pay no attention. The official side of this, Castang, all the mayor-and corporation stuff, the Prefect insists I handle that myself. And since there's a good deal of disentangling to be done in his remarkably complicated affairs, cut a long tale short, I'm taking Massip here with me, because if there's a hole in his budget or whatever, why, there's no more to be said. Quite an impassioned bit of homicide, and where there are signs of passion, my boy, in this beautiful country you're likely to find large sums of money." Richard lit his cigar, which had gone out.

"A character like this, lives . . . a great deal in public. Limelight . . . everywhere. All this public; what, no private? No lemonlight anywhere? I'm not going to hog any light, I'm merely there to put a good face on things. Massip does his imitation of a mole in and around the municipal castle: I'm a bit dubious myself about that football club. You, Castang, mole number two, and I enjoin you not to imagine you're a ferret. So much that is open, noisey superficial. Like the moon, there must be another side to all this. Today's the funeral, for God's sake, Castang, go home and get into a dark suit. Mingle. Look like a press person. Nothing fancy, you behave throughout in a normal procedural fashion, you get to know who is who, and why. I

22

don't have to spell it all out." Castang had forgotten all about the funeral!

"How are things on the terrorist front?"

"Rumours – and rumours is all they are. There's the usual pile of mysterious denunciation, which Fausta is making into a file for you."

Fausta! Now there was a Frenchwoman ravishingly beautiful, except that she wasn't French: half-Italian. Immense eyes. When she was tired, and she was always overworked, they started to blink in a nervous tic. This, in a young woman less intelligent, might have been thought a cheap effort at being sexy: it wasn't. Fausta was a decidedly puritanical girl: not that one blamed her really, with those looks. Her hair came down to her thin flat behind: both were kept exceptionally clean and the hair shone. Perhaps the behind shone: nobody had ever seen it. Fausta, as secretary (private) to the Divisional Commissaire was a very public figure, and an intensely private person.

Fausta was like Etienne Marcel. Everything was known about her public persona: nothing whatever about the private life.

A dossier could not be begun till after the funeral. Maigret always went to funerals: so did Castang; it was probably the only point of resemblance between him and the best-known fictional cop in the whole world, whom every French cop has cursed heartily upon occasion.

In the office he kept a 'circumstance' suit, for calling on bourgeois folk who wouldn't employ some scruff in jeans: also for funerals. So he didn't have to go home to change.

The local newspaper puts death notices in little boxes. If you think the dead person, meaning yourself, important you can with payment increase the size of the boxes.

A couple of the boxes were half-pages. With small boxes added one had nearly three pages. They'd done Etienne Marcel proud.

The family: there was a great deal of family and Castang, who had to talk to them all, groaned inwardly. Father, Mother, Wife. Two sons, one daughter. Innumerable in-laws. Lots of children.

The Municipality: Mayor and Corporation struck and

23

stricken to its innermost. It doesn't he thought really have an innermost except in death notices but there it comes out very strong.

The Sporting-Club and the Football Association. The Harmony-Group 'Concordia'. The Majorette-Group 'Rhythm': young girls in short skirts and high boots, who hi-step and twirl batons, in strange hats like pre-war Belgian gendarmes; a phenomenon copied from America. The Management – and Personnel – of the brasserie 'Crown of France': the pub. The Friends of the Opera, and the choirboys, classifiable as what Vera, born a hundred kilometres from Vienna, called the Sing-Verein.

The Association of Dealers in Liquid Refreshments, called in French the Lemonaders. The Guild of the Artisans. The Syndicate of Les Commerçants du Centre.

Und so weiter.

Everybody's deepfelt loss and sorrowing regret: not a single one of them, according to Richard, that wasn't delighted to see the back of the bugger. Richard knew everything; it was his business to know everything.

"To hear everything," he corrected. "Make the knowing your business please. To speak nothing but good of the dead is a precept people pay lip service to, and I'm wondering what I mean by lip. Man cannot live without myth, or so say the anthropologists." What has Richard been reading?

"You mean what made Sammy run?"

"Come back when you know who Rosebud is," said Richard looking out of the window, where it was raining again.

The funeral was as good a place to start as any. See who all those people are: hang identities on them. The man was a politician, lived in a whirl of multiple activities. What were the areas of sincerity, if any? Where did the man put his heart? He was trying to remember who Rosebud was – wasn't it finally a child's sled – when Maryvonne arrived.

Women in the police divided into easily recognisable categories. Nothing racist about this remark; so did the men. Tall or short, they're all sado-masochists, as Richard said gloomily.

Agricultural, with massive rears; lesbian with massive

shoulders; cavaliers with massive hands and feet, and you're by God the horse. Maryvonne did not fit into a category and this was nice. Very little was known about her; also nice. Very professional; lots of energy and concentration on her job. A bit under thirty, unmarried. She had perhaps love-affairs, but not with anybody in the department. Thinnish, average height, a neat build. Her tests showed her well-co-ordinated physically – she ran and climbed well and was a goodish shot, and a fair squash player – and mentally agile. Marked by the shrink, bless him, a well-integrated personality.

She had a bunch of blonde hair, reddish but not so as to be called carrotty, greenish eyes not too close together, a sharp nose, a good figure. Given to sweaters that came to shallow points in front, and Richard, who liked her, spoke of Maryvonne's unsuccessful breasts, but with no wish to be nasty.

She'd been posted to him a couple of months back with good school marks.

"What was the idea, becoming a cop?" Richard asked, tilting his chair back and wedging a foot against the desk.

"I liked it and thought I'd be good at it."

"Ideals?"

"Some I suppose, or so I should hope."

"Ambitious?"

"Yes, very. I don't want to sound cynical about it."

"What's your conception of this job?"

"Doing what I'm told is the textbook answer, I suppose, but if I can get given any responsibilities then I want to take hold of them."

"Okay," said Richard, more pleased than he showed. She'd passed Fausta too, a stiffer test. She hadn't done much yet but paperwork, which she did with a humourless attention to precise detail.

"We're going to this funeral," said Castang, using a rag on his shoes, which were always kept polished. "You look all right. I want you to find out who everybody is. I suggest you mingle. You can be press if you like: there'll be quite a lot and nobody will ask for cards."

"Everybody is a crowd, isn't it?"

"That's exactly the point. Not the professional civic mourners. Family in particular. As far as possible, friends. Several hundred people wearing expressions of circumstance, and I'm wondering whether any when asked why they've come will say 'I knew him, I liked him, I'll miss him'."

"All right," she said, sounding neither pleased nor bored. "I'd better buck up then, to get a good place."

"See you at the grave-side," unsmilingly.

The church was brim-full: the French love a good funeral and feel that by going to one from time to time they accomplish their religious duties. Candles, incense, flowers: we are Catholic after all despite anticlerical sentiments. Prayers come, sounding odd and as though made-up-as-they-went-along to anybody old enough to remember the antique patined words of the Latin ritual. A few phrases familiar since all time, memories buried but never quite effaced, as though in the voice of one's very first teacher at primary school. *De profundis clamavi ad te, Dominum. Domine, exaudi vocem meam.* A solid good old-fashioned funeral; no nonsense about cremation, or any of that no-flowers-or-wreaths-please: there were staggering amounts of flowers.

The mayor made a long and flowery exordium in his level, practised voice. Difficult to associate with the man seen yesterday, ruffled and edgy, using the stately and elegant proportions of his private office in the Hôtel de Ville to recover his own stately elegance.

"Who's this?"

"I'm associating Inspector Castang with myself in this inquiry. It promises to be complex," said Richard colourlessly, "and it's as well to be ready to cover a widish field."

"As long as discretion is absolute, you understand me: absolute."

The man was showing under the mayor. He paced about, stared at things without seeing them.

"Marcel of all people. Why on earth? . . . terrorists – this meaningless striking with an extreme of violence against the most arbitrarily chosen . . . what protection can one possibly have? . . . it might just as easily have been myself."

He sat down abruptly at his desk.

"Marcel . . . damn the man. This is very distasteful. It's no secret that I've been intending not to stand again, at the next election. I'm getting on and all the rest of it – bullshit mostly; I'm seventy-two and fitter than most who're half that. I'll make no bones about it: I don't mind saying, recently I've been in two minds about going back on that decision . . .

"Damn the fellow, he was after my job. And he hadn't the capacity, he hadn't the brains. No kind of an administrator, no proper base."

He tapped his hand irritably on the wood.

"Whatever people say I haven't gone about fabricating a crown prince. The succession is open, when I do go, and I'll be very glad to go. I've kept myself a free hand on this condition, that I have not sought to favourise an eventual successor . . ."

The mayor came to himself suddenly.

"I'm saying ridiculous things. You'll understand, Richard, one is shaken. Seeing the man dead like that in the street, shot to pieces with his blood all over him . . . Poor Etienne . . . Good God, it could just as well have been me. From now on we're going to have some security precautions round here, Richard."

Yes, there were quite a lot of plainclothes cops swelling the ranks of the mourners, glancing about a good deal. It really resembled a state funeral for a cop shot in the line of duty: one quite expected the Minister to step forward and lay a medal on the coffin; posthumous citation to the Order of the Nation. Makes a bit more of a pension to the widow. Widow – not much to be seen of her; conventionally heavily veiled, and supported by a numerous tribe. He could see Maryvonne flitting busily about, talking to an obvious journalist he himself recognised – fat biddy from *France-Soir*. What would she be? – human interest story for a German magazine?

It went on too long. People were tired and bored by the time the graveside business was reached: many of the downcast solemn faces had become perfunctory, were stretching with suppressed yawns. The cemetery smelt of life instead of

27

death. The sand of the alleyways was moist and clung plastically to the shoe; the plane trees, pleached to give shade, full of freshly rinsed leaf. Arrows of afternoon sunshine shot gaps in the tall piles of cumulus cloud, and brought a wonderful scent out of the yews and cypresses, and the pile of crumbly, fresh-turned black soil. The over-varnished, over-ornate coffin slid down out of sight and Castang felt it was all wrong. He had not known Marcel, but had seen him on a number of occasions. The stocky figure bustled and bristled with vitality; one of those persons who brim with physical energy, have soup-ladles full of it ready to hand around to anybody who wants. To the last second one half expected the heavy lid to be pushed aside and the fellow to sit up, grinning and flexing his biceps. Even underground – he might burrow out sideways like a terrier. Be back at the pub, ready to lead the company in song, before anyone else had got home. As long as I want him alive, thought Castang, he'll be alive.

People were already melting away around the edges before the grave was filled in. Castang strolled off like a tourist around neighbouring stones. He wanted to see whether anybody lingered.

Only one person did: a tallish, thinnish woman without a family look. He could see little of her but a curl of greyish dark hair at the forehead: middle-aged but the face was foreshortened and he could make little of it. Silk headscarf, navyblue raincoat covering her clothes. She did not linger any length of time, stood immobile with her hands in her pockets, looking expressionlessly across at the row of poplars bordering the main road. Turned and walked away with a quick light step. Long thin legs, bony but with an elegant shape. Large feet, neat in black and white shoes with a look of being Italian and expensive. On an impulse he walked after her, saw her stop outside at an emerald-green Alfa-Sud, a bit dingy with a dented bumper and muddy wings. He saw Maryvonne loitering to be picked up, but when he did not look at her she turned well-trained away and made for the bus-stop. Most of the cars had already left.

Luck, fate, chance? Stage-managed in any case; when he reached his own car the little green one was just backing

28

out. She might have stopped to change her shoes. Still on impulse he followed her: it wasn't difficult. The traffic had thinned, the green car stood out brightly, she did not drive very fast. Erratically more than badly; the way a person drives who is preoccupied or absent-minded.

Certainly she didn't notice him; he kept well back. She did not head into the town but skirted along the edges, keeping to main roads like someone who does not know the way well. When she turned off into side streets she was getting back to the quarter she knew: Castang sharpened his attention, risked creeping up a little closer. She whisked through a couple of the villages far enough outside the city still to have a villagey look despite housing estates mushrooming in the fields, reached a village some fifteen kilometres out and stopped on the main street to buy bread before the shops shut. He knew the place slightly. A bit of farming still went on but most of the houses had been bought up by bourgeois who went to great pains to modernize within and stay rustic without: a lot of self-conscious restoration. The street had kept centennial trees, was wide and quiet – an old marketplace. That had put the prices up . . . Pubs had become expensive restaurants; houses with vines or a wisteria across the old stone fronts, a pergola with roses.

She started the car again but drove it only a couple of hundred metres further. He caught a glimpse of her: fiftyish, well-preserved-looking. Pretty face and vivacious. The hair had gone grey early as that sort of coarse dark hair often does. She put her key in the door of one of the tiniest houses, a cottage a couple of hundred years old, door and shutters nicely done in a dark olive green with a transparent effect giving warmth and brightness. He wasn't going to hang about: he turned and followed the main road back into the city. It was just to see where she belonged. Idle curiosity. There was nothing to do at the office, or nothing that he felt like doing. Let Maryvonne see what she made of it all. This old mole wasn't going to work in any further earth today. Going home, and wondering whether he'd find his wife still there.

29

6. All Aglow with Parenthood

Vera was still there, lying on the sofa, imposing great calm upon herself. She levered herself up into sitting and said, "It's begun." Abrupt finish to all the old moles.

"You're sure?"

"Oh yes, I've been timing them. Quite regular now. In fact I'm awfully glad to see you. I phoned but you were out at that funeral."

"Death and birth, all sorts of excitements."

Only now did he notice her coat, mole that he was.

"My God we'd better get you moving."

"Look, stop panicking. Plenty of time." One would think she'd been doing this all her life. But all the features were sharpened by tension; she was looking very turned-on, and extraordinary pretty. Been getting steadily prettier these last six months, come to that.

"I seem to have arrived in the nick."

"I was thinking of ringing a taxi." She had the phone on the sofa. "But I held on, thinking with any luck you'd be back. In fact you're nice and early." Well, he hadn't forgotten . . . Other things on his mind, yes, but nothing vital. Vita meaning life, right?

"Shall I help you?"

"I can manage. Give me my stick just in case." Vera's walk was a hobbly affair, but even carrying a heavy baby she walked. "Is it raining – do I need a scarf on my hair?"

"We'll dodge between the showers. I've got your little case." Nobody clamouring for the lift, thank goodness. There wouldn't have been room! But he felt disinclined for explanations . . . She stood on the step, looking young and extremely happy, while he turned the car; she got in with remarkably little trouble.

"You seem lighter already – sure you've still got it?" She giggled at this antique pleasantry.

"Oh yes; still hanging on."

The day concierge at the clinic, yawning through his last hour before going off, didn't keep them hanging about. Every girl the first time was always convinced it would come popping out any sec. Your room's all ready – find your own way up. The duty nurse, a quiet girl, young enough still to be amused at the excesses of young-fathers-in-labour, said placidly, "You can help me settle her in. What kind of rhythm are they coming in? Oh, lovely, plenty of time but I'm going to ring your gynaecologist because he wants to cast an eye, simply because you've had trouble with your pelvis in the past. Have you your card with the blood group and stuff? Fine; get into bed and make yourself comfortable: back in a sec."

"He told me there was absolutely no reason why you shouldn't have a completely normal birth." Castang being pompous.

"I'm not in the least frightened. He's conscientious that's all. I feel pleasantly surrounded by experts, and I'm going to be one too."

The nurse came back and caught him looking useless.

"If you want to stay I can't let you smoke."

"Uh . . ."

"Plenty old gynaeco-shnoks can't abide having fathers under their feet, but yours doesn't mind. Unless it's a Caesar or something, which we're not expecting."

Castang was embarrassed. He longed to stay. It had been discussed.

'Begun together' Vera had said 'and I'd like to finish it together. I'm ashamed about this, but I want to do it all on my own. May I? – do you mind awfully?' He'd yielded. It wasn't so much, he thought, an idea of privacy, though she made a great thing of privacy. Had she a little fear of letting him down? He didn't ask. But damn it, this snip of a nurse would think him one of those cowardly fathers.

"Not this time I think," said Vera placidly. "I'm not altogether sure about how I'll cope with my stupid back. Next time he'll come and do all the work himself – ooh, there it comes again."

The girl took her pulse, counted it and said, "Oh yes,

that was a nice one. Thirsty? Like some orange juice?"

"Well then, I'll leave you in good hands," he said, lighting another cigarette to give himself a countenance. As long as she hadn't got it all on her infernal card there – father's profession: inspector of police – mm, probably wears his gunbelt in bed.

The night concierge had just come on; was doing his little housekeeping around the desk.

"You'll give me a ring?" said Castang, deciding against a card, writing his phone-number on a bit of paper instead. He had thought he'd got over feeling ashamed of being a cop, by now.

"Of course. But don't ring me – I'll ring you." The classic!

"Always takes longer than the poppas expect, specially first time."

"Yes," humbly; furious. He went home. He was going to have a drink. Not orange juice. And smoke like a bloody chimney if he felt so inclined. The flat without Vera in it was horrible.

He surprised himself by going off to bed in the most normal way imaginable and feeling sleepy after reading for a quarter of an hour. And tumbling down asleep with no more than the tiniest twinge of guilt.

He wondered how many times the phone had rung. He had been disgracefully deep. Good Lord, two-fifteen.

"Monsieur Castang? – maternity clinic. All okay. Girl, you've got. Three kilo sixty. Your wife's fine, and is going to have a good sleep. No problems at all, I'm told. All right? – best of luck then. Oh, and we ask you particularly not to come in before ten-thirty, okay? Give her time to have breakfast and get a wash, right? Good night."

"Thanks." And surprised again, falling straight asleep.

Shave. Looking at his face. Now, unaccountably, nervous. What about? Have to go and declare a birth at the Hôtel de Ville. A girl.

The only trouble about this was that he couldn't remember what the girl's name was. The water in the kichen was boiling its head off. Will you please stop being struck by

32

panic. He succeeded in not cutting himself: that would have been the final end in banality. You stupid little man, go to work.

He made a mess, filtering coffee: didn't clear it up; Vera wasn't there to see. Drank coffee. The idea of bread induced nausea. The idea of looking at the morning paper induced nausea. Everything induced nausea; this wasn't at all what he had expected. Father left a great pigsty everywhere, telling himself he would have a good clean by and by, felt anxiously to see if he had any money. Sod it, where was Vera's purse? She'd taken it with her. Resod it, now he'd have to go to the bank. Made up his mind he wasn't going to say a word to anybody.

This all vanished the moment he got in at the office door. Maryvonne looking tidy and businesslike. Instantly he felt irrepressibly light-hearted and insanely proud.

"You are allowed to congratulate me; I've got a girl."

"Oh great. What's her name?"

"Yes, this is less good. I've forgotten. It was all decided, at enormous length, and now I can't remember."

"Oh, I think that's quite normal."

"Tell anybody and I'll bite your ass clear off, right? I don't want any coarse humour from Cantoni. All right, now we're going to do some work. What have you managed?"

"Here's the family tree," producing two bits of paper, scotch-taped together. "Just a sec; I left my bag in the wash-room."

Nice neat work; nicely-formed handwriting; lines drawn with a ruler. All absolutely clear. This vast tribe – good, now he knew where he stood.

The door opened and Fausta came floating in cradling a champagne bottle. Oh damn these infernal women; wouldn't you know it?

"What the fuck's that?"

"Now tut-tut-tut. Don't be unbearably stupid." He was seized by Fausta, unheard-of occurrence, given two large chaste kisses. "You're a good boy and we're proud of you." Infernal Maryvonne carrying a tray and three glasses.

"Where may all this have come from?"

33

"Fausta's been keeping it in her little fridge where she makes God's dinner. All among the tins of Kitty-Kat and the Mars bars," twisting the wire off with strong competent fingers. "Pop, goes the weasel."

"For Godsake shut that door and lock it before the whole neighbourhood appears."

"Just let me get through the keyhole," said Monsieur Richard, bland and abominable in the doorway. He picked up the telephone. "Hold my calls until I get back . . . Very nice. Bonds of discipline pleasantly relaxed, I notice. Well Castang, is Fausta to wear a blue ribbon in her hair today, or a pink one?"

"Or plaited into two tresses," suggested Maryvonne, the bottle meeting Richard's outstretched hand, which had a glass between the middle fingers. He had put his spectacles on and was reading her homework.

"A pink one."

"Splendid," ambiguously. "You'll be getting on with this then, in the intervals between drunken euphoria. That's what I want. How nice then, Castang; what's her name?"

"Yes, I've got to decide about that before getting down to the town hall."

"The twenty-fifth of May is the Sainte Sophie," said Fausta looking at the post-office calendar.

"Something Czech I think."

"Not I hope Ludmila."

"Why not Ludmila? – it's pretty."

"This is plainly going to go on and on," said Richard. "Here's to all three of you, dear boy, and my loyal and admiring regards to Madame, and let me know, won't you, when it's decided," floating out as elegantly as he had come in.

"Showing off," said Fausta. "I could have sworn he didn't even know I had the bottle there. Always rummaging in my affairs; have to tell him off about that. Our love to her, then, and we'll make a call of state when she's had a rest. What clinic is she in? – right then, it's noted. No, if I've more than one I'll be tiddly, and the Absolute Monarch would be cross. See you later."

34

"There are a good many of them," said Castang, absently holding his glass for the last drops of foam, "so we'll have to split them up. In fact I want them all covered two ways. No harm if the questions overlap to some extent. We're navigating in the unknown; in those terms two bearings give one a fix, and it's nice sometimes to know where you are." She was looking a bit dubious. "Small boat in the dark," said Castang, who was making most of this up as he went along; it might have been the champagne early in the morning. "Submerged rocks and stuff."

"The private life of Monsieur Marcel is what you might call a lee shore?"

"Rather, I'd guess."

"All right, but give me a general line to follow, so they won't get mad at too many repetitions."

"Let's try then," taking a bit of paper, "I take for a start the family house, and then this daughter. You start with the other son, the one that's married, and the two brothers, that'll mean the pub. Pub'll be full of old pals, or claiming to be. He went there every day; it was a sort of headquarters.

"Brief outline of questioning," watching her fingers shorthanding on the pad, "you work at the chronology; we aim to establish the movements of friend Etienne over the last forty-eight hours."

"That long?"

"We don't know what might prove important, assuming anything is. I want to go for the relationships: character, habits, whatever you like. You're filling in as many gaps as possible in the physical employment of his time. It's another metaphor, but warp and woof: we'd have a canvas; one can hold it up to the light and look at it."

"What about all his public activities?"

"That's pretty tricky ground and Richard's sector. Anything of a business nature crops up you make notes and write them up as a report for him. We've enough until tomorrow: I can't see myself doing much before this afternoon."

Left to himself he did his homework on the 'family tree'.

Etienne Marcel: fifty-five years old when cut off unexpectedly and, said the medical report, in robust health. Name, probably an unconscious coincidence, of a historic personage. Like most such, after whom streets in Paris were called, exceedingly vague. The Provost of the Something, in the reign of Somebody.

Both parents alive. Father, known as Pépé, named Florent, reputed gaga, did not come to funeral (Maryvonne had added little notes). In his eighties and shaky. Mother, named Reine, late seventies, said to be physically active but 'didn't feel up to' funeral. Both live in the family house, Rue des Carmélites.

Living under same roof we find: — the wife. Named Noelle. Robust lady, shading fifty. Ex-barmaid. Ran the pub (foundation of family fortunes) many years, these last ten putting a distance, very much so. Goes to much pains to dress and act bourgeoise, gives an impression of not knowing what a pub is.

Unmarried sister: Thérèse. Early fifties (younger anyhow than Etienne). Faded and effaced impression: conventional front of one given to pious good works, churchy activities. 'The housekeeper' – big house; cooks and cleans (outside cleaning woman I gather for rough work). Eyes downcast, did not (does not?) utter.

Also son, second son, unmarried. Thierry, thirties. Black sheep? Apparently without occupation and does not desire one, but evasive (rather naturally?). Easygoing, smiling, agreeable, smells of drink. Appearance uncared for, smartish but down at heel. Forthcoming but glib? Source of much of this info. Income? – 'rubs along'?

Outside the house: family circle: —
Two brothers (Bonaparte brothers?) aptly named Joseph & Lucien. Some way younger than E. (& Thérèse) but appear older: both like a drink . . . Both in small independent business, J. as joiner ('yr antique furn. restored' – that sort) & L. as small jobbing printer. Both married, some indeterminate children.

Eldest son, named Didier, 33-4. Independent houseagent business, 'Agence Moderne', appears prosperous, probably is (personal impressions suppressed). Married but divorced, two children custody mother. Lives alone (?) flat adjoining office.

Castang reached for the phone.

"Maryvonne gone yet? Put her on . . . the eldest son, your impression suppressed, let's have it orally."

"Well, very superficial, looks capable of any minor crime you care to name but as though he'd never have the guts for a major one. Thoroughly dishonest face but that's meaningless, so that's why I suppressed it."

"Okay."

The daughter (youngest child, about 28) named Magali. Assured, intelligent, striking looks (vulgar? – oh, all right), expensively dressed. Husband Bertrand, well matched in style, obviously doing well. Engineering background, technical job for rubber company (tyres, but I'm unsure). Two small children, rather horrid: Séverine & Jerome.

All 3 of E's children went to university & represent definite step up in social standing. Mag/Ber live in expensive bungalow residence with trappings. Car new Renault 6-cyl.

Nothing much to criticise about that. Maryvonne had strong feelings about people, and some trouble suppressing them. Would he have done any better?

Patterns there. Anything beyond what one would expect? Probably not. Nothing to be premature about, either way.

He was buttonholed by the charge nurse on the landing.

"She's awake, and very happy, and longing to see you, but don't stay more than a few minutes, because at this stage she's keeping herself artificially bright: wants another long sleep. This evening half an hour between six and eight."

"Labour all right?"

"A bit roughish – she was nervous and tense, and battled rather. All normal enough. A few stitches. Morchain is perfectly satisfied with her. He'll have a word with you if you want it – if you can catch him – but there's no need. If it's her back you mean, that's a totally distinct problem, but I can promise you quite unaffected by the birth. The baby's splendid, and the nurse will give you a peep."

Vera was sitting up, pretty, perfumed, much painted; eager eye and tender mouth.

"How're you?"

"Blissfully empty. Nice child. Naughty child. Oh, nice flowers."

"Not really your style. Best I could do. I've got to go and register her. Sorry, I can't quite remember her name."

"Lydia," reproachfully.

"Oh, of course. Was that what we decided? Well – nice name."

"Yes" reproachfully. He wasn't being much of a success.

"Comfortable?"

"Oh yes, I had a huge super breakfast." Why was he so stupidly tonguetied? Stop being monosyllabic. He struggled on as best he could for the regulation ten minutes. Vera was very far away and distant, secure in her new accomplishment. He didn't 'belong again' yet. Well, his first time too. Better leave her in this horrid female bower. It would go better tonight.

He put his face against hers.

"You've been very clever."

"Nonsense. We've been very clever. I'm sorry, darling. I feel so tired and silly. I'll be cleverer tonight. Good that you came. I'm dreadfully happy now. Don't you want to see her? Tell the nurse."

It was held up for inspection behind a glass window, through which came a lot of yelling, by a young girl in a mask. Ghastly-looking object. Get away, horrid child.

He hurried off, much ashamed of himself.

7. Rue des Carmélites

The Street of the Carmelites is an oddity whatever way you look at it. It doesn't even look like a street; a straggling series of elbows not going anywhere in particular and petering out into a side road. At the other end is a stretch of track: no other word seems suitable, for it is fifty metres of pot-holes and puddles bordered by a rich growth of nettle. Built on marshy bottom, probably. There is a rusty notice saying *Not Suitable for Wheeled Traffic,* to which, this being France, nobody pays any heed.

No sign of any Carmelites either but this is a commonplace. All expropriated at the Revolution, that disastrous moment when the dotty and the dishonest alike ran amok unchecked, and the more claptrap there was about Rationality the less reason prevailed. Somebody had laid hands upon a large desirable lump of real estate just outside the town as it then was (nowadays it is five minutes from the city centre) but dishonesty was quickly swamped by the dottiness which has reigned ever since. The convent of the holy fathers was razed with the utmost efficiency: there is no sign left of it but a small and awkward municipal cemetery, long overfull. The farm and garden, parcelled out as loot by a few geezers concerned with public safety and hygiene, can still be traced.

There are advantages: hardly any traffic and lots of trees. There are disadvantages: the roadway has never to this day been properly bottomed, the metalling is uneven bumpy patchwork, the pavements sketchy indications full of treeroots, there is no proper guttering and one would be pretty dubious about the drains. The fact is, France is full of places like this and a delight they are, though in wet weather the pools are chronic, in hot weather there are smells, and almost any time the Anglo-Saxon observer will be frightening himself with ideas of typhoid.

Castang had no such inhibitions, and no worries apart from getting his precious clean shoes muddy. He was seeing it at its best. May greenery, a great deal of it weeds, rioting about: overgrown hedges and sodden low-swinging branches that would slap you in the face if you walked too close to the rusty iron railings and decayed plank boarding.

Considered as a row of houses fronting the street it was equally dotty. No alignment. No damned nonsense about order, regulation, or discipline. There were huge rambling houses, gimcrack to start with and now in a state of advanced dilapidation, and there were tiny cottages. There was a huge monstrosity faced with stonework built by a fan of Baron Haussmann, and rural, very, sheds sagging under bindweed. There was a prim pebble-dashed suburban house with a privet hedge: there was even a dashing modern bungalow, with fake landscaping on a bulldozed hillock. Some houses were right on top of the street, others far away behind rural orchards with cordoned pear trees and knee-high wild grass.

Castang liked all this very much. Two hundred years of municipal bribery, and plenty of originality: this seemed to fit Etienne Marcel well enough. He approached Number Three. There wasn't any Number One that he or anyone else could see. A biggish house, though by no means the biggest; a medley of architectural fantasies but nowhere near the most extravagant: approaching from the wrong end he'd had everything already, including an immense Savoyard chalet with a slate roof and pepperbox turrets added . . . Quite sober dingy stonework. But a very elaborate front door, frothing with ornate carving. The door was opened to him by – plainly – Thérèse, though he could scarcely make her out, and coming in from the outside nothing at all of the hallway, save that it was big. God had perhaps said 'Let there be Light' but the builder of this house had decreed 'Let there be No light', and fortified everything to make sure.

There were the usual explanations about Police Judiciaire, and he was left standing, to wait for Madame. His eyes got used enough to the gloom to distinguish black and white marble, radiators painted dirty brown –

this place would take some heating – a clumsy, heavy, cramped-looking stairway of polished oak, a small cluster of feeble lighting, bulbs obscured by dust. He was getting so many impressions so fast that he wasn't taking them in, and when Thérèse came and shooed him into a big room at the back it left no mark till much later. French windows opening on a big, muddled, attractive garden.

"I'll tell Madame Noelle," Thérèse had said, like a servant. Not, I'll tell my sister-in-law. Perhaps it was to put him in his place. There was a lot of heavy mahogany furniture, much polished but dusty. Madame was opening diamond-paned cabinet doors and fidgeting with a lot of decanters and stuff. He didn't really want a drink; it was too early. And he loathed those sticky dark apéritifs. However, he needed a drink. There was too much of everything.

A good deal of Noelle, for a start: bosomy and hippy in a black skirt and a fussy white blouse. She didn't look like an ex-barmaid, but once you knew it, you could see it. A lot of jewellery: the clothes were expensive and well cut, but over-elaborate. There were many tables and lace mats, a great many lamps and a great many flowers. But Noelle was very businesslike. Remarkably shrewd blue eyes. It would take three auctioneers to catalogue all the stuff around, and she compelled all the concentration he had.

"We dislike intruding on your privacy."

"Yes," with no particular inflection.

"But we're faced with a complex situation."

"Really? I thought it was simple. Wasn't it terrorists?"

"I don't know," said Castang. Everything was complicated including this woman. He needed to give himself time. "May I smoke?"

"Of course," Damn, mistake; swamped at once in boxes of cigars and lots of huge ashtrays. Extricated himself with a maize-paper Gitane: thank God he didn't smoke a pipe. She was heavy, but quick and decisive in her movements.

"If it was terrorists there's no direct lead to them. Nobody claims responsibility. Who are they, where do they come from, what purpose can they have had? You see?"

"Yes."

"Monsieur Marcel led a very busy life, a very varied

41

existence. I should like, indeed I must, learn all I can of the different facets. Includes his home life, indeed that's where one has to start. You knew him best. I can take it you would have known more about his life and activities than anyone?"

"I suppose so."

"You're not sure?"

"No, I'm not. About some, not all. About certain things more than anyone, yes. Other things very little, maybe nothing. It's hard to say. About municipal business . . ."

"Yes. Commissaire Richard is looking after that end of it. My present instructions are to get as complete a picture – this we think will help us distinguish relevant from irrelevant facts – so I'd like to learn what I can of his home life."

"You want to see the house?" unexpectedly direct.

"I'd like to, very much."

"I've got nothing to hide. I suppose I must expect this. He was a public figure and so on. Areas of privacy and all that – I'm not going to let it worry me. I was expecting it anyhow. If I refused, you'd just go ferreting, I imagine." There wasn't any answer to that.

The house rambled, as such a house will. Noelle, who seemed to have done a lot of modernizing, was voluble about bathrooms and the servants' staircase. He didn't listen to her much, didn't try to keep his bearings. Her own bedroom was displayed with pride: a fortress of long-haired rugs and complicated looking-glasses; two wooden heads wearing wigs and a tailor's dummy wearing her dressing-gown. Ivory telephone by her bed on a tatty pile of womens' magazines; a seagreen bathroom with a pearly pink bath, ough. Immense quantities of feminine frippery flung about with energetic, enjoyable untidiness: she was not unlikable. Strongly marked character, personality of much charm.

Marcel's bedroom was the other side of the landing on the sunless side; oddly dark, gloomy and severe. Old-fashioned country bed looking narrow and uncomfortable, an enormous mahogany tallboy. One of his dark go-to-meeting suits was hung neatly on a wooden stand. Everything was orderly, or would have been but for the obvious traces of his wife's passage, looking for suitable clothes in which to dress him for the funeral.

"It was the bed he slept in as a boy," said Noelle unemotionally, "and he was obstinate about it – refused to be parted."

"He didn't sleep with you?"

"Oh, the odd time," unembarrassed. "We got on better leaving the other to manage his own affairs. We were very good friends," a little defensively. "Nothing wrong with this marriage and I hope you understand me, inspector. Simply that we were both busy, active people . . . I won't bother showing you the top. Thérèse sleeps up there, and the maids' rooms, all converted of course. This one is our parents' room, won't interest you either – we'll go down, shall we?" Etienne's bathroom was an old dressing-room, small and without light. Cough syrup, a throat-spray, very few jars and bottles: no hypochondriac.

"In pretty good health," remarked Castang.

"Very much so – a bit overweight from all that eating and drinking, but he played a lot of tennis." They had got down again to the other corner of the ground floor, like the living-room with a French window opening on to a terrace, and the big back garden behind.

"This was the business-room: I use it too but here again, we kept our affairs separate." There was a baby grand piano, unexpected till one remembered that Etienne had been an accomplished amateur musician. Big room, probably been the dining-room in Third Empire days. His desk was bare and neat, with conventional presentation deskset and calendar.

"He had an office of course at the town hall: this was for personal affairs."

"Not just now," said Castang, "but I may have to ask your permission to look at all these papers. There may be things – you see?"

"You'd better take that up with the notary," said Noelle." I haven't even the keys. I've no particular objection, but I dare say the man-of-affairs would," with a bit of a snigger. Castang felt sure he would! Need to get authority from Colette Delavigne. It would be a boring, and probably useless, business. He looked at the desk. High-class modern affair, with good locks; locks that could be broken, but not without leaving traces, and could certainly not be slipped. A careful man, Monsieur Marcel.

Noelle seemed indifferent to his nosing about. She had sat absently behind her own table on the other side, where she got a good light; a table as crowded and untidy as her bedroom: she glanced at a few papers and shuffled them aside. He looked around. Nothing very personal about this, save the piano with its ragged pile of dog-eared sheet music. A few prints hung on the walls and a couple of lithographs that meant nothing to him. For the rest, tidy and chilly. Wastepaper basket empty. A glass coffee-table and two office-like easy chairs, in black leather: one might be at the town hall. It was on Noelle's side that activity was pronounced – her wastepaper basket was over-flowing.

"Did he do much business here?"

"Not a great deal. Sometimes people came. I know little about it, really. We weren't in here together often. We kept things separate as you can see – even the telephones are separate lines. Both unlisted, naturally. Mine's the same as the living-room and upstairs, but his was private." Yes; the man had lived in a series of boxes: they linked, but he kept everything in its own compartment.

"What affairs were yours – or do you mind telling me?" She smiled, showing good teeth.

"I don't mind – and again, if I did . . . you'd make it your business to find out, wouldn't you?"

"Probably. It'll be my business to look into everything until I find out why he should have been killed, and by whom." She had gone away, looking out of the window, thinking.

"As to that . . . I have no idea . . . simply no idea at all." She came back, looked straight at him, said "Etienne's affairs . . ." holding up her hands to show helplessness. "I miss him," simply. "I miss him very much. Just because life has to go on – but it does, doesn't it?"

44

"That's why we're here."

"Yes. Well, affairs we shared – the brasserie, that's really all. I was co-owner, which will mean I'm now sole owner. Joseph – my brother-in-law – manages it for us. If you go there – you can draw your own conclusions about that. Say that Etienne didn't really have time for that kind of detail, and most of the work devolves upon me. Naturally – I ran it myself for many years. He didn't want me to continue that, after he became adjunct to the Mayor. Then – the affairs of this house, which were mostly left to me. As you can see it is large, awkward and expensive and he wasn't the kind of man to be greatly interested in plumbers or electricians. Then – as to my own affairs – do you want to question me about those?"

"It's as well that I should understand once and for all."

"Right. Just the little restaurant – it's a secret but a pretty open one. Here," rummaging, "I'll give you a card. You can go there, ask what you like. Show them this," writing on the back, "and they'll give you a free meal. It's very simple really. I liked to have an interest, and an activity. My own money went into it. Nothing to do with Etienne. He would sometimes entertain people there, whom he wanted to favour. For the rest it was my pigeon, and will continue to be. There are no legal complications – it's all in my name."

"Then that's all, I think. Can I chat to the others here in this house – your parents, or his rather."

Noelle made a grimace, shrugged, smiled.

"For what good that will do you. Whatever you please. Just that you'll find Mémé – she's physically very active still – but her areas of interest, you must understand, are pretty narrowed nowadays. And Vieux-papa – outside in the garden, which is his particular terrain . . . he doesn't talk much at all. Not to put too fine a point on it, he's gaga, poor old dear. But you're welcome. Thérèse you'll find in the kitchen mostly: that's her real domain and I don't interfere with that much. You can talk to her; whether she'll talk to you is another matter. And Thierry . . . he's my son. I prefer I think not to say anything. He can speak for himself, and you'll see why I don't want to

45

prejudice anything or anybody. You will understand –
he's my son and I love him. That's all. My eldest son, and
my daughter Magali, live in their own houses, live their
own lives, and any approach to them is their concern.
You'd better not bother Thérèse now; she'll be busy with
her lunch."

"This afternoon will do for that. I've a few other chores
anyhow."

Right: a baby to register, at the Town Hall. While on
this little errand, no danger of crossing Richard's path!

8. Sisters, Sons, Daughters

Get it all over and done with. He didn't go home; the bed
wasn't even made and it would be depressing. He'd do the
housekeeping tonight. He had lunch, both bad and expensive, in a horrible beer-palace near the town hall, which
emphatically did not belong to Noelle. He thought he
might explore her restaurant this evening, see what the
grub was like. It was a place he knew without knowing,
never having had occasion to go there. Neither Vera nor
he – nor both together – went much to eat out – on a
'divisional inspector' pay-scale . . . He turned the card over
in his fingers. 'Cave Saint Symphorien' – the sort of place
that was indeed a cave, where you went downstairs knock-
ing your head on a beam, found yourself in a vault, rather
cramped, with bare refectory tables, bottles with candles
stuck in them, and a huge illegible menu in olde-gothicke
full of 'specialities' served in brass warming-pans. So what?
– he'd get a free meal out of it. Noelle's life seemed pretty
free from twisty bits. A few business fiddles no doubt –
she was certainly a tough and competent woman – but even
if she had a lover it wouldn't be any cook or head waiter –
and it was most unlikely to be someone with hostile feelings towards Monsieur the Adjunct Mayor. Commonsense
told one that Noelle would not be an underhand person –

46

that led to complications of a kind she would dislike and have no time for. Business was business, and good business depends largely on personal relations. And she hadn't looked very frustrated to him.

He got all the frustrations he wanted from Thérèse. The horrible meal of tough steak and dried-out chips, and a beer half of which was foam, and serve him right for setting foot in this dump, made him aware that good police work depends on a peaceful digestion for a start.

Thérèse's domain, the converted basement kitchen, was comfortable, sunless, but full of warm red tiles, polished brass, blue and white china, baskets, red cushions, and pictures of saints and the Pope. There were two dogs that took a dislike to him, and with Thérèse that made three. Given to pious works she was, but not any police charities, thanks. A good smell of food hung about, making him cross: she was plainly an excellent cook. She was extremely sharp. One kept falling through the strewn brushwood into tiger traps full of pointed bamboo stakes. One got little out of her save maybe the dog's plate to lick. He was treated as though he'd come selling encyclopaedias at the door and dismissed classically with a flea in his ear. 'You won't find any murderers in my kitchen, young man, nor by hanging round here.'

Thérèse seemed as uncomplicated as Noelle. Her brother had been to her simply her pride, the centre of her loyalty, the object of her devotion. Apart from pestering the local parish priest about the Tridentine Mass, and seeing to it that she was the scourge of the vegetable market, what else did she have in her life? What else indeed did she want? Now that he was dead she would stay on, because there was nowhere else to go. But don't bother me with your detective rubbish – go out and catch terrorists; that's what we pay you for.

While he was feeding off these assaults the old lady came pottering in, upon some errand connected with lifting the lid of a jampot and putting it back again; glanced inquisitively across.

"What is it, Thérèse?"

"Nothing Mémé. A young man about the gas." He decided that he was not going to risk appearing ridiculous. In every country house there is, or ought to be, a granny of this sort. They are always busily on the go, picking a bunch of parsley and setting it in a jamjar: *mettre le persil au frais* is a way of ensuring that things are as they should be.

"You've been most helpful," said Castang, ignoring the small smile of pure malice. "I'd like to see Thierry by the way."

"Monsieur Thierry," making sure the police stayed in the social class in which God had been pleased to place it, "won't be back before this evening."

"What do you call this evening?"

"Most people," patiently explaining to an imbecile, "get back from work between five and six. Unless of course they work in shops."

He had better not ask what work Thierry did, though he was a little curious about it. What had Maryvonne said – 'no visible means of support' – not quite the same as doing nothing and getting well paid for it, which is a commonplace phenomenon.

To pester Thérèse he went out through the back, into the garden. Big garden, surrounded by a high wall. And virtually in the centre of the town! Well, what use was it to be – to have been, he corrected himself punctiliously – a municipal councillor and the Adjunct Mayor if you didn't see to it that you were pretty damn privileged? Not necessarily a proof of corruption! Castang was as urban a person as you could get, but there is no soul, male or female, of French blood that looks at a garden without the heart beating faster. He loitered for a good ten minutes, enjoying it, stopping to pick off a caterpillar that was eating the leaves of a black-currant bush. Vieux-papa, accompanied by a small wheelbarrow and extremely well-cared-for tools, was lifting out old rooftiles forming the border to a bed, one by one, weeding very deliberately round them and putting them back. He paid no attention whatever to Castang, who hadn't the heart to disturb him. That his son was dead, and moreover assassinated, had or quite possibly hadn't sunk in. He would have heard the news. Yes, so they

48

tell me. I'm worried about that frost last week having got at the melons. The old man did not deserve a cop saying useless, senseless things.

Etienne Marcel had been no doubt several different sorts of crook, and aroused acute loathing in all sorts of quarters, and no doubt deserved it, but he had done well by his family. Even for him this house must have been a troublesome burden. But he'd seen to it that his old parents, and his unmarried sister, as well as his wife and children, were well looked after. Castang couldn't help thinking that it was much to his credit. There wasn't anyone here with reason to put a bullet in the boss. The whole place breathed harmony and comfort and settled, secure patterns. Rough winds there might be in the public sector where Richard was a-prowl, but nothing shook the darling buds of May within this wall: nicely maintained, observed Castang, a solid seven foot tall. And topped with broken glass against marauders.

"Is this house burglar-alarmed?" he'd asked Noelle.

"Certainly," she said briskly. "Not that there's anything of outstanding value. But I don't take unnecessary risks." Marcel, from what one heard, had had no aversion to taking risks. But in the right place.

This was surely a nonsense. If there was anything to discover it wasn't here. Still, such were his orders. Made for a nice tranquil day. He shut the gate carefully after him and wondered whether Magali would be at home. It did no harm to go and look . . .

In the car he glanced at Maryvonne's notes. Rather vulgar good looks . . . expensive bungalow res. with trappings . . . he'd see what he made of this.

The district was outlying, of no great interest, flattish being on the valley side: villages long swallowed by suburb. Along the riverbank were clumps of woodland, where the rich had seen to it they stayed undisturbed. The President-Director-general class, the captains of industry had houses along here with river frontages, nice English-style lawns, moorings for their boats under the willows. Magali's Bertrand, something in rubber making good money, wasn't in this class. But there had also been manor houses of previous centuries, *gentilhommières* with nice enclosed parks but too big, chilly and draughty for today's living. Two or three of these had been cannibalised by astute promoters. Knock the house down, but leave at least a few trees, carve the park into lots of a half acre, flog them to the rising young executive. Not quite the cream, but your standing is assured; these are exercises in elegant-and-relaxed living, and you can say you're living quite close to the rich. Buildings, roughly the top end of levitt-style-American. Veneer of Ile-de-France style, meaning a row of French windows opening on the terrace. Three bathrooms and a two-car garage. No cellar, no attic, and a colossal profit.

When you have small children, you see, it's much more comfortable having a house with a garden than it is in a flat in the city. Certainly, agrees the middle-grade police officer, mentally reviewing his salary scale and the potential for bribes . . .

The private road – Route Sans Issue: Uniquement pour Riverains – wound about and decanted him by a thuya hedge, a wrought-iron gate, grass, young trees, a clump of canna lilies and an immature rock-garden. Magali was on the terrace in a red-and-white striped sailor top, white trousers tight over the behind and flaring below. Good figure, probably excellent legs. Face handsome and often would be pretty, a French jolie-laide with too wide a mouth, too sharp a nose, eyes too close together, tanned dark skin, hair tied with a ribbon, alert expression of vivacity and intelligence. Barbaric earrings too big to be square-cut emeralds, but only just. A perceptible and somehow touching resemblance to the little old lady who trotted round with parsley. She had looked like this once – in the clothes of 1914.

Magali listened lazily to his patter.

"Sit down," pointing to a swinging garden-seat. "No school today, so I have to keep an eye on them." The children were playing by the pool. Water still a little cold, but they were dabbling, in shorts and no tops: their skin, dark like hers, would not scorch in the May sunshine.

"A drink? Perhaps a long drink?" He agreed happily.

She went off into the house. He sat in the sun and swung himself. This was a better way for the police to spend an afternoon, definitely. Why aren't there more inquiries into the rich, and fewer into Arabs-living-in-squalor? Don't answer that question. He got a tall misty glass, with too many iceblocks, not quite enough whisky, and sodawater: Magali inspected his maize-paper cigarettes and said, "Yes, give me one of those, would you?"

He sat and said nothing: let's see what she would make of this.

"Let's see if I get it right then: you don't seem very convinced by the terrorists."

"They're a possibility."

"Or does it occur to you that somebody might pretend to be a terrorist – adopt might it be a terrorist technique?" She was intelligent enough that he only had to cue her. She talked willingly.

"Mm, might not be altogether as easy as it sounds. Have to have accomplices and steal cars and all that, and hire a mercenary with a big gun. One reads of such things; wouldn't have much confidence in it myself. The accomplice would turn straight round and blackmail you, I'd have thought . . . Mm, profitless speculation. That drink all right? So you're checking up on the family. Oh. I can speak with detachment, you see I was educated and everything. You're intelligent enough I think to see that my speaking with detachment does not mean I loathe or despise my family: far from it. I rather like that absurd hugger-mugger of a house. I like them all, I'm much attached to them. Okay? I was attached to my father. An absurd person really, a great one for systems and different personae. You get like that in municipal politics. Terribly old-fashioned. Still, that was his life . . . I suppose it could happen that someone was keyed up enough to want to kill him: he'd certainly plenty of enemies. Bertrand – my husband – thinks that a very unconvincing theory. I suppose I do myself. I don't know what I think. Not beyond the bounds of possibility? Mm, you're not saying, of course. Let me talk, hope I'll drop you a clue. I haven't got any clues. I'll talk away if that's what you want."

"Give me a picture of your father's character."

"Didn't have any character. Or had too many, which is much the same thing. Like the house; ancient and modern, simple and sophisticate, naïve and elaborate. He had to be the big-shot, always bustling about. If I sound cold, perhaps it's that I saw little of him as a child – he hardly noticed us – and really I've seen little of him since. Occasionally he would bellow at us, or slap us, or pick us up and kiss us – me, anyhow, I'm the youngest, and a girl. But he was hardly ever there. Like a sailor, he would come home on leave occasionally. These episodes were noisy, and initially glamorous, but it soon wore off. Really, you know, I know very little about him."

"And your mother?"

"I love my mother very much: don't think I'm going to give you any backstairs gossip. She's a good woman, loyal, honest; no lovers or anything like that. Extremely single-minded and determined. I'm much like her."

Castang sipped his drink and said nothing. The young woman sprawled in her chair, relaxed as a cat in the sun, apparently without a care in the world. The surroundings made for a loose informality, almost a familiarity. He wasn't writing anything in little books. But she was talking too much. Still, she did resemble her mother; Noelle had met him with the same easy, uncramped openness.

Experience told a cop to be cautious of the ones who talk too much, who are so anxious to show they have nothing to hide.

"I can talk," said Magali suddenly, as though the same idea had crossed her mind, "because I'm detached about Noelle too, of course. She wasn't a demonstrative mother: we were under her feet a good deal and she didn't have the time to play with us or tell us stories. You have to understand that she married very young, and got her childbearing over early, and was pretty relieved to have it done with. She's not greatly interested in children; she's fond of mine but doesn't really notice them. Having us was a nuisance – there, one didn't have much choice in the matter in those days. I was brought up largely between Thérèse and my granny, in one way or the other. I'll get you another drink, shall I?" uncurling gracefully.

She'd swigged her own pretty quick. His was still half full. So she wanted another.

While she was gone he felt his strong physical awareness of her. Certainly she was not acting sexy; nothing about her suggested anything but the honest woman. With her perfume as she jumped from her chair came a sharp attractive tang of sweat. There was a smudge of sweat on her lips. The May afternoon sunshine was warm, and enjoyable after the cold rainy days, but not hot. Movements graceful, well co-ordinated. She set his filled glass on the table, looked to see that the children were not bickering. Beautiful body; high waist, long fine thighs. Noelle was much broader and thicker.

"Your mother has a strong character," to be saying something.

Undoubtedly she was wound up. Made too slow and elaborate a business of sitting down, reached too deliberately and negligently for her glass, took too big a sip. All this slowing herself down had, as it often does, the opposite effect. Her voice was faster, more emphatic.

"Her mentality too is different from my father's – how my father was. Etienne was terribly old fashioned. She wasn't interested in that political stuff. So antiquated. I mean 'smoke-filled rooms' and shifty-eyed ward-heeler types. He was a thorough provincial, you must understand. He would have liked to stand for a national election and gone to Paris as a Deputy. But he never felt at ease there. Realised I think that he'd never build any sort of solid base at that level. Concentrated all the more on the local scene, gladhanding everyone, being very thick with every sort of petty power. I suppose it wasn't really contemptible; just that it seems so to our – my – age group." Do I look so old? thought Castang. She's the same age as Vera. But I'm a cop. Part, and a shady part, of local power-structures.

'Who do you think killed him?"

She stared as though taken by surprise. Her face went absent and then came back and concentrated upon him.

"I've no idea. How on earth could I? I don't even know

53

all the facts. I'm not stupid enough to imagine the paper prints them all. If it's not terrorists then, then – a mafia of some sort. It's all so professional – or so it sounds – or am I mistaken?" Fishing. He wasn't going to say that he didn't have the remotest idea.

"You get on well with your brothers?"

"I don't really see a lot of them." Being evasive now. "Well, you know, my husband's not that friendly with them. I mean they're my brothers of course. We have a kind of family unity."

"Being detached, as you were before."

"Well . . ." She picked up her glass, twiddled it, drank off the watery remnants. "Thierry's a bit of an ass; Didier's a bit of a bore. What more is there to say? They're both of them intelligent enough. Thierry's too bone-idle to use his brains. Didier's a sharper. He's a rather bad copy of his father in some ways. I don't really want to say much more. Put it like this : I'm not really very greatly in sympathy with the way they live. I've my own life," defensively, aware of being a scrap disloyal, "my own family. My husband lives in a different world, and I see things with different eyes."

"Does your husband get on well with your family?"

"Pretty well. He never asked my father for any favours," voice sharpening. "Has this lasted long enough now? I've really told you all I can."

"I'm sorry," said Castang, getting up at once. "I've no wish, and of course no right, to press you at all. All this was just background, and routine if you like. Character – mentalities as you called it yourself. In talking to members of your family I didn't want my big feet getting obtrusive. You've been very patient. I got rather roughly handled by Thérèse," grinning. She broke into a laugh at once.

"Oh, she's an old terror. She's like that with everyone. Domestic tyrant."

"If I want to get in touch with your husband, can I give him a ring here?"

"Oh, yes. I'll tell him. But he always kept himself a bit aloof, you see. He doesn't know any of the family well – with this notable exception," smiling.

"Goodbye then, Madame, and thanks again."

"You're welcome," she said formally.

9. A Son, Specifically

The sunshine hadn't lasted long. Big lumps of wet greyish cloud had come quietly up over the horizon and were filling all the westerly sky. Drops were falling already as he got back: he struggled into his raincoat before climbing out of the car. Thérèse kept him waiting a long time on the step, but probably she did that to everyone.

"Monsieur Thierry's in the kitchen," curtly. He should have gone to the kitchen door! Houses like this still have a tradesmen's entrance . . .

Thierry was in the kitchen all right, making himself at home there, comfortably having a cup of coffee. He seemed younger than thirty. Dressed to match; jeans, and a scruffy pullover. Tall and lanky; it was not the square thickset build of Etienne Marcel. Took more after Noelle's side perhaps, but the same sort of sharp pointed nose as his sister Magali. Long legs; longish hair. The legs were sticking out, with big, dirty, trodden-over shoes.

"Take them out of my way then," said Thérèse indulgently. Castang got a previous impression reinforced that Monsieur Thierry was her ewe lamb.

"We can talk somewhere for a few minutes?"

"Sure," amiably.

"I'd like to get out of this lady's way." Sniff, from Thérèse.

"Aha. Private conversation?"

"Oh, it's a routine sort of ruling. You aren't a witness or anything, so we aren't formalising. I'm having a word with everybody, and don't want to be a nuisance. How about your room?" Thierry considered this.

"Pigsty as usual," said Thérèse, still indulgently, "but I don't want him here."

55

"No strain," said Thierry coolly. "Just finish my coffee."

Castang followed up to the second floor. Unhurried, easy walk in front of him. The movements too were like his sister's, in a sloppier, scruffier fashion.

Castang hadn't seen the inside of Magali's house. Hadn't found a pretext – would, if he wanted one. This was different: if he hadn't seen this, there would have been a lot more that was puzzling about Thierry. A cool card, putting on an act. He wandered about with his hands in his pockets, studying things. Nice big airy corner room. On the cold side of the house; that was the only drawback.

"Make yourself at home," said Thierry with mild sarcasm. "Any drawers you want to peep into – don't embarrass yourself."

"Training, instinct, what you like," said Castang to the figure behind him, "all adds up. Nosy by definition." Thierry chuckled.

"Like a drink?"

"No thanks, I've had one." Clink, glug-glug. Maryvonne had smelt whisky on his breath too. The morning of the funeral, one takes a brace, but she had been right. Whisky; expensive whisky in a square bottle. One had a quick brace when it was needed, and that could be any time of the day.

He went on wandering about, reading the titles of books on the shelf, studying the pictures on the walls.

"You'll find it, I imagine, normal," he said over his shoulder, "that I have some questions to put." The boy was supine in a big armchair, its upholstery worn bare and dark, but looking comfortable. Why did he think of him as a boy? Only a few years younger than Castang. Because of the student-type clothes? Is it true that once you are thirty you don't wear jeans, because they make you look ridiculous?

"I gather you've had questions for everybody – even Thérèse." Mild amused drawl. "You struck a patch of rough water there – I'd have guessed even if she hadn't told me. You were busy with my mother as I learn. Are we all under suspicion of smoking opium? – I've often wondered what Vieux-papa was getting up to there in the garden shed. Why be surprised at your chasing after me?

I should think certainly I was a likelier dope fiend than my dear old Auntie T."

Castang sat on the divan and took a cigarette out.

"You got any pot?" he asked amiably. Thierry heaved with silent sniggers through his nose.

"I've got all the vices," he said, enjoying himself.

"How about shooting at people?"

Thierry considered this idea with apparent seriousness.

"Now there I wouldn't agree. If anyone in this house shot at anybody, I'd have to say in my considered judgement that Thérèse would be the likeliest candidate. Except of course," as though the idea had only just struck him, "if you mean my father. Do you mean my father? Mark you, she threw things at him sometimes. But I don't see her shooting him." Shaking his head gravely. Castang had decided to give all this comedy plenty of rope.

"So let's have your considered opinion."

"Oh. Oh, you think then it wasn't really terrorists?"

"You know any terrorists?"

"I know lots of would-be terrorists. With their mouth, you know. I'd have to think, if I know any real ones. I'd be inclined to doubt it. Is it interesting? – the categories of people I know?"

"Suppose you tell me."

"Really I'd have to say all sorts. I'm like Kim – or my father come to that. I'm the little friend of all the world."

"Try not to act the imbecile," softly.

"I beg your pardon."

"I said don't play the mental deficient with me," shouted Castang at the top of his voice. There was a small pause. The laddy had to have time to get his back patted.

"That's not imbecility, Inspector – is that the right title to call you by? I don't, you notice, call you an imbecile, though it might be thought a police inspector provides an admirable characteristic specimen. I'm just universally sceptical. I have the habit of raillery. Sorry about that."

Castang got up and put his cigarette in his mouth, stared for a moment, and said, "I've no questions for the witless." He stopped in the open doorway. "You know what happens to the universally sceptical?"

57

"But do tell," pouring himself another shot from the bottle.

"They don't have anything left to live for, and put their head in the oven," heading for the stairs.

He was glad Thérèse wasn't in the hall to chase him with her broom.

10. Reports

"What sort of a day have you had?" A pleasure to see Maryvonne; bright, serious, sitting bolt upright. Quite nice looking, too. The gingery fair hair was scraped back too abruptly for the narrow face: too many pins and then a ribbon too. Effect sort of scraggly. But she wasn't there to be glamorous.

"I don't think I've got anywhere very far," worriedly flipping back pages of her notebook.

"Neither have I. I didn't in fact expect either of us to, much. It would be too good. You see the elder brother – the Didier?"

"Certainly. Very polite and co-operative – smarmy even. Not a very nice person, or am I being too subjective?"

"No, it's what you're there for."

"Tall, handsome, I mean well-shaped features, good figure. Sallow though, a nasty colour, hair going thin. Horrible eyes like wet stones. I wouldn't trust him as far as I could throw him. Bright, cold, crafty: puts on a warm charming act, with a lot of jokes and little laughs, but it does look perfunctory. Was the father like that?"

"Less perfunctory. Went to a great deal of trouble. Looked and sounded interested, always."

"It's the same politician's performance. He did give me a lot of time and trouble. Can't help it, I found him dislikable and dishonest. Very earnest about the terrorists: urges us to use the utmost diligence and he'll be of service all the ways you can think of: squirmy person but I mustn't sound prejudiced; he gave no trouble."

"Funny he should be so anxious for there to be terrorists – nobody else believes in them or pretends to."

"Didier states he was on excellent terms with his father but kept a certain distance between them. Values his independence is how he puts it. Father wanted to put his finger in all the pies – interfering in a helpful friendly way, giving unwanted advice."

"Quite believable too. And the pub?"

"The brother's the complete figurehead, wood all the way through. Madame Noelle's the key to all that."

"That's what I thought. Okay, let's go see Richard."

Commissaire Richard was smoking a cigar, with several piles of paper arranged neatly over his desk, studying them with the same affable calm as though it were nine in the morning and the day just begun, instead of six in the evening. Shirt fresh, face fresh, hair impeccable, suit unrumpled.

"Ah," he said when he saw them. "The character students."

Castang sat down and turned a cigarette around between the finger and thumb of the two hands, intent on getting it round and even.

"Bearing in mind I know nothing about Etienne Marcel's public life, I'm not likely to find out much. He kept his private existence separate. It's oddly impressive. A generous person. Family provider, who took his responsibilities as head of the clan seriously. Went to a lot of pains to see that his elderly parents were secure, comfortable, happy, occupied. Recognised his wife's skills, respected them. Treated her in fact as an equal, which I wasn't expecting. She had to act the bourgeois hostess a bit, he insisted on that, but nothing forced. Used his sister as unpaid slavey housekeeper – or so I had thought. In fact he gave her a generous personal allowance and allowed her to have a sort of domain of authority. Cranky cow, but she was devoted to him.

"Relationship with his own wife – impressive in its sense and balance. There was a mutual respect there which made for a good partnership. His daughter. who is a sensible and intelligent young woman, got on well with both, speaks well of both. A bit strained and tense, but I don't see any reason to give much importance to that. The younger son is a kind of layabout, his auntie's tame canary and she's full of little indulgencies. The mother likewise has a soft corner for him. He milks all this shamelessly. The father saw almost certainly that he was useless – I'll have to check this a little further – and accepted it as just another fact of life. No cutting him off with a penny, and no sign of friction. Closely united, warm, affectionate family unit. First impression, but they're rarely wrong."

"Very well," said Richard. "Maryvonne?"

"Mr Castang and I arranged to split the family between us. I haven't been to the house yet. I've been in this brasserie thing which is the family business, where they started. The wife used to run it: these last ten years it's the brother who runs it for them. I can confirm what Castang says, that he looked after his family. The brother's an indolent self-satisfied lunkhead, and I should think they had to put up with a lot of incompetence there. It didn't – doesn't – matter much because the wife keeps a sharp eye on all the details, goes there every day, and so on. Oh yes, and she also has a restaurant in her own name, which isn't generally known about. Open secret – they buy in potatoes, say, for the two places together. Etienne never missed an evening there – an hour at least – when he could help it. Shake hands and say a word to everyone. Shrewd – a popularity base: anybody with a grievance could buttonhole him there."

"That's confirmed," interjected Castang, "by his not encouraging people in his own home much. He could use the pub both as office and for entertainment, except for Important People."

"Between nine and ten at night you could count on an audience," she went on. "The staff say he could lose his temper and yell – an act to my mind to keep them in line – but was generous, especially if they were ill or in trouble, then he'd look after them. Like Boussac staff, swearing by 'Monsieur Marcel'. He knew how to mix familiarity with

60

authority. It's difficult in this world to see anyone with a grudge, let alone a motive for ambushing him."

"Any more?"

"The second brother, the furniture business – well, he's a competent craftsman, but workshy as all hell. I wouldn't say Etienne kept him afloat – he wasn't the type to throw good money down the drain – but he sure as hell threw him a lot of goodwill and patronage. If you came there with the right word you'd get a good job done. Otherwise you'd wait six months and your chair would still be sitting there untouched. Then the other son, that's the eldest, in a lot of little estate-agent deals. He almost certainly got a start in that through pa's helping hand, but I'd say he's worked it up since on his own: he doesn't lack talent or ambition. Probably he relied still on inside info about municipal projects and contracts. One can't conceive of him not finding the relationship rewarding and valuable. I thought he might bear looking at a little closer in his personal life: he seems to be divorced and lives on his own there. Mr Castang suggested we might reverse the operation next day: get two levels of observation, which might shed a bit more light."

"All right," said Richard, waving smoke away from his face. He thought for a moment.

"I don't want any superficial or premature conclusions. Do as you suggest. We don't want anything in the nature of a neighbourhood enquiry along ordinary lines: that would only arouse gossip and speculation. Try to broaden it into – old friends, habitual guests – mm, love affairs, he sounds the model husband, and knew how to be discreet, but you never know. I leave it to you. Put your heads together tomorrow; give me a brief précis then. I'm meeting the same pattern. An onion; we go on peeling off layers, and each looks much like the one before. We have to go right on down, to make sure there is, or was, no flaw or crack where something could have gone rotten. Very well, the two of you can go home. Our love to Lydia," he said to Castang. How did the artful bugger know her name?

Monsieur Castang – Henri only to intimates and there

61

were not very many – Divisional Inspector of Police Judiciaire and newly a father, a fact which procured strong and disconcerting sensations, got home rather late but in high fettle. His wife and his daughter were in fine shape; the daughter in fact a great deal more attractive than she had appeared that morning. He himself had been a good boy; had tidied the flat most conscientiously. He'd had a good dinner; most important.

As for being a cop, why, even this – generally unpleasant – fact of life was less of a drag than usual. Vera would be home in four or five days: she'd slept well, was resting comfortably; everything was normal. She had a few stitches, and the gynaecologist would be deciding when to take these out, but it wouldn't hold matters up unduly. An amiable conspiracy involving Fausta would stop any of Commissaire Lasserre's nonsense about time off. He would get his days off when he wanted them, when he needed them, when Vera came home and he would have to look after her awhile. This was all cut and dried.

To be sure, he was on a job, which might, in fact did, get more and more complicated. But he felt quite sure it amounted to nothing. Look, go digging into anybody's private life and you'll find complications. People, under the most banal exteriors, can and do construct weird and elaborate areas of privacy. All the more somebody cunning, secretive, discreet like Etienne Marcel, who had kept his life in carefully watertight compartments. A day or so, and it would all be classified.

Well no, it wouldn't be classified. The inquiry would go underground, and might prolong itself a long long time. But that was a worry for the Procureur and the Prefect, for the Mayor, for Madame the Judge of Instruction, for Commissaire Richard . . . Not for him; he was an understrapper. All these people might think up persecutions and torments for unhappy police officials but he would be saying Kiss My Ass. Birth was more important than death. Meantime, he'd been an extra good boy. Feeling free, feeling fresh, feeling energetic after a good meal, he'd done some quite useful extra work. He'd acquired merit. He had something to spring on any clown, be it Lasserre or

Richard or even Madame Delavigne, who might take it into their heads to accuse him of primrose dallying on this job, of not being very Zealous.

He felt in fact – what had that ass Thierry called it? – that's it; the little friend of all the world. He put his key in the street door, lock going tralala, tralala, but silently because it was after eleven and this was a Respectable House, was borne up in the lift to the fourth floor, stepped across to his own front door, virtuously conscious that the apartment was tidy, and the bed made. He would sleep well. Damn, that stupid phone was ringing.

Nothing had happened to Vera surely? He shut the door quietly, hideous nightmares jumping about and shrieking at him in the dozen steps across to the obstinately yacking phonebell.

"Yes; Castang."

"Maryvonne."

"What? Look, do you realize it's after eleven?"

"I'm sorry; I've been trying to raise you for some time. I'm afraid I'm in the shit." Her voice was weary, strained. He took hold of himself.

"I was out, and what's more I was at work. Very well, let's have it."

"It's Didier: I'm afraid he's dead."

"WHAT! ?"

"Marcel's eldest son, the one I interviewed today. Been found dead; it's a long story. I haven't been quite sure what to do. I tried to – I mean I felt I ought to ask you, and your phone didn't reply. So I got Richard, and he said yes, you'd have to – and to get Lasserre if I couldn't raise you, but I thought you'd want –" She was a bit incoherent – he realized that she hadn't much experience and was plainly out of her depth. He realized too that he did want to know. He was a cop. There was no discharge in the war. Whatever this was it was no business of Lasserre's. Or Richard's. This was his investigation.

"Tell me. First of all, where are you?"

"I'm in the flat. I mean his flat. You see, they – I mean the firemen – found the card I'd left, saying PJ, and they thought this is funny, so they thought they'd better get in touch, and whoever's on guard put them through to me and –"

"Maryvonne. You're forgetting your training. I realize you're distraught. But put this in the shape of a verbal report."

"Water was dripping through. The man downstairs noticed. He couldn't get in to the flat above. He had to call the firemen. They forced the door. They found him dead. In the bath. Electrocuted. You know, like the singer – who changed a bulb while in the bath. People do such stupid things. It's more complicated than that actually. I'm trying to simplify . . ." It was quite natural that there was not only weariness and strain in her voice, and anxiety about a cock-up, but relief. She'd got the responsibility on to him. He was, after all, the senior officer concerned. Her superior.

"Right, girl, I've understood. Be right around. Meanwhile, your standard procedure, okay? Stand fast, hold fast. You know what we used to say in the army? – if it moves, salute it. If it doesn't move paint it." It pulled her together: she gave a laugh, a bit off-key. Still, a laugh.

The body was gone, in the fire-brigade's ambulance. The doctor had been and gone. The press – he was sorry to hear – had been and gone. Alerted of course by the neighbours and the hullabaloo. He'd better cut that off straight away, or the Lord alone knew what they'd be printing. Pull rank, boy. Richard's rank. He got the paper's night desk on the phone.

"Yes, I know this links to Etienne Marcel's death and you want to make it a splash. Get one thing straight and make sure you have it. This matter comes under judicial control. Outside the one fact, this wouldn't rank above five lines ordinarily; this is a coincidental accident. You will confine yourselves to that, right? Any speculation about suicide or any reference whatever to the homicide under instruction and you've got the instructing judge and the Proc with the chopper on your neck. You can't print a damn thing without authorisation, got it?"

Maryvonne, of course, had only arrived after it was all

over and gossip already running rife. Never mind. He had one rock to cling to. An unimpeachable professional witness, a genuine expert. The lieutenant of the fire-brigade was still there. Maryvonne had asked him to hang on. He would have hung on anyhow: he knew his job.

"When I realized who it was . . . and then hunting in his pockets, wondering who to notify since he was alone here, I found your card. So it had her name written in, your girl here, so I thought I'd better ring your people and the duty guard put me through."

"You were quite right. Routine of course on the family, but this will blow the lid off: we're in the shit now whatever happens. Never mind; it's not irreparable. Can you give me your breakdown, the way you'll be writing it up in the report."

"It's easy enough to reconstruct, I think," leading the way back into the bathroom. "Look, he was running the bath, probably going to dress and go out again – around eight. There's no sign of his having eaten. The autopsy will tell us whether he'd been drinking; there's a glass in the kitchen. Okay, the water's still running; he undresses, steps in. Stepped in awkwardly, or slips, and, the way one would, he grabs at something. In the event, this bracket. You reel a bit, you grab – as you see, it's just the right height. He falls, and he brings down the shower curtain. It's possible he grabs at that too. He has both feet in the bath; that's the way we found him. Half in, half out.

"Now observe this building. This is all old, this plasterwork is old. Enamel paint over, above the level of the tiling, but shaky old stuff and softened by the steam. Look, it's like cheese. The curtain rail, and this bracket, might have looked firmly fixed but weren't: quite a slight pull sufficed to fetch them out. He may have grabbed the curtain while falling forward, and bumped into the bracket, but I say he grabbed the bracket too: which came first and helped the other down is of small importance. Now look at the silly idiot – he has this little electric fan plugged in on the bracket. Had never put in an extractor, the window's shut for warmth, heavy condensation collects here. Habitually, he puts on the fan and leaves the door open to dispel the steam. Right, the fan stands on that shaky bracket . . . Floop into the water, it shorts of course, blew the fuses out but too late, he gets it in the worst possible way, standing ankledeep or more in the water. End of a very unfortunate tale which should, but won't, discourage people who will frig about with flimsy electric appliances in bathrooms. Little heaters – hairdryers – curling-tong things, toothbrushes and crap, seven-tenths of the plugs in these old houses aren't even earthed. If that wasn't enough they plug in extension leads, three-way adaptors, radios, record-players – anything you like that will leave lengths of flex around to trip over. A classic way of killing yourself, the files are full of them. I'll send you a copy of my report, Castang, since it's tangential to a thing of yours. I'll buzz now, okay? I was kept hanging about but I phoned in to explain."

"Is there anything one can still do?" asked Maryvonne. "I'm sorry, Henri. When I got here they'd already got the body out, there was no chance for photos or anything *in situ,* they were charging about mopping up – the water came down into the flat below of course after overflowing; that's what alerted them. There was nobody here; they had to break the door open. I couldn't see any point in calling technicians – prints everywhere of his own, of course, and firemen, and the doctor. I spoke to the doctor. Classic electrocution death, a bruise on the skull where he tumbled and caught his head on the side of the bath. This shelf here where he had shampoo – awkwardly placed. He might have got shampoo in his eye or something – the shower was on too, they told me. It's just a bloody stupid coincidence, surely. I mean there's no homicide picture; there was nobody here, and it couldn't have been rigged up. And no suicide either. I mean, nobody commits suicide in such an awkward way as that, least of all a person like this. What do you think?"

"I don't have any thoughts."

"I mean, is there anything you want me to do?" asked Maryvonne carefully.

"I don't feel at all like a detective in the middle of the frigging night."

66

"So when there's an official report from the firemen that this is accidental death ..."

"So they know a great deal more about it than I do."

"So I report to Richard in that sense."

"You report to Richard in one line. That we fell out of the frying pan. Or got tipped."

11. Marie Touchet

Yet it had been a good day. Vera much enjoying 'being spoilt'; she was stuffing herself happily with expensive fruit. And expensive chocolates!

"Where do these come from?" stretching out a greedy hand.

"Richard! He came in, even. I thought that dreadfully nice."

It was, rather. Castang was touched. Like most departmental chiefs, Richard could display steel-jacketed egotism and blinding insensitivity. He was also capable of small charming unselfishness. He knew, too, how to engage loyalty. Grapple you with hoops of steel, thought Castang.

"How's the child?"

"It screams and squabbles with its dinner," said Vera lovingly.

"Tremendous fighting with my nipple: it gets horribly frustrated at dinner not coming fast enough." All was well here.

His own dinner had come fast enough. In Noelle's restaurant as promised. Well enough cooked and well enough served: things seen to by a quiet, competent young man who knew what he was about. Castang did not try to milk his free pass, and ate an unostentatious meal, but it would still have been a lot too dear for his pocket. But she's giving reasonable value, he thought. Here, as elsewhere, Noelle knows what she's about too. The place was clean, the atmosphere good, the lavatory spotless.

"You enjoyed your dinner, I hope," said the young man, bringing his bill.

"Very much. You're the owner?"

"No, no – simply the manager."

"Sit down a moment and have a drink," said Castang showing his identity card.

"That's kind of you but I'm afraid I haven't time . . . I think you'd better come outside service hours."

"Now," producing the other card, with Noelle's writing.

"Jeanne – can you manage for five minutes? No, if there's a drink wanted I'll get it . . . Try to make it brief. And I may have to interrupt you."

"It's not complicated. And needn't worry you. Just the way things are put together. You're in partnership with her?"

"I wish I were: she drives a very hard bargain, the patronne. But she's fair. She gives me a good salary and a good percentage. She realizes I need an incentive. She knows I've my way to make, that I won't stay long – unless I get a partnership. Well – hard but fair. That answer your question?"

"Thanks, I don't want any more to drink. She's a good-looking woman still."

"No, Mr Castang, there you're up the garden path. And if I may say so politely, don't try to put salt on my tail. I might add, you plainly don't know the patronne at all well."

"Elaborate on that a bit."

"I'm not a fool, you know. Trying that way of getting a partnership would be a stupid trick. You have to understand her and I think I do. She has a great deal of charm, and uses it to get people to do what she wants. A very feminine charm, next door to sex appeal. So you start drawing conclusions. You're wrong. She does have plenty of sex appeal; in fact she's a warm woman with a lot of juice, and she does a lot on impulse. Make no mistake, she has it well worked out in her own head. Impulses all over the place, some of them foolish. A big potential for affection, or love if you call it that. But that's kept in her family. You can believe me: I've got to know her pretty well in two years. Try anything on with her and I'd be out, but in a flash. I've no hold on her. What's more I've seen people try this – and get their chair kicked out under them. She can be extremely ruthless. I shouldn't tell you this but to get you quite straight . . . there was a cook who tried that. He thought he was pretty good, and he was good. I can tell you; that evening I did the cooking. And she served. She'll do the washing-up, she'll clean the lavatory, but she won't take any nonsense. All right?"

What's the secret of success for her?"

"Quite simple, she takes immense pains. Tremendous energy. In here with flowers every day, unpacking crates, taking the curtains to the cleaners . . . Getting people to do things for her – charm the birds out of the trees. I've seen customers clear away their own dishes, because she was short of a waitress. Didn't get a cent off the bill, neither; yet she'll be absurdly generous on occasion. Sorry a minute; I've got to serve those people over there." Said too much already, and regretting it, thought Castang. But that's the effect she has on people.

"I will have that drink after all. But I won't keep you. One or two small points. So if you were to sum the patronne up, a lot of pretty cold thinking, disguised as spontaneity."

"All right, I'll join you. No, that's not quite right. She thinks, yes, all the time. You might be talking about the weather or something, and suddenly she'll say 'Why were those cucumbers so dear this morning?' out of the blue. But it's a genuine spontaneity. She'd been treating me like dirt, and suddenly she sent me a rug for my flat. Weeks before, I'd said something about wanting one."

"She's been in your flat?"

"Of course she has. Oh fuck the fuzz, it thinks of nothing but sex."

"Just universal scepticism," said Castang grinning, thinking of Thierry.

"If I had a grippe she'd be there with aspirin. Probably make the bed while she was at it. She can be very bleak, and she can show much kindness – and now I'll say no more about my employer, all right?"

"Last thing – was her husband often in?"

"A rarity, and not with her. Didn't come checking up, if that's what you mean. Rung up the odd time for a table. A week ago – ten days? – he was here, with two men from Paris – business of some sort. They don't talk when you're listening . . . Paid the bill like anybody else: she doesn't give away free meals much – you're privileged. Okay now? Good night to you – yes, to be quite honest I want your table! Jeanne – lay up here." Castang left quite pleased with himself. But don't be pleased with yourself now, will you? You were fortunate. Intelligent young man. Intelligent too of Noelle, to know how to hang on to him while giving so little away . . .

It was no trouble finding his way in the dark to the village where he had left that woman the day of the funeral. Curiosity had been growing . . .

He couldn't recall ever having been out here at night. Quiet? – yes, relatively. Plenty of movement, plenty of cars. The restaurant up the road, and the pub, were doing good business. The farmers go to bed early, but how many farmers are there left? Tax farmers, most of this crowd.

The battered little Alfa-Sud was not there, but light showed dimly behind the curtains in the cottage. Wrought-iron antique knocker. Didn't look faked but you couldn't tell. Lot of very clever fakes about, a lot of them much too smart for mere fuzz. Especially around here. Nice, this country living. Between cars there was good still air. In the gaps between car exhaust there was a smell of lilac, and wet lilac bushes.

She took her time. Cautious too. The light did not go on in the hallway. There was quite a fair amount of light on the street, that way. He was being scrutinized through a judas. When the door opened – good plain slab of oak, that – it did so a crack, on a solid chain runner.

"What is it, please?" Soft voice, low.

"Police Judiciaire, Madame, good evening."

"Good evening – good heavens, Police Judiciaire? How very odd. Do you mind showing me some identity?" She turned the light on. He saw an elegant hand, another black and white skirt but a long one this time, in chevrons.

"Thank you. Come in please. I'm sorry, but I live alone, and people say all sorts of things at the door, and at night..."

"You're quite right to be so careful." It was the old kitchen of the little cottage, and there were antique roasting-jacks and stuff, and not much room. "I'm sorry to bother you. Thought this might be a good time to catch you quietly, shall I say? It's unofficial."

"You'd better come in then, and sit down." A small but cosy sitting room. Tiled floor, wooden presses and things smelling of beeswax. Irregular plaster walls. Overhead beams. He wouldn't crack his head – she was taller than he was. Being thin, and the long skirt, made her look taller still. Oddly attractive. And somehow lots too of sex appeal. Not like Noelle but yes, like. Different style... Silk jersey top, black down to the wrists. And then those huge horse-woman's hands, strangely well-shaped, very competent looking. She sat upright on a wooden armchair and looked at him calmly. Large clear brown eyes. "I have to take it, I think, that this must be about Etienne Marcel."

"Why so?"

"Because I think I saw you at the funeral. I am observant, even in moments of emotion."

"So am I. That brought me here. To be frank, I followed you home."

She laughed.

"Do you know, I wondered about that little car."

"Yeck, I didn't know I was that bad at being discreet." It put her at her ease. The soft voice rose to a soprano caw when she became animated. Harsh but clear, attractive, a ring to it.

"Good then, you've Tracked me Down. What now?"

"I thought we'd have a talk. And I know it's a boring subject but I expect it might be about sex. The fuzz is obsessed with sex, or so I got told about half an hour ago. We're all Irish parish-priests at heart." Uninhibited laugh.

"You know Ireland?"

"No, except that judging by the tourist literature it's impossible to find more barefaced liars."

"I've been there about horses. All right, sex is a subject like another. Whose?"

"You know about the black chief, filling in the immigration form? – when it came to Sex he crossed out M or F and wrote in 'Immense'." Her upper body was slim and well-shaped; bent gracefully to the laugh. "Etienne's, I should imagine."

She didn't waste time, nor try to prevaricate. She didn't bother offering him a drink. She did not stiffen, showed no hostility. He knew nothing about her intelligence, but this was a sophisticated woman. She was going to keep her distance. She didn't mind laughing at his stupid jokes. What struck one about her was her balance. The time she took was no more than that needed to get up, take a small cigar from a box above the carefully restored cottage fireplace, and strike a match.

"I won't tell you any lies. If you want to push me over into the mud, it's your affair. I've fallen in the mud all my life; face first, pretty often. I'm used to it. One gets to expect it. It's up to you. Don't push me over, and I'll be grateful. Yes, I was Etienne's mistress."

Said very naturally. It was not unlike Noelle's saying 'If I'm not frank with you you'll only pester me' but both less provincial and less material. Castang tried to choose his words in answering.

"If this has a direct bearing on his death, or if you have any knowledge about that circumstance, even a knowledge of a likelihood or a possibility, then you're a witness. Your story will have to be heard by the Judge of Instruction. Try to conceal or distort such knowledge, then I couldn't help you, and I wouldn't show you any sympathy. I'm doing my work. But if, as is perfectly likely, you can help me, and are willing to help me, then I can respect your discretion. Give me your promise, and you'll have mine. Don't break it, and neither will I. As for the Judge, it's a woman, I know her fairly well, she's not an inhuman woman. She won't throw you to the press, and a statement to her can be arranged in confidence. If it came to a trial, and having to bear witness in a courtroom, I can't guarantee your privacy there, you realize. That's about

72

as far as I can go without knowing more."

"That's pretty fair, I think. Let's say I can promise you that I know nothing about his death. Wittingly, that is. If it came out that I knew something without knowing it – I'm putting this badly – something I didn't know was germane, is that the right word? – it would be in innocence and you'd have to accept that."

"All right. Now I'll put this in formal terms, so you know where you stand. Code of Procedure. I'm an officer of police judiciaire, meaning I'm under oath. I'm acting in this inquiry under a mandate from a judge of instruction. Means a statement made to me has evidential value, I can make notes, write it up into a statement, ask you to sign it."

She drew quietly at the little cigar. When she smiled, her eyes, much lined at the corners, crinkled up attractively.

"I like putting a horse at a jump. I like doing it at a high or awkward jump, without really knowing whether he'll clear it. I'm like that. All my life, every time I had two sous I had twelve cents' worth of thirst."

"Fire ahead in your own words, taking your own time, I'll make a note or ask a question if I have to."

"I'm married to a Belgian, a businessman. I'd like to keep him anonymous if I can, because it's nothing to do with him and he hasn't deserved any trouble at my hands. We're not divorced, we're separated, by consent, and he pays me an allowance just the same as an alimony. So write me down if you will as Madame Touchet, Marie Touchet. Because that's really who I was. You don't understand? – you've never read Dumas? Of course but you've forgotten. King Charles the Ninth takes the King of Navarre for a walk at night and shows him a secret, a cottage with a young peasant woman in it. She has a baby, I don't have a baby, but the parallel is close enough otherwise. You see, Henri, says Charles, this is the only place in the world where I can be myself, and am valued for what I really am. It's historical, in fact. The baby grew up to be a celebrated royal bastard, the Duc d'Angoulême, and occupied quite a prominent position at the court of

Henri Quatre, and later of Louis the Thirteenth. What happened to Marie Touchet I've no idea. She got forgotten, I dare say. I hope she wasn't persecuted. As for Etienne, I met him at the riding school on the outskirts of the town here. I was living in a flat in a footloose way; I'm an aimless, silly woman. He sat on a horse like a sack of spuds, because it was pure pretentiousness on his part: no feeling at all and moreover he was frightened out of his wits, and rather pleasantly he admitted as much and well – we became acquainted. I don't want to go into details of the sex thing unless you oblige me. Just it didn't happen as trivially or as casually as you might believe. Whatever you've been told he wasn't a skirt-chaser or whatever I might look, I'm not a mantrap. There was struggle, and on both sides. When it took place it took place – no I won't talk about it, or not now anyway. I may be able to later. Etienne got this cottage, through pull I suppose, but I pay the rent. I wasn't a whore and I wasn't 'kept'. I pay my own way. I've taken presents from him because he was happy to give them. Nothing elaborate, no jewellery or stocks. He was quite well off. I don't know how rich he was. I have never asked," angrily. "My furniture is my own and nearly all I brought with me, and you can check on that."

"I'll have to check on a lot of things, but rest assured I'll be discreet. How often did you see him?"

"Fairly irregularly. Once a week, once a fortnight – a month sometimes. Nearly three years now. I have my income. I supplement that by part-time work, I can tell you my employer, but if this comes out I'll get the sack. Perhaps I'll go anyway: it would be best; I've been thinking about it. If you let me, now." A little bitterness: resignation. "You'll ask when I saw him last: exactly a week ago this evening. Whether he behaved as usual: yes, precisely. Whether he said or did anything to lead one to believe he was menaced, or had enemies, or was engaged in anything unusual or dangerous or – I don't know, anything to interest you, that might suggest or explain the reasons for his being assassinated – no, no, and no. A bolt from the blue, totally. I know nothing whatsoever. I didn't look for confidences or get any. He'd talk about anything and everything, but he didn't gossip. Either about his affairs or his home. I know something of both, inevitably, but quite certainly a great deal less than you. I was just – a woman, whom he felt he could talk to freely. Who would make no exaggerated demand on him, wouldn't have an eye – I think this is it – to her advantage all the time, seeking all the time to turn the relationship to profit. Which is what pretty nearly everyone wanted of him in the long or short run, and that's just what he'd got sick of."

He'd got her moving now: question of keeping the flow up till he was fairly sure there was nothing left.

He was a cop of some seniority by now; with considerable experience: had learned to be wary.

It rang true. He had however known other women who rang true. She looked, felt, tasted good. Her atmosphere, her surroundings felt right.

He had, too, taken her by surprise, at night, in her own home. He had, however, in the past come near being stung. Did one ever know? And if she thought that she had him in her pocket . . . A woman of experience, skill, a clever woman. And brighter than she looked. She acted stupid. Women act . . . and he, undoubtedly, was vulnerable. He could see Richard's face. Richard would not say much. He had said it already. 'You realize, Castang, in an affair like this, just how vulnerable we are.' The Mayor, the Prefect, the Minister of the goddam Interior. Talk about being inside nutcrackers . . .

He felt ashamed of his own cynicism, and found himself thinking of Vera. This was not, repeat not, the moment for any of the little armoury of tricks – they are all dirty tricks – a cop can reach for. But boy, you better be sure what ground you're on.

"Well – Madame Touchet – we can probably manage to be pretty discreet about all this. There's a good way of making sure – mm?"

"I don't quite grasp."

"You're an attractive woman, you know." Perfectly true; she was.

She said nothing, looked at him awhile with a meaningless, expressionless face. She got up and went over to where a drinks tray stood on a side table. She poured herself a glass of something, added nothing to it, drank it off in one, stood looking at her reflection in a round glass that distorted. Her body looked suddenly too heavy for her: the long arms and bony hands hung limp and numb. "Inevitably," she said in a dull limp voice. She moved over towards the fireplace and put her elbows on the chimney piece.

"Do you want me to undress?" she asked without looking at him, "or will it be enough if I lift my skirt?" Without bitterness; as though she were exhausted.

"Neither," said Castang without budging. "I wanted to see what you would do. I haven't any intention of breaking my word."

"Ah, I see . . . A sort of test. Yes. I deserved that. The police . . . I can't blame you." She turned round to face him, propping her elbows behind her, as though she still needed the support to hold her up. "There isn't any truth or honour anywhere." No, alas. Save in Vera.

It was too late now. She would not trust him, really, again. But how does one tell? he thought bitterly. You follow your instinct, but the cop in you tells you it's not always to be relied upon. That is one of the things that is vile about this job. The inability ever to trust anyone.

"I beg your pardon," he said formally.

"I'm just so damned accustomed," wearily, "to having advantage taken of me."

12. Against Bad Fortune, a Good Heart

Richard put down the local paper, which said, 'Tragedy strikes again at bereaved family' and said nothing. The face was of bronze too. It wasn't, thought Castang, the face of the Commander come to dinner, about to tip Don Juan down the trapdoor. There was a silence. Castang knew better than to break it. Maryvonne fidgeted slightly with her skirt.

"The one thing," said Richard," that we know for sure, concerning the death of Etienne Marcel, in the present state of the inquiry, is that it was a homicide. If, Maryvonne, please do not scratch your stockings, you fall out of a high window, which if we all fail to control ourselves will be a distinct possibility, what would one do about that?"

"I suppose probably one would start talking about vertigo so as not to upset the relatives. I haven't looked at the statistics about high windows. I suppose there are some somewhere. I'd suspect I think a lot more suicides than were in the book. I wouldn't believe a great many people fell out of windows by accident. I dare say too there are quite a few homicides that aren't on the book because they could never be adequately proved."

"Exactly, and in particular if it were a Czech Prime Minister. If you've finished making faces, Castang, we might have your opinion?"

"What you're saying, at least I suppose so, is that shooting people in the street isn't just homicide, it's a loud noisy proclamation that it's homicide, meant to be, and can't possibly be mistaken for anything else."

"Precisely so. A point that seems to be getting itself underlined. Would you like to go on?"

"If this next death were a homicide it isn't underlined, is that what you're getting at? That if the deaths were linked they're not so by method and the break in the pattern is arresting, but I don't know where the hell I go to next."

"A sadly confused mind: can you do better, Maryvonne?"

"Well, falling out of a window might be anything, but the likelihood would be a suicide. Getting shot is labouring the obvious; there isn't any possibility of anything but homicide. And getting electrocuted in the bath is again on the strong balance of probability an accident: leastways I would suppose so. Has anybody ever committed suicide by such a weird complicated manner? I might wonder, I

77

think, whether a person wanted to mask a suicide, to avoid the stigma, maybe spare pain to the relatives. And, oh yes, I'd look at his life insurance, to see if there was a catch because of them not paying out."

"Now you're beginning to use the brains God gave you. The hypothesis of a homicide did, I presume, cross your mind."

"Well, in general sort of terms. Isn't it a very complicated and elaborate sort of method? Like an English detective story?"

"Particularly if you're in the habit of straightforward simple procedure like shooting people with a huge big pistol?"

"Yes, it isn't a way terrorists would choose, is it?"

"Welcome back, terrorists," said Richard pleasantly, "haven't heard from you in some time. Now, Castang, you're an investigating officer of experience, it says on your dossier. I realize you've been jolted in your domestic tranquility and are vexed about that, but I presume you've given this matter some thought."

"A homicide would depend on two things. Since you're being sarcastic we'll leave out the death-trap mechanisms, the thread attached to the soap dish and so on. A fellow has to be there to heave the electric thing into the bath. Answer, yes, a fellow could have been there; the door was only a spring lock. Firemen didn't break in any bolts or stuff. That is, a fellow could go out, shut the door after him, walk out unobserved onto the street and be in Marseille, probably, before the water leaking alerted the people downstairs. If the judge or someone wants it to be a homicide there's nothing to stop him. I'd think a suicide, masked or not, a hopelessly strained interpretation and if Maryvonne hadn't had the bad luck to leave a card on the bugger the same day nobody would have such a silly idea. Man threatened with police inquiry takes the short way out – it could make tomorrow's headlines if that's what you want."

"And the second thing you forgot to mention while carried along by this tide of eloquence?"

"A homicide in the bath – I'd have to postulate somebody who knew him pretty well. I don't know whether any judge would like the idea of dotting the chap with a soda syphon in the living room, dragging him into the bathroom and happening to notice there was an electric fan on a shelf."

"Go on with that, Castang."

"Because of condensation, I think he was in the habit of leaving the bathroom door open. Postulate a person present who knew him well and was familiar with that bathroom. He was divorced from his wife: as I gather he wasn't living with anyone but he had Friends. Maryvonne didn't get any further, I think."

"He didn't make any secret of it," she said. "I asked in the usual colourless way what about his domestic arrangements, and he grinned amiably and said he led a bachelor existence in the little flat next door to his office. I asked did he object to my drawing conclusions about that phrase and he said he couldn't stop me speculating but he'd object to me prying into his privacy and would make a complaint if he had reason to suppose, blahblah. I left it at that."

"And now he's dead," said Richard with the air of one making a discovery. "You see, Maryvonne, we, or rather the judge, can in this instance make a feint of believing anything we please. Like the next Czech Prime Minister said, maybe the man was on ellessdee and thought he could fly. Anything would do to keep the press quiet, and the Mayor, rather naturally, wants to see me this morning. But in reality . . . Accident in bath, as the Mayor feels, comes a bit pat. As you justly remark, a fellow is not going to commit suicide simply because a police officer walks in and presents a card. Is there even any sign of family upheavals or tensions? – you both say no, and we're left high and dry with terrorists.

"Postulate one or more persons who'd like it to be thought they go shooting people. That they, in secret conclave, decide to make another hit – yes, it's supposed to sound ridiculous. That they would decide to make the next hit Marcel's son – declared the vendetta, what. They then adopt this exceedingly weird way of terrorizing the populace – you're quite right; even the Mayor won't swallow that, even if he's careful not to tread on any soap these coming days.

"But there's one thing, my dear, that I never like to hear in these domestic affairs, of people who fall off step-ladders while hanging pictures and so on. That's the glancing blow upon the head so dear to the story-writers. One may get glancing blows on the head of course; I get them myself from time to time. But if, Maryvonne, you are standing in the bath. Or getting into the bath. You slip, very well. Now whereabouts would you expect to get a nasty rap?"

"Funnybone. Hip, knee, hand. Maybe shoulder."

"That's right; your head is the last thing that's going to collide with a surface, am I right?"

"I did think perhaps that shelf – the one the fan stood on – because it's about the right height."

"How sharp is its edge?"

"There's that."

"I think in your shoes I'd cultivate Professor Deutz at the Pathology Department. Now there's been a seal put on that door, and the judge as you'd expect wants a complement of information. You'll take the technical squad, I'll say a word to Lasserre, and let them do what they can with that flat. Fingertips tell one nothing, whereas the absence of them in a place like that might? This will upset the family – yet another funeral, but this one, I imagine, strictly in private. Your bad luck as well as theirs. Slings and arrows. Against the outrageous fortune, a stout heart.

"I think it as well, Castang, to be quite firm with them about the accident. You don't want them getting hysterical. Maryvonne, you'd better see the secretary or whoever looked after the business in his office, and get what line you can on his playmates. If he was as secretive as his pa . . . if the phone numbers are all in the little book then count yourself lucky.

"Apropos, Castang, this Pony Club idyll you have uncovered . . ." Richard made a coarse joke about Castang's attractions for horsy ladies. Everyone was fond of picturing him with a straw in his mouth and dung-fork at the ready. Lasserre, who disliked him, talked about the bullet-headed little bugger mucking out the stable. Maryvonne, who liked him, laughed a little because he was given to waistcoats and caps, and words like natty and dapper did spring to mind a bit. Castang, who'd never been near a horse in his life and didn't intend to try, was used to it.

"I don't think there's anything in it at all. Another of Marcel's private compartments. But just what she said it was, a place where he could forget his large and at times troublesome family, and all his elaborate systems and personae, and be uncomplicated. She's naturally a gay cheerful person. Likes to laugh, is excellent company, has always a new funny story: I think she suited him very well. Better than a safety valve. If one wanted a generous, open, attractive and kindhearted mistress – I think she deserves to be left in peace, and I should hope Delavigne will agree."

"He didn't have any private papers or stuff out there, Castang, did he?"

"I never thought of looking. Or even asking, I'm sorry."

"I think I'd better make a visit out there in your company. I've had Massip on of course about safe-deposit boxes and the like, and I had an exceedingly boring time with his notary. Several tangled skeins, but no thread of Ariadne. He was given to hidey-holes though, and this might be one. What's her name?"

"Clothilde."

"Why is everyone's mistress always called Clothilde?" enquired Richard.

Castang felt there were enough questions as it was.

13. Hard Day's Night

Everything had been leisurely and orderly and really rather cosy, and there you were again working like a dog and nothing to show for it. The whole morning was just what you'd expect . . . he was late getting in to see Vera.

"She's got to feed the baby," said a nurse severely. "Don't you go exciting or upsetting her now: a child has to be quiet and undisturbed."

Having the Police Judiciaire come heaving up over the horizon, flying a Jolly Roger, always does turn the milk sour: he didn't need nurses to tell him how that went.

"Come and sit down," said Vera cheerfully, unperturbed by his being late. Routine. "I'm in fine form. You don't have to work at amusing me. I've lots of everything, books, chockies; stuff away all day. How's it all going? – tell me what it's been like, without wifey there darning the socks."

"Much as usual. Boringly. Picking up a foot and putting it down again. Boots, boots, boots . . ."

"A soldier musn't ask, must he, what all those pointless manoeuvres are about. Trained not to think about it. He's there for the Defence of the Realm and that's it. Never seek to know who you're defending, or what against."

"Yes; the point about a disciplined body is that it should be disciplined."

"This Marcel . . . I've read the paper of course. The nurses talk about it a lot. I maintain a discreet and disciplined silence. They look at you and simply burst with curiosity."

"Marcel . . . Well, he enjoyed power."

"Power," said Vera, who was decidedly over the hibernating period and wanting again to sharpen her wits, "means having a lot of people anxious to do you a favour."

"Yes. I haven't had much to do with all that. Richard's doing all that in person, having been instructed by the Mayor that the fewer people there are knowing about the corridors of power the better. And thinking likely enough that Castang's a pretty shaky defender of society and had better be protected from nasty surprises. So I got the family enquiry. Which is in a way quite complicated and troublesome enough. The said Marcel was a complex person, who kept things separate. The general idea has been to build up a synthesis of these elaborately arranged personalities in the hope that it will shed light upon persons with an interest in attacking and demolishing him. This side of him shows up well, I'm bound to say. Good to his family, and generous."

"So, or so it's always said, are Mafiosi. Send their beloved daughters to expensive convents, show the utmost faith and devotion to their wives, and cherish their old ancestors. I can't see any difference."

He recognised with pleasure his sharp and sceptical Vera, who had the ferocity of all very gentle people and who generally managed to sharpen his wits while busy sharpening her own. This particular point hadn't occurred to him before. But it didn't do to get excited about it.

"He had a mistress too," lazily. "Quiet, respectable bourgeois woman; she's rather nice."

"He'd no business having one at all: it doesn't improve my opinion of him." There wasn't anything to say to that . . .

The baby appeared, in the classic phrase 'falsely genial in a knitted coat'. The moment it caught sight of him it started to yell.

"Can't stand the sight of me."

"Oh, you look no worse than most fathers," said the nurse; "your main problem is you've got no tit. All right all right, a moment's patience you." It laid hold in a frenzy of greed, with an open hand solidly implanted upon Vera's breast.

"Just look at its great paw," she said fondly. "It will settle down in a minute and then you can talk."

"Wasn't going to talk anyhow with a nurse there. Sit gazing admiringly at all this magnificent arrangement."

"Its main trouble is it drinks much too fast and chokes itself . . . there, what did I tell you," dragging the child away; it let go with a sticky plop and showed symptoms of frustration. "Full of wind now: you stay quiet, you hear, and stop bashing me in that aggressive manner. Yes; go on . . ."

'Sorry," he said, catching a yawn. "There were alarums in the middle of the night."

"What, at home?"

"No no, at work. Another affair altogether," mendaciously, or so he drearily suspected. "Young Maryvonne got into a slight flap and I had to go bail her out."

"Is that the foxy one? I think she's very nice."

"I didn't know you knew her."

"I don't, really. She came to see me with Fausta: I like her. She said she was working with you. Thrilled about that, Fausta says."

"First time she's had a chance to show her paces." Vera could get all sorts of weird notions in her head, but wasn't going to be jealous about policewomen.

"Now sit up, you, and stop falling asleep." Not him – his daughter. He could see the point. He would be all for drifting off with a tit in his mouth right now.

"I'd better go and have something to eat too: my stomach's rumbling something chronic."

"See you have an early night. My dinner'll be coming soon but nothing to offer you. I even lick the yoghurt pot out."

"I'm delighted to hear it. These girls looking after you all right? No nurse, I'm just off; I'll be in this evening. Makes me hungry, you know, sitting admiring that monster shovelling down the steak and chips."

"Can I have some cotton wool?" asked Vera. "I'm all milky here."

Noelle was in bed too, Thérèse had told him sourly. But if he called, she admitted with reluctance, she'd asked that he be sent up to see her.

"Who is it? Oh it's you. No, I want to see you. Open the shutter, would you? Draw the curtain back. I know I'm a sight: I just don't care."

He let fresh air in on all the perfumery. It was raining outside steadily with a moist fresh smell. The rain falling had a calming, incantatory effect.

"No, leave the window open; it'll do me good," sitting up in a lacy nighty. "Chuck me my woolly, will you? No, I'm not in the habit of receiving strange men while in bed: once more, I just don't care." Her face was puffy and patchy, her eyes red. "Take a drink. No, I don't want any. I'll admit I've been drinking, a thing I seldom do. When you rang up in the middle of the night . . . and later when you sent that young woman around . . . this, I may tell you, just about takes away my last resources. I'm going to stay in bed, and I'm going to pray for sleep. No, I wasn't asleep. I thought you'd be coming: I asked Thérèse to tell you . . . I want the true answer to one question. Are these two deaths linked?"

"It's too early to say, and we don't know. The most I can tell you – no, believe me, it's all I know myself – is that it can't be excluded."

"Is there anything that will help you tell?"

"It's barely possible the autopsy will give us some pointer. No, there's always an autopsy in cases of sudden death like this. No, please don't interrupt for a minute; let me make myself quite clear. There's no sign of this being anything but an accident, and it's not unheard of in circumstances like these. I mean a person who has had an emotional shock like losing a close relative in violent circumstances may very easily be carrying unsuspected fall-out from that shock. It happens. One may be distracted or unusually clumsy. Do you understand? There's an accident-proneness, to use a piece of professional jargon, that might not otherwise exist."

"So why an autopsy?"

"You'll read it in the paper and for once it'll be true: in the circumstances of Monsieur Marcel's death we are conducting a routine enquiry into his meetings and acquaintanceships: that's natural, we've been over every aspect of this, you and I. This enquiry is controlled and directed by the examining magistrate, the Judge of Instruction appointed by the Procureur in all cases of homicide. The Judge does not know whether any conceivable link may exist beyond the one I've just mentioned, which the doctor calls traumatic shock and which is just what you've got."

"I know. I'm not calling him; they go ploop-ploop and give you a sedative. Tell you not to drink. I drink very rarely but when I drink I DRINK," yelling. He gave her one.

"This is thus an extension of the same routine. Judge wants a post-mortem. Okay? When I know – this evening

– I'll phone you. Now get some sleep. There is nothing you can do. I'll ask Bertrand to look after the business details for you; is that a good suggestion?"

"Yes it is. Sorry I yelled. Thierry's no use in a situation like this; he just gives way to it. Perhaps you're aware that he is my favourite."

"Yes. Has it any importance?"

"None. He needs me more. Didier – was – always a self-contained character, much the stronger of the two. I don't know why. We've always got on well . . . He was my son, Castang, my son though: you realize that? Oh well, you can't do anything I suppose and neither can I. Wait and see, and suffer it all passively: I'm not good at that. Leave me then, would you? Be a dear and tell Thérèse I don't want anything to eat."

"Where's Thierry?" he asked Thérèse.

"In his room."

"Boozing?" His voice was too knowing and too tolerant, because every bristle on the porcupine rattled menacingly.

"Is that something for you to feel superior and humorous about?"

"No."

"He's in no state to talk. The boy's sick."

"Yes."

"His father and now his brother. Dead people are just like cabbage to the likes of you. Something to poke at with your foot, while looking to see if there'll be more rain. To us – our family. Thierry is a human being, and he takes it hard."

"You, too."

"I stay on my feet. With the help of prayer. I try to do that which is asked of me."

"And I, Mademoiselle, do exactly the same."

Magali opened her front door, looked at him without surprise, said simply, "Come in." She showed him into the living-room, went out again. Bertrand was sitting at a large flat desk in a bay, where you might put the piano if you were inclined, or the television set if you weren't. This was not a musical family, but cultivated just the same: low bookshelves painted white and no television set to be seen anywhere. In the kitchen, where it could infantilize the populace to its heart's content while the children ate their supper.

Bertrand was busy with a few handwritten notes. One has funereal *faire-part* cards printed, and the envelopes typed by one's secretary, but some one does oneself, with a proper pen and not a ball-point.

He looked up.

"Will you forgive me for two moments? Please sit down." Castang sat, studied him, slid idly into day-dream. The look thought proper to ambitious middle management; that formerly found suitable for headwaiters. Nervous and fatigued, knowing and disillusioned; the voice slow and deliberate, the manner elegantly indifferent yet alert to whisk into tense activity at the hint of a vice-president (Marketing) approaching with heavy tread and bilious expression.

Not for them the pathetic eagerness of the juniors, rushing to pull out chairs and click lighters, unfolding starchy napkins with a snap of the wrist, bending forward to catch an abstracted mumble with the smartly-shaved and aftershaved face from which intelligent willingness must never, never be absent because make no mistake, the subject of conversation may sound like a glass of Chablis but it's really MONEY.

'Good morning, John.' This one's name is known, he's been tapped. The rising middle executive is known by the spareness of his speech and waistline, the gentle turn of his head and fine smile in appreciation of a witticism-that-wasn't; his relaxed readiness to speak upon his cue and only then.

'I think you'll enjoy the langouste – it's exquisite this morning.'

Just so too, at the (enlarged) Council of Ministers once a month, will the State Secretary for Posts and Telegraphs remain smilingly alert. He is less important than anybody, barring always the S. Sec. for Former Freedom-Fighters, and nobody gives a farthing for Him. But he is there; admitted to the magic circle. At some moment, a very great man may say 'Now how many phones was it we installed in the Oriental Pyrenees last year' and he must lean ever so slightly forward and unhesitatingly, in low well-modulated perfectly audible voice, deliver the good word.

'Three thousand seven hundred and thirty-one, Mr President.' Lean back very quietly with the silent prayer that is always the same. Loving Jesus, don't let me be on the shit list; let it be someone else's turn to be given Rat Week.

"I beg your pardon once more," said Bertrand politely. His face might in fact be stamped with the rubber goods once you knew, but looked, to the stranger, human. He was the same age as Castang but dressed much better. A cop may be bald, thick, or sweaty, or even smell not very nice. An executive may be none of these things, unless of course he's a technical wizard liable to be hired by the opposition. "You can imagine, this is a very trying day, and these must go off. Magali, surely you can find something to offer Monsieur Castaing." They always make sure to get your name right and very slightly wrong. It was not offensive; nearly everybody with this quite common name is called Castaing.

She had been sitting silently behind him; floated up.

"Nothing, thanks."

"I've been anxious to meet you. Thanks, I don't smoke. Please do."

"Thanks, I prefer these. You know my function and purpose, and you don't need tedious explanations. The judge wants more information as was to be expected. There'll be a post-mortem report by tonight in all probability, and it will confirm the Fire people's report of unlucky combination set of circumstances; of course it is a silly thing to do, having an electric gadget near the bath, but it is an old cramped building. I've just come from Madame Noelle Marcel, who's feeling badly under the weather as was also to be expected, and I've understood that you've taken charge of formalities, which is a weight, simply, off everyone's mind. It is not my superior's intention to create any publicity, any disquiet, any public – or private – rumour. Commissaire Richard, in conjunction with the municipal authorities, is determined to keep all this on an even keel with no inflated emotion, while we see that the admittedly obscure motives for the assassination are disentangled. Authors brought to book, goes without saying.

"My instruction is thus clear, to conclude this – we generally term it a neighbourhood inquiry – as soon as may be without pestering the family. Inescapably, I'm a pest. Since I did not know your brother-in-law, and my colleague had only a superficial meeting with him, I'd be most grateful for as exact a portrait as you feel able to draw for me." Ouf, the hard day. Drawing along, and night would come, and would it be less hard? Kind night, don't bring anything but home and music – chosen by Vera – and plenty of Sleep. But first – Didier.

14. Didier

Bertrand took his time. He settled himself in the armchair – creamy pale leather, nicely chosen to fit his personality; light, modern, uncumbrous, of good design and execution – and crossed his legs.

"Magali, I'm tired, and so are you, and I think we might manage to overpersuade Monsieur Castaing; I suggest a bottle of champagne. To make one thing clear, Inspector, there's nothing I could or would say on this subject outside my wife's presence, so do not be tempted to interpret the notion as a manoeuvre – it isn't. I'll be totally frank, and it may be somewhat bleak, and you can make – will make – your own interpretation. Didier was of course my brother-in-law, Magali's eldest brother: quite a few years between them, not very much in common, and he was a person who confided little in others. Even as I gather in childhood remote, self-contained, and cool. Thanks, darling, will you see to opening it; that will do us all good.

"I've little enough to tell, really. I knew him very slightly, and he did not seek to enlarge the acquaintance. In family gatherings he had the habit of appearing as late as he decently could and staying as short a time as possible. He showed no enthusiasm towards his sister, nor interest in her family; he never, for example, took notice of our children, their births, our anniversaries. If we met him, it was at our father's house. Personal contact was thus at a minimum. In business our paths did not cross: I can recall seeing him on the odd semi-public occasion of a chamber-of-commerce nature. I've never been in his house, he's never been in mine – when we met we both uttered the usual social formulae of artificial cordiality. To say thus that I detested him or he me would be a crude exaggeration: we didn't know one another sufficiently well. You can take it that I didn't like him, and I can take it – I always did take it, without seeking explanation – that he didn't like me. Both Etienne and Noelle were well aware of this, and had too much wisdom, or sense if you like, either to comment or to interfere. With them I've always been on a comfortable footing of mutual respect and cordiality, and wherever the relation touched Magali, of affection. I liked and like them both. Whereas Didier I do not know, and was never curious enough to wish to know..."

"Would you attempt any definitions to the antipathy, which was more instinctive than anything else? Here's to you; I could wish the occasion happier but you understand it's my misfortune as a police officer to be uncomfortably close to disasters."

"It won't cause him embarrassment," said Magali in her low voice, hard but attractive. Yes, in this light you'd call her pretty; even very. And competent; the bottle had been opened without fuss or noise or nonsense about 'a man's job'. "But perhaps it's my rôle to answer. Didier never was an attractive person. Selfish with toys as a child, as I recall, cold at all times, and with our mother's charm but quite without her spontaneity, and our father's quick friendly way without his vitality and genuine interest in everyone. There was always something unpleasantly self-seeking. He had a nice wife. Salome, I always liked Sally and she did her best but he was deplorably insensitive towards her and I had every sympathy when she said firmly she'd had enough. We weren't close and she was too proud to seek sympathy, and didn't confide in me – I've no details. But he did not behave well."

"He remained close to your parents?"

"With ups and downs – on the whole perhaps it's fair to say yes. They weren't too pleased either about Sally, but there was a family loyalty too. With Noelle he always got on well, but he was her eldest son and she never forgot that – to his credit, nor I think did he."

"And his other brother?"

"Their characters are so different . . . Didier was determined not to live in Papa's shadow and held him at arm's length as soon as he was able, whereas Thierry's abiding characteristic is of course his laziness which is colossal."

"What's your view of Thierry?" inquired Castang of Bertrand, whom he was beginning to find sympathetic. Not that his heartbeat was noticeably quickened, but racist tendencies were simmering down to manageable proportions. The man was talking naturally; had unstiffened. It might be the champagne, which should really be classed as a valuable social medicament, and reimbursed by the Sécurité Sociale.

Had he known, Bertrand was thinking exactly the same. Frankly, one had thought earlier that the least this man Richard could do was come himself. Said, by one or two golf-playing acquaintances, to be someone with his head screwed on the right way, who could be trusted to know his way about. Magali's account of this one hadn't been too reassuring. Not perhaps a total farmer; knew how to hold his knife and fork, and wouldn't knock glasses over. But . . . However, it seemed that Richard's collection of rugby-playing barbarians had perhaps an exaggerated reputation. Fellow looked like an orangoutang, but had reasonable manners, if stiff. Had loosened up a lot: a glass of good stuff hadn't been wasted on him. Was sitting back now unwound, with an ankle crossed on his knee like the English . . .

"Thierry . . . in a way I quite like him. I oughtn't to say that, because really he's a barefaced parasite, but he carries it off well."

"Does he do anything at all?"

"He's brains enough. Forever starting things, but never finishes them. Been in half the faculties of the university and out again. A smattering of knowledge in half a dozen subjects, and a clever trick of appearing to know more. He uses people. The truth is that he discovered early on how to sail skilfully in his father's wake and get towed. He does well at that. Did – what he'll do now, I wonder: his father's death will have been a blow to an accomplished parasite. Etienne got him a job once in the administration; he claimed he couldn't work in offices because of an allergy to dust, gave him hay-fever he said. Came up with a doctor's certificate to prove it. Recently he's been adopting a drop-out hippie stance, says he needs nothing and has no use for money. Philosophizing he calls that. He's Noelle's pet, of course; Thérèse adores him; Etienne was absurdly indulgent to his every caprice. Four square meals a day, plenty of comfort, plenty of pocket money. He can be extremely good company when he rouses his wits. I've something of a soft spot for him, which Magali says just shows how he gets away with murder – sorry, that remark was in bad taste, wasn't it. Just the sort of thing that would make Thierry dissolve laughing."

"It wouldn't be quite so funny if it were the truth."

"You can't be serious. If you had a permanent free sleigh-ride, and never had to pay for the horse, you'd see to it that the horse was well treated and got plenty of oats. But I realize of course you were being sarcastic. In fact Thierry's not an uncommon type, and I think quite often met with in families where the father was a self-made man of great energy and push."

"Also he's a gentle and timid creature really," said Magali. "Highly sensitive, as you often find behind a pose of cynicism. He used to write a good deal, and could still I think make a career for himself in that. The hay-fever might have been psychosomatic, but was quite genuine: he couldn't stand the pettiness and materialism of the

Customs and Excise or whatever it was. Lots of people with high ideals pretend to have none."

"I'm idling here, and abusing your hospitality." Polite remarks were made, but no one stopped Castang going.

The technical squad had tidied up and gone. The secretary, with much ostentatious rattle of keys, was waiting impatiently to close the office. She started a tirade about not letting a perfectly good business collapse simply because 'one of the principals' had a tragic accident; Maryvonne, who had come in quietly, winked at him behind the woman's back: a spare bony soul with an improbable bosom, much overdressed and wearing a lot of sexy perfume. Castang told her to sort out the business details with Bertrand, who would be 'administering the estate', got rid of her at last and went to look again round the flat next door. There was nothing much to see. The walls were hung with a lot of dimmish-looking landscapes in Victorian gilt frames. Didier seemed to have been an amateur of this sort of art. Done perhaps a bit of dealing in a small way; he had done doubtless a bit of dealing in anything that came under his hand. The flat was furnished with quite good semi-antique pieces, showed little individual taste, was tidy, neat, and on the whole clean. The technicians, said Maryvonne, had found no striking break in the pattern. She had been trying to find out about women: there were oldish prints of at least two women, and a woman had been on the phone, the secretary said, the day before 'but it might have been a customer'. She kept her trap well shut, said Maryvonne. "Wants to try and carry on by herself, if she can find a 'suitable partner' – there are prints of hers in here; she says she tidied a bit from time to time out of kindness. She slept with him too of course, denies it but I wasn't going to make a thing of it." Castang nodded.

"We'll lock up. These keys can go back to Bertrand tomorrow, in all probability, if Madame Delavigne agrees. Buy you a drink in the pub?" looking at his watch.

"I don't have anybody identified," said Maryvonne. "I think he might have been fooling round with some married woman. I got his ex-wife, I've spoken to several other people in the business, I think I've got a pretty fair pattern of his conduct and general movements, but I'll put it all in the report shall I? – anyhow, not to bore you with it now. This is nice, I could just about use it," taking a gulp. "It seems much like the father somehow; plenty of people with solid reasons for disliking him but no adequate motives for killing him that show. But we've no adequate grounds for a homicide, have we?"

"Don't suppose so. Have to ring Deutz when we get back to the office. Just it doesn't fit. The accident-prone thing would satisfy Delavigne, doubtless, if nothing else shows. Let's try and make it an early evening if we can." Maryvonne took the hint and drained her glass.

"Phone IJ would you?" said Castang, sitting at his own desk and scribbling memos to himself. Colette Delavigne will want a long exhaustive written report, he thought gloomily. Have to do that on the typewriter at home, preferably after supper.

Identité Judiciaire had nothing to contribute. Yes, there were a lot of vague old prints everywhere, kitchen, bathroom, where you like, that hadn't been wiped or polished recently, and the last good clean-up had been some days ago. Fresh ones of the fellow himself, meaning made that day – he didn't wear gloves to make a cup of coffee. But if anybody else had been there, let alone an assassin, well, they'd kept their hands in their pockets. Sorry, Castang, no handy bottles wiped clean.

"God, I hope Deutz isn't gone yet," in a panic hunting for the Pathology Department's number among a lot of scribbles on calendars. "Would you put me through please – Castang, PJ." Professor Deutz was the medico-legal expert, referred to by Richard as 'Our Spilsbury'. He was an eccentric and gifted teacher, and his personal interest in criminology, which was his hobby, made him a source of light a great deal brighter and richer than that of the average staff pathologist in a university faculty.

"Castang. Oh yes, finished ages ago. Not the report, have to wait for that. But you can tell the judge; who is it? Young Delavigne? I don't know her. She can ring me if she's not satisfied, or wait for my girl, who as usual has a

94

mountain to type up. Perfectly straightforward. Cardiac, vertigo, brain arteries – all my eye, fellow absolutely healthy, youngish man. Didn't fall down in a fit. Sober-living too, no heavy meal, no high alcohol level. Stomach wasn't empty; he'd had a bite of bread and cheese to stay the pangs. So you're left with did he slip on the soap. Maybe he did, I haven't seen the bathtub."

"Old-fashioned, enamel worn and rubbed, nothing remarkable either way."

"Hm, makes no odds. If he fell and hit his head on the bath then the bath was upside down."

"Huh?"

"Don't be ridiculous, Castang, of course I paid close attention to the bruise. Bruises are always interesting; come and see me next time you get a black eye."

"I'd be there daily."

"Quite, and your diary would make boring reading. A microscope on the tissue tells one all one wants. Now when you fall and crack your silly head on something lower than waist level you'll find the bruise most pronounced on the lower peripheral area, I'm not going to bother blinding you in technical jargon. Glancing blow going upwards, and if I take a swing at you with a copper saucepan underarm your black eye will show heaviest on the lower edge. Whereas if I grip it like a club and bring it down overarm from above shoulder level – you follow. So if the bath hit him the bath was suspended upside down like it was there to keep the rain off."

"At head height there was a shelf. The electric fan was on the shelf and the shelf jarred loose from old plaster."

"Richard told me about this shelf. How thick is the shelf? Wood is it, or plasterboard?"

"Wood, the usual, two, two and a half centimetre. But I had thought there was a sharp edge but there's not; bevelled round, so no profile. Old hard wood, covered in cracked old varnish; the tech. squad makes nothing much of it. I mean an impact enough to stun someone wouldn't make an impact on the wood; was there any skin lost?"

"No no, it won't do, Castang, your wood. Something slightly rounded yes, there was no sharp edge. But a lot wider in surface than your shelf. The bath would do nicely but sorry, I won't accept that he fell on it. It reared up and downed him."

"Oh fuck."

"Yes quite, I agree completely. But I'd testify in that sense and I'd have slides, photos, the lot to bring into court. It's serious, Castang, you've quite certainly a homicide there. He was bonked, slid down in the water, and the electric shock thing flung in on top."

"And that caused his death, did it?"

"Adequately. The fire-brigade diagnosis is unimpeachable. Electricity deaths they see a lot of, naturally, and all the clinical signs are present. If it hadn't been a PJ job to begin with it might well have passed unnoticed. So a clever homicide, Castang, intelligently carried out."

"Was the bonk hard enough to make him lose consciousness?"

"I wouldn't risk an opinion on that. A solid dose of household voltage produces alterations enough to make much of what went before unreadable. Judging by what we have, it was a dint hard enough to make one see stars and sit down, no more: it didn't come near fracturing the skull."

"Nothing to show he was transported to the bath?"

"The point occurred to me. He wasn't manhandled in any way. It would depend more upon your scenario, whether he was bonked in the next room and hauled into the bathroom. I'd prefer it that there was someone in the bathroom with him but I'm not prepared to say he couldn't have lost consciousness long enough to be hauled about and undressed. With your permission, I'll be on my way home now."

"An ingenious idea," said Castang putting the phone down, "defeated by the perspicacity of Sherlock: a pathologist is about the only real one there is, and Deutz has always been a tremendous reader of detective stories; his office is full of them."

"Ingenious fellow too," said Maryvonne, "keeping as IJ assure us his hands in his pockets. That electric fan, smooth plastic surface, prints would have shown up nicely on that. So you push it off the shelf in a plausible, natural way, with your elbow maybe?"

"We aren't going to get anywhere much along those lines. We'll call it a day; it's knocking-off time. If you want something to be going on with, stick to the classic approach. Once we accept this as homicide, what are the possibilities, I mean the number and likelihood of authors, the probability factor."

"I see, yes – you mean somebody in the bathroom is somebody he would have known, and well."

"And somebody familiar with the bathroom. It isn't very likely somebody invented that gag with the fan on the spur of the moment."

He sat by himself a moment. This is the second full day Vera will have spent in hospital. And am I any further?

15. Boots, Boots . . .

He buzzed Richard's line but there was no answer. He clicked the bar and got the switchboard.

"Raise the boss when you can and give him this message: I rang Deutz about the electricity death, and the medico-legal evidence says homicide. Got that?"

A sort of psychic chemistry took place with Vera. Her antennae were always sensitive; in these circumstances more so than usual. When you are in a maternity clinic, well protected from worrying or upsetting influences, and a cop of all people walks in, you sit up and take notice, because of all the sharp disquieting smells that come in with him. There are disturbing electric currents, to say the least. He did of course his best to be placid and emollient, and made things worse, because she knew at once that events judged unsuitable for the Nursing Mother were getting withheld. She became, quite naturally, cross, edgy and tired, with long jagged silences and sudden mono-syllabic interjections. Brave flows of talk about flowers,

97

weather or the book she was reading fell horribly flat. She summoned resources, to no avail.

"You'd better go home, darling. Whatever bothers you may have, they don't have to include me. I hope that may be some small consolation. I am extremely peaceful and quiet, and concentrating on getting strong as soon as ever I can. I'm doing lots of leg exercises. They want as well to get me up on my feet. The old idea of lying like a log is greatly discouraged. I'll be home very soon, and you can take your days off." He smiled, got up, kissed her, left. What was the use of making a fuss? He went to the supermarket on the way home, cooked himself some supper, watered the plants, went around solemnly with a duster, washed up the supper things, and that morning's breakfast things, with plodding humourless exactitude. He took up the current book, with a ballpoint pen marking the place – he was a massacrer of books, one of those people who annotate in margins and leave lists of page references on the back endpaper – and fussed a good deal making himself comfortable. The television set, its face dusted but no further attention paid it, sneered at him silently from the corner with a hostile unwinking gaze. Stupid cop, it said; intellectual snob. Foolish little man.

There was a loud, peculiar, unusual ring at the front-door bell. He paid no attention to it. It was repeated, bossily. He sighed, got up, pressed the catch, stood waiting to hear whether the lift stopped at his floor. He stood staring vacantly at his door. Good solid door of an old house; thick old-fashioned hardwood. It wasn't armour-plated or anything. Vera had a chain for it, for when she was alone.

The lift stopped; he opened the door. He was considerably taken aback. Of all people, Commissaire Richard had not been expected. Wreathed in a crooked social smile, looking – if it were possible – diffident.

"Hallo, Castang. I dropped in. My wife has gone out to some boring function." Richard never mentioned his wife. Come to that he never dropped in. This was all so wildly out of character as to be breathtaking, but he wasn't going to be breathtaken. Richard, who had never been here before, looked about with approval at the high old room with vaguely Greek motives, acanthus leaves or something, in blackened stucco on the ceiling, at handmade rugs on the floor, at Vera's drawing board and windowboxes, at pictures, most of them her drawings and some hung to hide bad bits in the tatty wallpaper. Finally he sat down and looked at Castang. "I got your message, incidentally." Yes, of course it was business that brought him here. He hadn't brought any flowers . . .

He was dressed in his clerical dark grey suit, rather tight, a bit precious, generally a hint that he was in a fussy, niggly mood. The skin of his face was smooth and fine as usual, with a healthy colour and a slight tan on the bridge of the nose; his straight silvery hair, fine in texture, unruffled. Looked in fact much as usual. But the thin lines were sharper, deeper than ordinarily. And he had always an upright carriage: when he walked in had he been round-shouldered? Yes, undoubtedly. Richard was looking older than he did as a rule. In fact he looked like an old cop; to wit an old bastard. The word, certainly, was 'unusual'. Monsieur le Commissaire Divisionnaire, who looked at all times like the brisk and mordant businessman of mature years and incisive judgement, was looking knocked about.

"You feel like a drink?"

"Yes. No. All right, yes." He was wearing his gold-wire reading glasses, over which the china-blue eyes stabbed shrewdly at Castang. He took them off and tucked them in his pocket: he'd done enough reading.

"Another day spent snuffling into municipal politics. I've done a lot of it. It doesn't come new or anything. Mistake, to believe one might uncover complicated turpitudes. They exist, to be sure. Much like those you'll find anywhere, but in no greater quantity or flagrancy.

"Corruption? It is now difficult to ascribe a precise meaning to this misused word. Marcel was no more corrupt than anybody else, on the whole.

"The stuff out of the code, corruptly inducing for gain or interest – knowingly uttering or accepting – uttering or altering the written word knowing it to be false – tja, what

99

does everybody do, all the time? Little vanities or impor-
tances, that's the fabric of municipal politics, the game
of little clans and alliances, the preservation and promotion
of self-interest. Just like everybody else . . .

"Well, we've uncovered nothing, Massip or I.

"Nonsense all this is. Obviously, the mayor didn't have
any choice. Neither did I. Fellow gets assassinated like
that, you're bound to look for scandals. Frightful big hole
in the football club treasury; shameful feeling-up of choirboys; illegal abortions of thirteen-year-old choirgirl, what.
In short, something for the press.

"There isn't, of course. Etienne Marcel was an astute
and experienced official, who took pains not to get dipped
in any scandals. And took pains that none of his associates
should either.

"Of course there's any amount of what makes the wheels
go round. Semi-public or semi-private featherbedding and
barrel-rolling. Incompetence winked at, nepotism indulged. A brisk trade in tiny items of knowledge. Pilferage
of paperclips. I could go on for weeks tugging at who gave
the order for sixteen hundred litres of paint flagrantly unsuitable for its designated use. Who altered the specifica-
tion, who juggled procurement forms, how much paint
was used, and where's the rest?

"Petty dishonesty: but what we're looking for is a man
with a gun. Not a finger in a porkbarrel; a finger on a
trigger. I couldn't give a rap about the fellow having gold
in a Swiss bank or shares in a holding company in Liech-
tenstein. Why the hell would there be any integrity in these
ward-heeling affairs? Is there any integrity in national
politics? No, of course there isn't. Is there any difference
between the seven sisters flogging oil to Rhodesia and a
procurement form for three hundred and fifty wastepaper
baskets? Less interest involved, so if Mr Veesohn didn't
get shot why the hell should Marcel?"

Since this was roughly twenty times as long as any
speech Richard had ever been known to make, Castang
was puzzled. If he made tirades, they were at Fausta, about
telephone calls or his tea being cold. They lasted fifteen
seconds.

"I've gone back," said Richard in his normal voice, "to the essential physical facts in this killing, to the technical inquiry carried out. None of it tells me much, and nothing's come of it."

"Didn't Cantoni find any terrorists, then?" tactfully.

"Found far too many; the word's a meaningless platitude. We could fill Fresnes prison with what we've got. Officially there aren't any: Special Branch will tell you blandly there are a few loony lefties. Doesn't want attention drawn to them, on the perfectly sound grounds there's nothing they like better than free publicity. The Minister isn't keen on terrorists at all, having declared openly that this is not a French form of amusement. It's as though they got turned back by the Customs, at the Italian end of the Mont Blanc tunnel. You see the hole I'm in? What they're really afraid of is that machine-gunning politicians might become a popular sport, something like skateboarding. Little notices would be going up: Assassinations on the Public Footway will be punished with a fine of fifty francs. Exactly like rinsing out oil tankers."

"You mean otherwise one would have to build gigantic concentration camps?"

"That's it: a use found at last for the abattoirs of La Villette, the Lorraine steelworks, the Château de Rambouillet and numerous other monuments to national prestige."

Richard frustrated, Richard in his nutmeg-grater mood, launching sarcasm to 'ginger up the peasantry' was quite a common occurrence. A safety valve for both boredom and hazard: as he had been heard to say, the Royal Navy grew great on rum, buggery and the lash. Scurrilous pamphleteering in no way endangered governments, nor relaxed the bonds of discipline. It was indeed a carefully controlled performance, and trodden-down underlings could relieve their feelings by saying 'Have you heard Richard's latest?' In much the same fashion, the *Canard Enchaîné* is read, and quoted, with the most fervour by the employees of government departments.

What was new, unheard-of, not to be thought of in the office, and not to be tape-recorded, was Richard staying all evening, Richard drinking a lot, and between long silences Richard carrying on a long monologue, sprinkled with scraps of conversation with a subordinate who – or so Castang thought – wasn't even there half the time.

"How old are you, Castang? Thirty-three, -four? . . . Good age to be, mm . . .

"Good age to retire. Like an athlete. Jacques Anquetil was thirty-four. How old I wonder is Gareth Edwards?

"No, the point is that if you go on longer than that you risk becoming pathetic. You know too much but you've no punch left. And the government sends you back to school, to be recycled. And of course indoctrinated. Renew your vaccinations, lest you catch the very fatal disease of thinking for yourself. Mm, dangerous age . . .

"I haven't pulled your file in a long while. Full of stuff about your small arms proficiency, your tendencies to paranoia. Let's see though, you've a master's certificate, right? And you're still second mate, on the good clipper ship under Master Mariner Richard. And you're not anxious for command of a coasting steamer carrying coal between Fishguard and Rosslare: well, I understand . . .

"But you want more. And you're a family man now.

"I'd not recommend any son of mine to become a cop, now. What, if you're really anxious to work evenings, week-ends, and other people's holidays become a cook. In Switzerland, naturally. It's airy now, and hygienic. Not even as hot any more. You've seen these magic stoves that don't give out any heat? And the money's excellent. Somebody asks your profession, you say Gourmet. Kiss enough behinds and get your prices up high enough you might get asked to lunch with the President of the Republic. That's a thing never happened to a cop yet. You have that perfume of money being made. Whereas a cop of course, the day a Minister comes to lunch is the day you're laid out in your coffin.

"So that in five years' time, when I'm gone, you'll still be under forty.

"Stay till then and you're up shit creek. Too young on the one side and too old on the other. Though you needn't think you'll be stuck with Lasserre. He'll get his step, and he'll be sent to command the convict hulks at the Ile de Ré.

"You assume that I keep him and cherish him because every department head needs a real bastard as his enforcer, and childish as it may seem, you're quite right. Lasserre is my Haldeman and my Ehrlichman. One also needs several Gordon Liddys: you're well acquainted with them.

"With money, of course, you can do anything you like with the French.

"When I was a boy I wanted to go to Spain. We had a Popular Front Government then. Great, I thought: we'll whip in there. We didn't, as you know. Non-intervention has been the name of the game for too much of my life. My generation, Castang, is like the SS, we have a tattoo on our armpit we never get rid of, and ours says 'Munich'. And the police commissaire of Munich, that's me.

"Oddly enough I met the real one once. Interesting man . . .

"Spain was the country to belong to. Still is, oddly enough. It would be sentimental to say that they at least don't get down on their knees for half a crown. It is fair though that there are some who don't."

Bemused, Castang still understood several things about Richard's house, and about the mysterious Madame Richard, who was never seen and was reputed not to speak French after thirty years in the country.

Most shattering of all; was Richard getting coolly drunk?

"In its natural resources, Castang, this is the richest country in Europe. The most varied, the most beautiful, the most balanced. The ideal marriage between north and south. Is it on that account that we are the most mediocre?

"The curse of futility is upon us. The General knew that, secretly. It's the explanation, I believe, of the strain of hysteria in him. He needed badly to believe that we were worth something, and he had such contempt for us, and so justified.

"In fact we have plenty of talents, including some very good ones, if we were allowed to settle into our component parts. That's right; our antique provinces. We haven't been allowed to do anything worth doing, for five hundred years now.

103

"But take a look, Castang, at some of our best-known Patriots, hammering and screaming with their veins standing out about the Nation, and notice how hard they have to scream, because it sounds thinner and more unconvincing with every month that passes.

"It's argued that Germany or England rival us in mediocrity. Don't believe it.

"Our twin qualities, of vanity and avarice – they're very unattractive you know.

"This town – of course it's far too big. Anything this size, anywhere, it's the pest and the cholera combined, in permanent, endemic state. But it's a natural, old, good provincial capital. I wish there was something I could do for it. Our tragedy, in the PJ, is that we're nothing. We're the agents and slaves of a centralised apparatus. The Nation. Which doesn't deserve to exist, and doesn't in fact exist. We're nobody. Hated by the people, as we deserve, treated with contempt by Paris, as we deserve, underpaid little informers, dressed in shoddy clothes, armed with shoddy guns, with shoddy little minds. We do nothing, Castang, but keep in power a crew that isn't worth powder and shot.

"We're the Guardia Civil, and that's just our speed. We're – just barely possibly – less bad than we were.

"Keep that in mind, boy. That's your job. Try to leave things less bad than they were.

"Well, thanks for the drinks. A pleasant evening that: a gossip from time to time."

Castang watched him go, strolling loosely along the street to where he had left his car. Drunk? Not a bit of it. Monsieur Richard was as always; perfectly self-possessed.

16. Reorientation

Polish those boots, boy, and examine them for roadworthiness, because there's no discharge in the war.

Castang, dapper, was met by a summons to Richard's office. Richard this morning very dapper. A new suit, of a creamy beige colour like oatmeal, a gay tie, a clear healthy eye, an air of just having had his hair cut.

Present Lasserre, with a lot of horribly healthy flourishing hair, blue-black and shiny, needing cutting; neck full of Assyrian curls. Unshaved, would look like the Guardia Civil. Overshaved, as he always was, and smelling strongly of attar of roses or something equally Bulgarian, looked like a colonel in the KGB. His suit the colour of the blue in the French flag, a perfectly hideous shade.

Present Cantoni, hair dry, brown, wavy, here and there in tufts, looking as though he'd had a fight with a Harridan who'd pulled a lot out. Tight pursed wicked mouth; quick roving blackish-grey eye. Muscles loose and ready: a dodgy rapid sidestepper, a clever elusive runner. Looking as sinister as Gravedigger and Coffin Ed rolled into one, and armed with both of their guns. A good man to have on your side in a scuffle: you wouldn't worry at finding him behind you. Chocolate brown suit with little white lines, rather dressy.

Present – a rarity – Massip-the-Fraud, in pale grey, looking like a banker: his protective colouring was almost perfect.

Present the Secretary, a model of discretion, who never lost files and always knew who'd had how much leave. Big broad shoulders, huge in a scratchy great tweed jacket with leather elbow patches, and a dreadful knitted tie. Pockets full of pencils, erasers, calculating machines: a deep trustworthy gruff voice.

Present – rather oddly – Liliane, the senior of the

women. Tough well-shaped legs, broad Polish shoulders, massive bosom husked in an iron brassière, square humorous face and springy dark curls, pretty grey eyes and a Lille accent. Short pudgy hands, hard. Our Karate Queen.

Present finally, and everybody had been waiting for him, Castang the Bookmakers' Friend, neat rather than small, not really in the least like a jockey; no smaller than Cantoni but more compact and not quite so like a chimpanzee.

"Late," said Lasserre.

"Had his bicycle pinched again," said Cantoni.

"Let's be grateful," said Richard, "that we don't have to listen to the minutes of the last meeting. To come straight to the point, in this matter of Marcel, we've got nowhere. On the ground, nothing; some ejected cartridges of which we can only say that they're a common make and belong to no weapon that's on the central file. Professional in that whoever loaded them left them wiped clean. Gun fairly old, rifling somewhat worn, but clean and well cared for.

"The car used tells us nothing either. Every indication is that it was lifted there because it wouldn't be missed for some time; further that it was a commonplace model that would attract no attention. No handy prints, threads, loose buttons or any of those comforting short-cuts. We did perk up a little at finding some sand, until learning that the owner's brother-in-law had been mending his garden gate.

"No clear description of the two men concerned at the scene, and none where the car was left: at the airport of course nothing was noticed. It was in the car park half an hour; we recovered the ticket. We have thus nothing but obvious premeditation, a planned conspiracy, an ambush. Carries a death sentence; much good may it do us.

"Marcel's movements tell us nothing either. They picked him up at one or another of his well-known haunts, followed him around till a good opportunity was present, and made a thorough job. He does not appear to have known or recognised the gunman, according to our eye-witnesses, and seems to have been taken by surprise. He himself had received no threat, showed no sign of anxiety or preoccupation, had been behaving normally, made no break in habitual patterns on that day or those preceding. One can say that all the routine threads of approach break off short in the hand. Any comment or question so far?"

"His mail? Or phone messages?"

"At his office of course it all went through his secretary: he had only an interphone direct and an outside line goes through the switchboards and through her: normal shield against the importunate. Mail marked personal, confidential or whatnot she put on his desk, and he went through it with her. He was a careful man, and experienced: he kept every scrap of writing.

"Mail and messages at his home passed his wife, who saw nothing attracting his or her attention. We're short once again of any handy cliché like ash or torn-up envelopes. At the pub he got plenty, especially local people who knew him. We can't thus say categorically he got no letter or message, but we can say that everything passed through other hands first. I'm not giving any weight to this point.

"Incidentally he had a hidey-hole – Castang, did he get letters there?"

"I didn't think of asking."

"Check on it, though," making a note. "Right, finance next. No unusual payments either made or received: no peculiar or unnaturally complicated dispositions. Once more, careful and prudent man, who kept everything, took witnesses to transactions, knew how to protect himself. This takes away, naturally, a promising line of inquiry, or what seemed so. Bank, notary, advocate, everything sewn up. Anything to add, Massip?"

"Careful, and quite naïve, or should I say unsophisticated. He didn't try anything tricky. Bought a few shares but didn't dabble. Bought a bit of gold. Nothing speculative. No trouble with tax. He wasn't rich. Plenty came in, but plenty went out. House cost him a packet, and he was openhanded. He made cash deals, like everyone, so that they would go untraced, but nothing that would arouse comment. I can sum it up: he wasn't a manipulator in that sense. He wasn't even much interested in money, nor

107

clever with it. He could have got a lot more milk, if he'd tried. The deals are standard, such as any adviser would recommend, and in fact did: all his business connections confirm. He was interested, and skilful, in the traffic of human beings, in influence, information, contacts. But money – no."

"Multifarious doings," Richard took up, "official or semi-official. But in none of them do we find a financial interest as such. He liked to be a queen bee, a key figure. Would scatter little favours, football tickets, a word in someone's ear. In return, his car would be fixed or his plumbing mended, it's fraudulent in the sense that when he was handed a bill he got a ruddy great discount. Some fraud . . . which of us stays out of jail?" It got a snigger round the table.

"As for vice – the Mayor's been rather puritanical about that. Fabre, in confidence, put through a trace. Negative: neither boys, children nor decorative stimuli. One wouldn't have expected any: he wouldn't have lasted as long as he did. Ditto gambling. None of this surprises me. It wouldn't be in the pattern. A prudent man, and secretive, but balanced, extrovert, no oddities.

"What are we left with? The terrorist thing . . . there's been a lot of dotty anonymous mail, but nobody claims credit, seeks to build on it or try to make leverage out of it. We've a blank, and DST say there's nothing in it. We've thus a general loss of momentum. Fantasy begins to reign: the mayor sits there in his office, reads terrible stories about people left weltering in their gore in bars in Marseille, and rings me up with dark tales about Settlement of Accounts. He begins this fearful screenplay of the hired gun riding into town with the cold eye and the slow voice. You may all snigger: I have to listen to stuff like that. What Accounts? – I don't know of any. To which he replies by urging me to go out and find some. I may remind you that while the Mayor is a clown he has too many friends in Paris to be treated like one. We're under pressure; I may tell you strong pressure. We've got to start again with what we have, in the light of any new fact, and have we got a new fact? Castang?"

"New in the sense that the Mayor doesn't know yet that the death of the son of night before last is homicide." At which, suddenly, the conclave woke up and conversation became general.

"The judge doesn't want the fact made public at present."

"We've nothing to base it on but expert opinion in the path. lab."

"The expert opinion – crackpot theories of Deutz . . ." Lasserre.

"What's this? – one fellow's shot in the street, and another's sliding about on the soap in the bathroom?" Cantoni, moustache bristling.

"Yes, there's a complete break in pattern."

"Look mate, the first is professional, right? This Marcel gets shot, and we're all high and dry? No amateur is going to do that. Then you come along with this, which is straight out of Agatha Christie, and you expect us to believe they're connected?"

"What you mean," Liliane said, "is they're connected by happening within the same family."

"Yes. Why should Marcel be killed? – I mean Etienne. We haven't the remotest idea. Why should Didier be killed? – a question nobody's had time to ask yet. As a revenge killing? That he was in some way behind his own father's death? And somebody guessed it, or knew it? Or found it out? That too far fetched? Would it account for the break in the pattern?"

"Or a quarrel with accomplices, since there obviously was more than one? A falling-out, say over money?"

"I've never heard of anything as crappy as this," said Lasserre disgustedly.

"That doesn't interest me," Castang said. "If we've two unsolved homicides, the pressure on us is that much greater, and if the explanations are crappy, that's too bad for the explanations. Sure, the super Criminal Brain is a bad comic strip. Any second now one of us will drop dead, and it will turn out to be South American arrow poison. There may be more than one person involved."

"Terror Reigns in Concarneau! "

109

Richard had had enough.

"That'll do. The inquiry takes on a new dimension, the inquiry must be put on a different footing. In consequence reorientate. The fact clear to me is that there's a family connection. I want the scope extended beyond the immediate circle. I want to know who they see; when, why, how. Without their being aware of it. Two light surveillance teams: now who have we got?"

"I've nobody to spare," said Cantoni.

"No; we don't want all this respectable crowd suddenly noticing they've acquired gorilla bodyguards. Castang, you plainly take charge of one; you've Maryvonne anyhow, now who else: Lucciani?"

"He's busy with that false numberplate fiddle," said the secretary.

"Well take him off it. We know all about it and it has no great urgency. And where's Orthez?"

"Back tomorrow."

"I'd rather have Orthez – he's a great deal brighter than he looks."

"Unlike some we know," muttered somebody; Lasserre probably.

"Liliane, you for the other. Maryvonne can brief you on the clan. You take Lucciani then, who's useful enough, and Davignon, who knows what he's at, and you coordinate this, Jean."

"Exactly."

"Davignon has done the paperwork for the judge, Castang, and Massip will brief you on the financial file. I'll talk to Madame Delavigne, and I'll talk to the Mayor. How long I can stall him for . . . I repeat; there's something there. Get hold of it."

Castang was thinking that Vera would be out of the clinic in another two or three days, and what about his time off? It was no misfortune to be on good terms with Liliane.

There wouldn't be much chance to get over to the clinic this morning. He'd have to give them a ring.

"What about a cup of coffee, Liliane?"

110

17. Light Surveillance

Much like a lightly-boiled egg. As light as you choose: exactly how light that is you will see when you come to eat it. When the police speak of holding so-and-so under observation the impression you receive depends pretty well on how many spy stories you have been reading recently.

A few hints are conveyed by the word 'light'. Not around twenty-four hours: that's 'intense' and needs three separate shifts; and all police forces are parsimoniously administered, and chronically short of manpower. It is indeed possible to recall off-duty staff and wring out a lot of largely unpaid overtime. Reasonably, the police has small stomach for this, and no officer in his right senses will order it more often than he has to. The fuzz in question will be cross, sleepy and not at its brightest. When you come to think of it most people (outside spy stories) have work to do, and most of their activities can be encompassed between eight in the morning and midnight. That is quite enough for two shifts, thanks, especially when you think of rotating them; and Sundays; and days off. Spy stories don't bother about that detail, but secretaries of police departments had jolly well better.

Light means not leaning on people: the surveilled aren't supposed to notice. There exist plenty of ploys like the 'open tail' where Dingus Is supposed to notice, and get all uneasy about it, but they depend on the controlling officer's discretion, and the beginnings of discretion, as Richard would say, begin with being discreet.

It will probably mean a tap on the phone, but not a bug planted: microphones and transmitters and stuff mean breaking-and-entering, and all sorts of procedures illegal unless ordered by an instructing magistrate, and he'd be a bit uncomfortable at its coming out in court unless he can talk loudly and emphatically about the Safety of the Realm.

In principle it calls for one agent at a time, with a flexibility about relaying and replacing same, and see note about My Free Sunday. This agent is there to observe, and log what he observes: she and he are supposed to use their common sense about meals and going for a pee.

It can be lifted off a subject who has plainly settled to a humdrum occupation, and moved to another. It is not, in fact, enormously ambitious. The essential aim is that of all police work: to establish a pattern, after which variations in that pattern attract a certain interest. Most people vary little in their patterns: hence the observation that life in Paris, that thrilling city, boils down to Metro – Boulot – Dodo; in London – Bore, Snore, and Stanmore. Or as the diarist put it: Got Up, Washed, Went to Bed; with the note on the third day 'Did not Wash'.

Lastly, light surveillance takes some time; a fortnight at least. This was achieved by Commissaire Richard explaining at some length to the Mayor that the enquiry was like the Bakerloo Tube: it had to go underground before popping out in daylight. To the Press, that printing anything further in attempts to whet public greed for sensation was contrary to the interests of justice. To the examining magistrate, Madame Delavigne, not only explaining that this was a good idea, but persuading her that she'd thought of it herself.

Light surveillance to Castang meant in fact not more than two or three days, which was not enough to show up anything at all interesting. After that, Vera was released from her clinc and came home proudly with the baby dumped in her lap, trembling a bit because this was rather a responsibility (there'd always been some nurse or another frigging about with it, annoying her considerably, holding it upside-down, shoving safetypins into its defenceless flesh, and so on; treating it in general with the utmost callousness and brutality, as professional nurses always do).

Castang pressed with the greatest resolution for his days off; got them with no trouble. There didn't seem to be anything much happening anyhow. He'd set up his scheme, and it was working smoothly.

With Liliane he had no problem. Since she came from Lille (her real name was Agnes) they drank lots of cups of coffee together. She was suspected too of going round her highly-polished flat with felt soles on (known in France as skates) but this might have been an exaggeration. Certainly the flat was full to the brim with potted plants climbing and writhing everywhere: you can see them through the lace curtains, said Maryvonne ('I swear it'). She was a good deal liberated, but so, Vera-trained, was he. Cantoni was an unliberated oaf, but what did you expect of the Intervention brigade? Lasserre is a phallocrat pig. Massip dips his dick in the inkwell to write with. But being Polish she was a believer in hard work and Christian charity, and Castang found her good to work with.

Maryvonne he'd got keen on; conscientious, observant and patient, a good cop. And brief readable well-written paperwork. Having two women – however liberated they were they understood what it meant having a baby – was a great help when it came to being missing.

The three men he knew of course well, and could appreciate their various talents. Davignon both quietly spoken and taciturn; nearly his age, and ambitious. Had susceptibilities you had to know about. Studious. Sleepy in the mornings, at his best in the evening. Experienced, and reliable; would be getting his step soon.

Lucciani, sleepy both in the mornings and the evenings, but given to sudden bursts of interest, energy and inventiveness at odd moments. Results irregular, said his dossier ('en dents de scie' which is expressive). A Southerner from Nice; intelligent, vain, sly. Talked enough to make up for Davignon; worse he was a tale-bearer, a back-biter and gossip-shop. But he had good qualities, too.

Orthez was a good cop because constantly surprising and unexpected. Looked a dolt, mostly acted like one; thick, tactless, woodenly insensitive. A gifted mechanic, and the best driver in the department. It was not a recommendation in Castang's eye: an interest in cars is a classic sign of a sub-normal intelligence, and Orthez could both look and act maddeningly sub. He often smelt not very nice, too. How had he ever passed his examinations? – the examiners must have got the papers muddled. Learning how unsafe, facile and stupid this opinion was had been a lesson in humility for Master Castang. Orthez could sometimes be much brighter than he was. He had Vera-like characteristics too: modesty, simplicity, common sense and sound judgement. A terrific worker, with tenacity, staying power. *Ausdauer* as the Germans say: he came from Carcassonne and looked like a bullet-headed Bavarian, particularly in dark-blue blazers, to which he was given in the summer months.

Surveillance, if to be continued any length of time by a limited group, means a good deal of masquerading. The cops do not dress up in disguises more often than they can help, and not as much as the public imagines, but a bit of camouflage is desirable. The personage with the dirty raincoat and the large flat feet, ostentatiously reading the racing news in crowded doorways, will not do. One has thus a couple of people on the technical squad, known as the artists, who are given a small amount of money and urged not to be too tricky. It shows up first in the cars used by the department. Beside the ordinary workhorses, medium-sized, solid unimaginative things of the Peugeot-station-wagon type, there is a litter of small tatty cars fixed so that their bodywork comes easily to pieces. Known in France, charmingly, as 'banalised'. There are one or two souped-up but most are, as the name suggests, designed not to attract any notice from anyone. If you are in a small grey mongrel Renault, with a few lengths of metallic piping on the roofrack, and a plaque on the side saying something unreadable and preferably unpronounceable, like say Chomfieh s.a.r.l. Technical Supplier, you can hang about anywhere without being asked your business. But the Artists are perpetually put to it to invent new ones, and must keep a repertory in hand, and be flexible. What will do nicely in a crowded city street would stick out like Fred Karno's Army in the leafy residential avenue. Start mucking about with the gas mains outside the Algerian Embassy, and you will become aware of this.

Above all be simple. The Red Faction stopped Schleyer's

114

car by pushing a pram in front of it. Avoid complex and ingenious technicalities. That black man with the nice face, in 'Mission Impossible' who is never seen without a swarm of conjuror's contraptions–he has a lot to answer for.

If Castang wanted gadgets, Lucciani, who had a childish passion for them, was handy : a great setter-up of infra-red binoculars, cameras in wrist watches, and tape-recorders in Gitane packets. And most technical squads contain someone with a taste for electronic doodads. Why have some cop outside the garage door all night, probably in the pouring rain, when a thing the size of a cigarette-butt will tell you all you want to know?

Castang, with no interest and small talent for gadgets, was mistrustful. He was sure that the thing, having once been dropped on the floor, would when activated have no effect whatever save to set off all the air raid sirens in the entire municipal area. But it was nice sometimes when Lucciani said, "I know a better way of doing that." His little repertory would have been bigger but that whenever he dashed in all excited with one of his catalogues the controller would make a prim mouth and say 'Too dear'.

His own instinct was to keep the affair very light-handed indeed. Better, to his mind, to miss a few things almost certainly trivial, than jar someone's funnybone. These are intelligent, observant, wary people. The whole of Etienne Marcel's family has had some training in prudence, discretion, carefulness, indeed quite a considerable wiliness, he dared say. Even the pretended naïvetés of such as Clothilde ('I'm a born pigeon; walk wide-eyed into everybody's gluepot') were to be taken with a big discount. 'If you want a good folklore phrase, the soup isn't eaten as hot as it's cooked.' On the likes of Noelle and her children were few flies. And one could not tell – in or around these cosy set-ups there is possibly a connection with some cool and cunning types. Otherwise what's the point of this operation? Don't let's forget, two people have been killed . . . And they know the police take a certain interest.

As for him, he had surveillance to do at home. At night too. That baby howled. Lucky the walls were thick, and as far as he knew there were no electronic ears a-listen.

18. Coming up for Air

"You're moving very well," said Castang admiringly. He himself was moving awkwardly, clutching the baby, a sleepy bundle rolled up in shawls and not objecting so far to this bony male presence, and with Vera's overnight bag dangling from a couple of spare fingers.

"Don't grip it so hard. It's this lovely empty belly. And being dressed again after so long. Morale is extremely high." Vera had her stick, and was pottering down steps gingerly, but with unusual freedom. The cramped stiff hobble that had been her lot since learning again to walk at all was now a walk. Halting, but a walk. "And I've been exercising like mad. Scandalised the nurses rather; always coming in and finding my bottom up in the air but old Paddy was thrilled." This was her gynaecologist, whose name was Patrice. She got in the car unaided too, holding out her arms and saying," Shove her over to me."

"Even so, unusually well," getting in beside her. "Are you all healed up?"

"There was a horrid moment when Paddy took the stitches out and fiddled interminably with my fan. But that's all very muscular you know, vaginal wall and I don't know what besides and it healed up like one o'clock."

"Your back," moving the car through traffic," I find it less locked."

"Yes, well, it was supposed to be a surprise but there's no keeping anything from the observant Detective. Not even one's fan. The fact is there are things I couldn't do before. So Paddy phoned Rab." Professor Rabinowics, a surgeon of a complicated and technical orthopaedic kind, had treated Vera after her accident. "And Rab came, and said God moves in mysterious ways, and so does the spine, and having a baby is sometimes even better than having a wonderful clean-out and he'd seen it before but one

116

couldn't bet on it, and all round you'd think it was him who'd been so clever and not us."

"But what exactly happened?"

"Oh, some nerve endings got unblocked or something. Very technical and I hadn't wanted to tell you till we got home."

"We are home," parking the car and getting the bundle back, which yapped faintly and then fell asleep again.

"How nice it all does look," she said happily. He had scrubbed everything, done his best with flowers – there was still an armful in the back of the car – and whitewashed a ceiling he'd 'never had time for'.

It was an old house, on a street called a quay because it overlooked a disused canal, with poplar trees and a former towing path. A bourgeois house and too expensive for an inspector of police, but having nobody on the far side meant quiet, as well as having trees and water, and quantities of rusty old iron beyond, whose colours Vera liked, and a neglected railway siding, and a general air of industrial decay, and the sun going down to one side. This was all well worth the money, when one has a wife who can't get out much.

Their flat was on the third floor, small and awkward, with the kitchen in a former passage. They had three rooms, two of them small, and a bathroom quite as antique and cranky as that in which Didier had been found. Across the landing lived the landlady, a thin and energetic widow who kept a close eye on her property. This was certainly a big black spot. But the rooms had balconies, and a lot of windowboxes, and the baby would be put out there to air, between the chives and the geraniums. These gave the house a gay look, said the landlady: by acquiring merit in this way Vera had earned small indulgences.

Inside, too, a strong personality had asserted itself. The furniture had all been bought in fleamarkets, until the moment when these got delusions of grandeur and started charging antique-shop prices. Chairs with no bottoms and disembowelled sofas. Vera didn't care, and had taught herself clumsy but efficient upholstery. As long as the frames

117

were solid wood, so that one could hammer tacks in, and a good shape. The latest was a large old-fashioned cot, and a high chair with by God a real abacus to play with. Castang who had spent groaning hours sandpapering all this started by being obstructive but ended up excited. There was even a cradle, with rockers. All too Brother Grimm for words, since already she had a rocking-chair. "All you need now is a spinning-wheel," groaned Castang, who was sick of hearing about her Czech granny's ingenious arrangements ('wasting good shit like that; go out and do it in the currant-bushes').

"There seem to be a great many flowers," said Castang, seeking jamjars, "and these are still quite fresh."

"Rab had some sent, which I thought rather touching," all a-beam and rocking the cradle, with the object in it, with her foot; it seemed to enjoy this, after all the clinical hygiene, "and Colette Delavigne brought more."

"I wondered whether she would."

"And an immense surprise."

"Who?"

"You'll never guess."

"Oh, stop it."

"Madame Richard."

"No!"

"Stop saying no in that imbecile way. I say, could I have a drink, or would it make Lydia pissed?"

"A spot won't do her any harm. Is her name Concepcion, or Encarnacion?"

"Stop being so silly."

"Then stop saying stop."

"Her name is Judith and she's perfectly sweet. She's shy and doesn't utter much, and her voice is barely audible."

"But do you speak Spanish?"

"This is bullshit, she speaks perfectly good French with less accent than I do, and I'm sick of this rubbish about nationalities, there's no earthly difference between being Czech and being Spanish. She was terrified of being indiscreet, and Richard isn't allowed to know, but she heard something from him and screwed up her courage and rang Fausta to know where I was."

"That cow Fausta never let on."

"No, and she won't either. And just look at what she, I mean Judith brought," rummaging in her bag. She unwrapped tissuepaper and there was a battered toy of rococo silver. One end was a grip of mother of pearl that a child could clutch and shove in its mouth – how many had not cut their teeth on it? The silver end was a whistle. Attached to this should have been five tiny bells, but two were missing.

"Oh, that's nice," said the sentimental father, all set to experiment and see what the baby did with it. Vera stopped this.

"Too tiny – shove it in its own eye. In a few weeks. It's a coral-and-bells, and it's made by a gipsy silversmith in the Albaicín where all the dancers come from. Very suitable, isn't it my poppet?"

"Now who's being sentimental?"

It was so farcically, so – outrageously – different a world that he felt like a diver, in the antique time before Commandant Cousteau. A Bibendum or Michelin-Man, with lead upon the feet and a huge copper globe that Screwed On, and a life-support system through a long fragile pipe that would snag all the time in things. Wonders of the marine world. You got down to maybe twenty-five metres, and thought it hellish dangerous, which it was.

He had a reasonable job. That's to say, a loony job. But makes more sense than being intent on Beating Last Year with automobile sales. And sorry; whatever the progress made (always called technological to make it sound more progressive somehow) somebody, in the ancient French phrase, has to empty the pot. Sewerage, dustbins and cops remain, and will go on remaining major municipal preoccupations. National preoccupations. You went to the office, and even thought it was a weird and hideous world full of corpses, frauds, hold-ups, everything for the Moral Pathologist – and stinks as bad as physical pathology, said Maryvonne disgustedly, there seem to be just as many samples of blood, pus, and faecal matter – someone had to do it, and be interested in it, be devoted to it.

He was. He liked the feeling, the atmosphere, the –

119

despite everything – comradeship. The odd police jargon. What, odd! No odder than any other shop talk. Odder than, say, television cameramen? Or the English when they talked about cricket.

But down there, in the great big submarine hunting-ground (vague childhood memories of reading Jules Verne) – that was the office. One didn't come up for air in the office. This was the real world, here.

"What's she like?"

"Who?"

"Judith of course."

"Plain, and very beautiful. Extraordinary huge eyes. Dreary hair in a plait wound round and held with pins. I can't wait to draw her." Vera, daring, had recently launched into drawing people. Very, very difficult. But drawing trees or flowers or stones is also very difficult.

"Where will you draw her?"

"Here. She'll come here. But you're not allowed to lay eyes upon her. Richard is not allowed to know. There are things that none of you are allowed to know." Conspiracy was multiplying like dry rot around here. Mutterings and scuttlings and secret threads a-spinning underneath Richard's very feet. If Fausta got caught at all this her arse would be on the grill: St. Lawrence would be nothing to it. There would be hideous, primitive martyrdoms that started with being tied to a wheel: extremely Spanish. And Czech too. Who burned John Huss? Castang couldn't remember, but felt sure Czechs were mixed up in it. Nasty goings-on with melted lead. Human beings have always done unspeakable things to one another. Still do. Ask – well, ask Amnesty International. Is there much difference between today and the year – say roughly 1500? The main difference would be that things today are less public. The Police Judiciaire . . . Cantoni would look very well in a Guardia Civil hat. Come to that, Castang my boy, try one on yourself. Might look more becoming on you than you realise. Let's not have any foolish talk though. The PJ could become a powerful instrument of oppression, and was certainly unpleasantly pliable in the hands of its masters in Paris. But believe me, it's necessary to any semblance of civilisation. Which is more, Castang suspected, than you could say for Electricité de France. And that is a body which is every bit as fascist, and a good deal more oppressive.

As for killing people in nasty ways – try addressing yourself to the State Tobacco Monopoly.

19. Shellburst

Sleeping was one of the first things to be reorganized. If the telephone rang at night; worse, if he himself got routed out, and it did happen – it had to happen without disturbing Vera. Who had enough on her plate in the middle of the night. And if the tiny one started yelling in the middle of the night . . . he would lend a hand. But he needed his sleep too, said Vera: there have to be arrangements that you are not disturbed.

Well, when it's hungry . . . But if it's going to yell out of sheer naughtiness . . . It's a thing they do do, or so I read in the book.

Experience, said Vera: a hunger yell, a pain yell, sounds quite different to a caprice yell.

It all sounds like yelling to me.

Nonsense, said Vera.

You'd think she'd been doing this all her life.

This all was not too late, though he was in bed. Half-past ten: he looked at his watch automatically. Damn. He had to be at work tomorrow, but was still officially 'off' and who was ringing him at this hour? The way to find out is to answer, instead of looking at the thing and damning its infernal insolence.

"Castang."

"This is Mademoiselle Marcel." He had trouble remembering who this was. Yes – Thérèse. Thérèse! . . .?

"Yes?" How had she got his home number?

"I'm worried. Something has happened that is disturbing. Something for the police."

"I'm not on duty."

"I know you, at least. I'm not going to ring up heaven knows who."

"If you'll tell me what's happened, I can advise you who'd be the appropriate –"

"No," said Thérèse inflexibly. "This is a private matter. I'm not going to blurt it out to just anybody. Nor to you – but I've thought it over. You're concerned."

'Tell me then, and I'll see what would be the appropriate –"

"No. Come here. You'll have to come here. I'll expect you. It's urgent. Come to the side door," and rang off before he could protest.

"You've got to go out?" said Vera.

"Sorry," looking for his socks.

"No – I was awake. Don't bother about me. I'm fine."

There was no point in wasting words. To complain about Thérèse, to roar at the night guard, who had plainly given his number when asked . . . if that good lady had her mind set on something it was not easy to put her off. She 'knew him'. They'd been introduced. So she wouldn't tell anyone else what it was. And what was it? Coup d'état, or coup d'éclat?

The streets were full of traffic still. It was not late. Not raining but windy, with low racing cloud.

The house in the Rue des Carmélites was dark and quiet. There was no 'surveillance' going on. There was no particular reason why there should be. But having been 'off' he wasn't up-to-date on developments. Assuming there were any developments. But plainly something had happened. He had to come and see, no doubt of it. As he had been telling himself ever since getting out of bed.

There was light in the kitchen. He pushed the door open; it was warm here. Probably she kept the big solid-fuel cooker going all the year round.

She was in a woolly dressing-gown, madonna blue. The thin hair in a plait. Woolly slippers. Not looking like a

122

madonna. The dog was in its basket, but bounced out and growled.

"Quiet," she said. And to him, "I want to keep this quiet. Press people hang about. Other people I don't know. This house is being watched."

"There's nobody watching it now."

"I don't like it. Now that you're here at last – Noelle's gone out. Some time ago. She took her car."

"What's strange about that?"

"She never goes out at night alone."

"Sensible of her but it's not late: what's there to worry about?"

"Shut up," hissed Thérèse. "You know nothing, you understand nothing. Understand this. She's been very queer these last days. I know her very well. I use my eyes and ears. I watch her. Listen to me."

While talking she had poured him a cup of coffee. He took it without thinking.

"Keep very quiet. I don't want a disturbance. Enough upsetting things have happened."

"Who's at home?"

"The old people. Thierry's out. He'll be late, probably. So much the better. He need know nothing about this – or so I hope. Noelle ate no dinner, no supper. She's had a very strange look. She wouldn't go out. She'd tell me, if she were. She always does. So that I know where she is, what she's doing." Castang drank his coffee.

"Since you know everything," without sarcasm, "has she had any message you think might have upset her? Letter, phone call?"

"No."

"But at the pub maybe – or the restaurant?"

"Look in her room." He went quietly; Thérèse in her slippers soundless behind him.

He saw the point. Noelle had gone to bed, and got up again.

"What's she wearing?" Thérèse looked queerly at him. "You saw her you said."

"A housecoat. Over her nightdress."

"I see." He went into the bathroom. In the wastepaper

123

basket was a green cardboard box, empty. It had contained a hundred aspirin.

"We'll go downstairs again."

"Hush."

She poured him a second cup of coffee. Perhaps she thought he'd need it. He dared say he would.

"You think yourself she might . . ."

"I said no such thing. God forbid."

"You feel sure she's not gone to meet someone?"

"In her nightdress?"

"She took her car. What sort is it?"

"I don't know. It's black. It's quite small. It's English I believe."

"Try and think."

"I think it has a D on it. Sort of like this," Her finger traced a capital D in the air, in script. What? He couldn't recall seeing her car, and couldn't thing of anything with a D. A Jaguar? An MG? It was like Noelle, somehow, to have a conspicuous car. Get her better service.

"A small car? A sports car? Hard top?"

"Yes." Orthez would know. Where the hell was Orthez? An antique? An Aston-Martin? He was being dim, and it was not the moment to be dim.

Light, in answer to prayer, dawned.

"Ha! Has it got a silver radiator, with sort of wavy lines?" His turn to sketch in the air with his finger. "A Daimler?"

"That's right," said Thérèse with approval. That at least made things easier. There weren't many of these. Sort of thing the royal family went to race meetings in. That too was somehow typical of Noelle. A barmaid is as good as a queen any day.

"I'll see to this. You were right to call me. Say nothing to anybody. If she comes home make no comment – see that you call me at once. At the office. Like you did before."

"The young man didn't want to give me your number. I insisted." I bet you did.

He slipped out and got into his little car with the automatic gearbox and the brakes fixed so that Vera could stop with her finger if her foot went to sleep. Not at all like a Daimler. The mind thought, going fast.

She wouldn't have gone anywhere into the town. Too many people about.

The boy on guard looked up as he bumped into the downstairs office at the PJ which was the 'communications room.'

"Thought you were off. That old biddy who was on for your number? – she said it was urgent."

"It is. Gendarmerie headquarters. I'll speak to them. Get a move on. Got any beer, here? . . . Castang here at PJ. I want the cars alerted; every patrol on the outskirts and country districts — well, every patrol there is within the fifty-kilometre radius, on full alert, urgency one, suicide or attempt. English car, make Daimler, don't say I don't make it easy, sports type, hardtop coupé, colour black, silver radiator sort of accordion pattern. Model unknown, number unknown but how many will there be for God's-sake. Woman alone, fifty – middle-aged, idiot – fair hair, medium height, sturdy build. Wearing housecoat, sort of dressing-gown, dark blue or sapphire blue, gold or silver embroidery, over long nightdress. Like an evening dress, nearly. Concentrate, obviously, isolated areas, wooded or watered, waste ground. Particularly along the river. And upstream surely. Use your loaf. One more item – discretion. Not for the press. Judicial enquiry. Understand this, I have the woman's identity but I don't want it divulged. So no blabbing. Go by the description. Been missing only an hour and a half: she's probably quite close by. Call me here, the moment you get any signal."

If we have three deaths, Castang was thinking, in this family . . . but don't think about it; it doesn't bear thinking about.

Little surveillance had been done on Noelle. She was an uncomplicated person. She worked hard, and she played hard, at childish, innocent pleasures. Above all, she needed people round her, lots and lots of people. She thrived on noise, light, bustle. Not for her the husband's addiction to music: operas, choral societies bored her stiff. But she had a reserved place in the best seats at the local football

125

club: never indeed missed a home match. It wasn't the play that excited her as much as the atmosphere . . . She had an immense circle of acquaintance – they would call it friendship – among the businessmen and their wives. With the women there would be tremendous 'shopping expeditions'. Not a lot actually got bought, but every novelty or event would be inspected; gazed at, poked at, sniffed at, commented upon. Noelle needed lots of novelty.

When Thérèse said she 'never went out at night', alone was what she meant. In fact she was out most nights, but always with a gang. Men – never just one man – and women. A favourite ploy was an expedition to the spa town sixty kilometres off. Race-meetings there in the summer she never missed, and throughout the winter about every ten days they would have dinner and go gambling at the casino. A compulsive gambler, yes, but ruinous to nobody. On the contrary, both clever and lucky. Came out about even over the season, minus expenses and the house percentage. No harm in that. She was ready to pay, and generously, for pleasure, and had plenty of money of her own. Absolutely no scandal. If she went to other people's houses it was to play cards, or even Scrabble. For money, certainly, but the word 'play' was meant literally. It was for fun. She liked fun, pursued it, got it. She worked hard after all. With the pub or the restaurant she was never satisfied to take her cut and let things drift. She wasn't frightened of shifting beercrates or getting up on stepladders.

For exercise twice a week she went riding, to keep her stomach flat and her hips trim. Hereabouts her path crossed Clothilde's . . . They knew one another to say hello to, but there was no intimacy. Whether they really ignored one another, or pretended to – it came to much the same thing.

Castang knew no more. If anything more had been found out – but truly, none of them would have thought Noelle a likely candidate for a suicide attempt.

"Are both cars out?" he asked.

"Only Lucciani."

This was just the thing with 'light surveillance' of this sort, which might go on a long time. If you didn't have anybody to spare (and somebody too had to do these boring night guards, and the week-end duty when the office staff went home) you had to fit in days-off. This is a toss-up. Cancel days off, and then nothing happens, and everybody's grousing. Give people time off, on the grounds that it looks like a quiet evening – and that was the moment that things like this happened . . . With Castang 'off' Liliane had strictly speaking no business letting someone else go, but if you didn't they began inventing toothaches or saying they had the curse. He didn't blame her: he'd have been doing the same.

"See if you can raise him." They had officially two radio cars, or would if Lasserre didn't invent pretexts for borrowing them. Of course, if only one person at a time is out in a radio car, and busy surveying something (the word is vague; it has to be, covering the multitude of sins it does) she or he cannot be expected to stay glued to the handset: they are ordinary radio-telephones: the PJ has a different frequency of course to the urban police and emergency services.

If the she/he has gone wandering off on survey leaving the car parked you have the blipper, the gadget people carry pinned to their overall to tell them when they're wanted. The trouble with this thing is that it blips, and agents turn it off to stop it being a nuisance. There exist of course sophisticated versions which will tickle you gently instead of making a racket. These are dear, and grudged to provincial police forces: they are thus status symbols. The perpetual wail of the PJ is 'The Germans have far more money than we do'. If we (runs the argument) had a Red Brigade that did us a favour for once and kidnapped a few Cabinet Ministers, then we'd get some credits in a hurry. As things are, all the money goes to surrounding them with expensive precautions. As though anyone gave a farthing for those rabbits anyhow . . . Three armour-plated helicopters to open a flower show . . .

Of course Lucciani had undone his bleeper, damn him. Castang didn't even know where he was.

"The Tuileries was last I heard. Thierry went out that way on a pal's motorbike." Thierry had a car of his own but was hard to follow because forever borrowing other people's. Mm, it was anyway unlikely. Noelle would not have gone to Magali in her nighty. Nor anywhere much in that down-stream area, he thought. Desirable residential suburb, heavily built over and thickly populated, well-lit (local taxes were high) and no 'wild' countryside. Much-patrolled, and full of people up to midnight. Even the villages further out, such as where Clothilde lived . . . no, don't interfere with the gendarmerie. They do this sort of job efficiently. Indeed, most gendarmerie brigades are a lot less sleepy than urban police forces.

Most of the area in the plain – flattish, vaguely agricultural – was a poor prospect. Industrial, and working-class residential, where people went to bed early, save on a Saturday night. Farming country beyond and some woodland cover, but it would not be countryside Noelle knew well or was likely to seek.

In the foothills there was vine land, orchards, and plenty of forest. There were any amount of possibilities out that way.

Look, there is no use getting into a flap; and stop smoking so much.

"Whip out very quick to the pub and get a couple more beers. I'll watch the switchboard."

The river banks upstream were surely the likeliest bet. He fidgeted with the switchboard, but hell, any gendarme knew this as well as he did.

The river comes out of the hills in a turbulent irregular fashion. In a rainy month of May, as now, it is full of water and has never been easy to control: it floods fields, slops up side alleys, creates boggy areas full of scrubby alder and willow and shitty undergrowth, interesting enough to local duckshooters, not much good to anybody else. Some engineering has been done on it, but in a desultory fashion: the water is too irregular to be good for hydraulic power. And there are three or four little side-rivers that come carting in . . .

He'd just got a beer uncapped when the phone rang.

"Castang – we've got the car. Empty, locked. At one of the worst places for a search. By the island, you know, just above the power station – she could get lost in there. And if she's gone in the river..."

"No use worrying about that. I'll be there in under twenty minutes. Get any spare cars you can. If we don't get her quick we won't get her at all. She may have swallowed a lot of aspirin, she may have other stuff I don't know about, and she may have done other silly things."

She was a healthy woman, and no compulsive pill-swallower. But with the double death, any doctor would let her have sedatives, and they are so easy to get. 'I'm not sleeping very well at present; have you any I could borrow?' All the bourgeois had cupboards of dangerous rubbish. Practically nobody has any confidence in their doctor unless there are six items on the prescription form, of which four serve no purpose. A hundred francs at least or it won't cure you, and a thick satisfying dossier for the Securité Sociale, full of complicated notation, before you can feel it's really doing you good. Tell them to stick to senna-pods and they'll go to another doctor. Or more. As Ray Chandler once said: 'Go jump in two lakes if one won't hold you.'

The dark-blue Estafette van of the gendarmerie is recognisable a kilometre off, even without its blue winker on the roof. An officer's car and a second van drew up as he did. Little enough for a job like this. Deal out a few walky-talky sets. You don't want to shout or make a todo. Such things have been enough upon occasion to send hesitating suicides over the brink.

They'd got a fire-brigade ambulance too. Not as well equipped as a 'Samu'. But they were not far from the town. If she were alive, quicker than the helicopter. There was nothing for it but to beat the bushes. The May greenery was thick and lush and wet. There were paths made by fishermen, poachers, gipsies. Not so many out-of-door fornicators as in Castang's youth. They had to hope she'd got tired before going far.

Luck for once was with Castang. He'd never been particularly lucky. But some people are, and Noelle was one. The good gamblers. A gendarme in leather gaiters (better equipped than himself) found her, only two hundred metres from where he was standing sweeping a clearing with his torch. He took shortcuts through bramble-bushes, doing his trousers no good. Soaked to the knee already anyhow. The real riverbed was a couple of hundred further, but the ground was bog from there on.

She was in a bad enough state. Half in coma, flat out from loss of blood – she'd cut her wrists too. Hopefully they've been too sloppy; they've tried three or four ways, and got muddled. One can sometimes save them that way, if they haven't got pneumonia too badly on top of the rest. The poor bitch; she'd been crawling round in circles, on her hands and knees, with no clue what she was doing. The gendarme had got his jacket off and over her, trying to warm her, trying to get her out of coma. She was alive though, and making incoherent sounds.

"Poor cow. She was tumbled down in the ditch and couldn't get out. Nighty rucked right up her back. Shone the torch an' thought what the hell's that? Big white bottom. Still, it showed up! " He had 'made her decent', was holding her up, warming her, wanting to shake her up, not daring to, because of her wrists. She was plastered with the thick mud of the alluvial riverbed. Who knows, thought Castang, it might have helped stop or at least slow the bleeding.

20. Picking out the Splinters

By no means at the end of his troubles, Castang. This fatal conscientiousness over small details – Richard called it the itch to have things tidy . . . Why on earth worry about that car? It was off the road, wasn't it? And locked. Either it would get stolen or it wouldn't, but either way it was not important. Noelle might have thrown the keys away, or she might have lost them: if you go crawling about in undergrowth the shallow pocket of a dressing-gown is not the best place . . . well you aren't going to find them, he told himself while they were wrapping the woman up and hooking her to the life-support system.

Hospitals are always a pest. It's not that they aren't well used to the cops blowing in in the middle of the night with people in an extreme state of dilapidation: smashed up road-accidents go to Surgery Two: drug overdoses go to the resuscitation block at Medical One: heart attacks to the Cardiology-Special annexe of Surgery Three. As for the badly burned, they should never have been brought here in the first place. There's a special unit for them in another town: what did that stupid ambulance driver think he was doing?

It is an understood thing too that much of the flotsam-and-jetsam 'belongs to the police' and gets tucked away in a private room with a cop on guard. It's a system; familiar. Try and deviate from any pattern in a rigid, centralised, and so-called Cartesian society like France, and the bureaucrats get restive. Once the elementary tagging was accomplished, and the doctors being a bit reserved about things – 'One wouldn't want to predict: this is going to be touch-and-go for some hours' – an administrative ape with a clipboard was pestering him. What's all this anonymity stuff? Is this patient under police responsibility? If not who are the relatives, what's her status (once her sex was settled)? It's PJ business, is it? Castang, who didn't want the PJ dragged into this, damned his own stupid eyes; should never have set foot here; should have left it to the gendarmerie but was afraid of somebody selling the coconut out of sheer stupidity. As it was he was making things worse by drawing attention to them.

Thérèse was in bed, but out at once when she heard a ring. She heard his news with a stony face. No, Thierry wasn't in yet. There were spare car-keys somewhere and she'd look in the morning. She didn't exactly say so, but this was what came to a people de-christianised and ceasing to live according to principle. Prayer might save Noelle: as for hospitals . . . He should have brought her back here: they had an excellent doctor two minutes away. Nobody, explained Castang laboriously, could take that responsibility. And sorry, the night was getting on.

131

It wasn't much after two. Vera woke up, of course, however still he tried to be. It didn't matter, she said: she was alert anyhow.

"You got back on duty rather abruptly, huh?" said Richard. "You've seen this, I suppose?" A nasty headline in the local paper.

'OVERWHELMED BY HER TRAGIC DESTINY, THE WIFE OF ETIENNE MARCEL ATTEMPTS TO PUT AN END TO HER DAYS.'

"I did my best," said Castang bitterly. "The combination of blabbermouth imbeciles and bloodsuckers beats you every time. Someone recognised her – or me."

"Can't be helped."

"What beats me – too – is that the moment one forms any hypothesis about this affair a new fact arrives to contradict it."

"Then don't fall in love with hypotheses. These ones that have no pattern – or seem to – are waiting for a new fact. You've got a new fact; welcome it. Being hit on the head by a welter of loud publicity is a turn of the screw. I'll handle that: it's my role. You've come back to this with a fresh mind; use it. I've other things," tapping a dossier Fausta had brought in. "This was one of yours and I'm taking it off your back. Concentrate totally upon this Marcel thing."

"What is it?"

"Raphael – the legitimate defence." It was indeed a nasty shell-splinter picked out of his back. Mr Raphael was a tobacconist. His shop had been broken into twice. The third time he had taken a shotgun and popped three vandals; one died. The judge of instruction had pegged him with unjustifiable homicide. His case had been taken up by the law-and-order brigade, anxious for a test case. The instruction had 'gone wrong'. Much would depend, at the trial, on expert police evidence. The investigating officer had been Castang. Richard didn't want anything 'going wrong' at a trial promoted to the Assize Court.

Well, there were lots more splinters.

"And Castang: I don't want to sound academic. But

it's the very absence of pattern that creates one. You follow? – this succession of oddities means there is a pattern. Go on watching your crew. There's something twisted there. A twist means a weakness. Something there will give."

It was sound advice, even if undoubtedly academic.

It would have been more logical – wouldn't it? – if Richard had taken this business over, and left him the was-it-or-wasn't-it legitimate defence? But that was not the way Divisional Commissaires worked. Quite, they were under political limelight, and had themselves to protect. But it was his throat too. There are sharp splinters. There are also large jagged fragments, with uncommonly large areas of razor-sharp edge.

Before he got to his own office the phone was ringing. He sat, heavily, wishing he'd had more sleep.

"Castang," said Colette Delavigne's voice, and on the icy side.

"I'm only just in, you know."

"Commissaire Richard informs me –"

"Yes, there's a lot of detail. We're what's it, evaluating it, processing it, as quick as we can. It's coming to you as fast as we can write it up. Events overtake us."

"Yes. Good God. You're under pressure – what do you think I am?"

"I'll be up to see you this morning." He punched buttons. "Liliane. Will you come to me or shall I come to you? Very Well." Another.

"Get some cowboy to pick up that Daimler car. The good lady at the house has keys, or if she hasn't fix it your own way. If the car's gone that's just too bad for the insurance company. It's not evidence; I just want it tidied up. Search it, naturally."

An outside line. Clothilde.

"Madame Dierickx? – Castang, PJ. I'd like to come over and see you this afternoon: would you have the kindness to be at home? . . . No . . . Yes, if you would, please."

Liliane, with a lot of paper. Fausta, with more paper: stuff that Richard had read and initialled, and 'belonged in the dossier'. Well . . . the best way of dealing with a restive judge of instruction is to feed her lots and lots of paper.

"Let me attempt to get this clear," said Madame Delavigne, tapping on paper with a nice birthday-present silver pen. "Are you trying to build a case against one or other of these people? Is the idea that if you all go on long enough one of them will turn into a suspect?" Very magistrate, the tone of voice. To your real dyed-in-wool jurist, the Criminal Code is something viewed with dislike and distrust. There is sound law, and unsound law: very little that's sound about this. They are fond, indeed, of saying that the Criminal Code has no meaning, and doesn't know its own purpose. Furthermore, the whole area surrounding it is riddled by termites: these impossible social-sciences people. Yet Colette was still young – his age or thereabouts – and a humane thinker. Not the kind of judge who thinks that anything to do with human beings is basically unsound, creating a grave flaw in the legal process.

"Everything that has happened, since the original assassination, has been in the family. I argue, to do with the family. It ties up somewhere there. Even the first death, so elaborately public and outside the family circle. There's some correlation we haven't understood yet. They're out of focus."

"Don't waste my time with metaphors. If they're your suspects they're a singularly unconvincing crowd. This wife who has attempted suicide; pass that for the present . . . These two brothers, whom – I agree with this girl inspector of yours; they sound like dimwit members of the Bonaparte family . . . The sister; middle-aged pious female . . . The children; surviving children I should say . . . daughter shows no sign of instability, and the son, mm, every sign of instability, but not energy enough to do anything but drift about cadging on his father's credit. What motive could he possibly have? What motive could any of them possibly have? On your own showing they're united, affectionate and loyal. The father was the mainspring, kept it all running. Kept them in jobs, in comfortable situations. They've everything to lose from his death, nothing to gain

. . . This son-in-law. Energetic, ambitious, climbing. Has obvious qualities of his own, but it wasn't doing him any harm, was it, having a pa-in-law prominent in local politics, powerfully influential in all that concerns local business? Nothing here carries conviction.

"The terrorist thing is totally exploded, I grant. I've here a confidential report from DST, to the effect that no local extremist group, and they're categorical, is more than talk and hot air. A group from outside? Marcel was not prominent in anything but local affairs, the assassination is unsigned and unclaimed. Where's the point in it, what would they be attempting to show or gain kudos by?

"To my mind it points to personal vengeance by some envious and disappointed ex-competitor, collaborator, whatever. The Mayor poohpoohs this – he has reasons of his own for wishing to play down such a notion, of course. Commissaire Richard sends me a long detailed report attempting to demonstrate that it isn't so. I've no complaint of his police work, naturally: I'm talking about wilful obstinacy. Won't-See is a lot blinder than Can't-See. I'm getting no real support from the Procureur on all this."

Castang, feeling muzzy, and unenthusiastic about the way he'd chosen to get back to work, had no ideas and no comments to offer. A tirade about Richard was banal coat-trailing and she didn't even expect him to react: her opinion of his intelligence wasn't that low. As for scoring points off the Proc, there was only one thing a cop could do when his feet got set in the mazy path of Parquet politics, and that was act stupid.

"I can only follow where a thing leads me. This inquiry's barely begun and what do I know? – beyond the awareness I have to know a lot more about all these people." A glance of extreme acidity welcomed this platitude. Madame Delavigne turned pages of her dossier, and made a noise like Tchaa, with a lot of fricative and sibilant in it.

"This suicide – a genuine attempt, or a self-dramatisation?"

"It's just this minute happened, right? And aren't they all? If you mean a fake attempt taking damn good care that she'd come to no harm, I can only answer, not according to what I've seen or been able to judge of her character."

"Yes, yes, yes, I'm not asking for a lecture on psychology. I'll get a long cautiously-worded report about nervous depression and what am I to make of that?"

"Is she a criminal or has she criminal knowledge you mean? – nothing at present to support that."

"This Thierry . . ."

"Nothing about this Thierry; he's a pain in the neck, I should guess to all but a few middle-aged women."

"He sounds too wet to be true."

"Very likely that's so: I'll have to see whether we've turned anything up. Young Lucciani was taking an interest in him last night: obviously he's not had time to write it up yet. Try to recall that I've had some days off, and I've had other preoccupations."

"Yes, Henri, I know. Try to enter into my problem too."

"Put it that Thierry is an expert consulter of his own interest. Has a nicely feathered nest, and wouldn't do anything to disturb it."

"Is that a bit superficial?"

"I've twenty people whose behaviour patterns we're attempting to establish. To do that with the resources at my disposal . . . get more people on it and we might have results quicker. You see what happens – this woman has a nervous depression and it monopolises our energy. If among this group of people there's a candidate for homicide I can't help believing we've more promising horses than Thierry. He might have all sorts of weird grievances. He could imagine, maybe plan an elaborate scheme for assaulting anyone from the mayor down, but would he be able to carry it through?"

"It's a point."

"People like Thierry defeat their plans – won't say voluntarily even if unconsciously since you don't wan't any police psychology – by making them too complex. We've two assassinations. Assuming the second one is, but Deutz is unusually categoric about it – still, that's only one expert opinion, then they're linked because they can hardly be

136

anything else. Then the second follows the pattern of the first. To wit two simply-planned and expert crimes, carried out with skill and resolution. Simplicity and efficiency. Do you see those as characteristic of Thierry? – I'm damned if I do."

"Yes, now you're strengthening your argument, I'm bound to say."

"I'll tell you frankly I'm not happy with any of our present candidates. This Bertrand – he's smooth, and there may be a lot more to him than meets the eye. I mean there might be a drama of jealousies or conflicting interests; it isn't beyond the bounds of imagination. I can only say his life and marriage seem stable, he follows conventional patterns. The reports on him are those of a person with settled habits. Tuesday bridge; Thursday the freemasons or the frothblowers or whatever. Saturday take your wife to the theatre. And his wife, the daughter, is much devoted to both her parents, gives a good honest feel. If she's foxing me I'd like to know about it. Again; what interest is there, what motive? Etienne Marcel and his son Didier – it's fair to say they could both be hard, sharp, and tricky. Any number of people who'd be quite pleased to see either or maybe both slip on a banana skin. Richard's got more people working on this. I've this family investigation. That's all."

"You think he's using you as a stalking horse, do you? To create a distraction and get people off their guard? That would make sense."

"I don't know it, and don't think it. Not my work to think any such thing. Where would I be, every time I did a job, thinking it was a set-up? You've no business saying it to me. Think it by all means, and then go see Richard about it, or the Proc."

"All right; don't get on a high horse. To my mind the whole problem lies elsewhere, but I agree I've no power to alter the instructions given you. What about this mistress?"

"Clothilde?"

"Extraordinary name for anybody's mistress," said Colette, with the first sign of humour shown that morning.

137

"I'll be seeing her afresh today. I'll have a report on her. There's been a bit of surveillance done on her: I'll see what Liliane has to say. I agree, she may not be as simple-minded as she likes to suggest."

"There might be a pattern of conflicting interests there. Banal as the suggestion may seem, the obvious is frequently the truth. Her act of being very open and naïve may be just that; an act. Furtive in ways, she could be furtive in others. Look up the background of this separation of hers. I'll give you a rogatory commission for Lorraine or wherever it was. See if there's any link between her and these other people. We know for instance she went to the same riding school as Noelle: there may be more."

"Very well."

"That'll do for now then, Henri. I won't put any untoward pressure on you, Inspector," with a glimmer of smile. "I remain convinced – the problem lies elsewhere. This Didier – he got to know or hear of something – threatened to blow the gaff on it."

"That would be a likely motivation, all right. I'm off then, and I'll keep you posted."

"Do just that."

She'd had a little anti-personnel bomb there. Thing with ball-bearings in it. Or, more accurately, splinters. Be a cop, and you wish you were an armadillo. You'd know what to do then, when jaguars come patting at you with their soft velvet paws. Curl up, and stay still. Don't excite the nasty beast.

21. Secret Societies

He'd read a report, by some sociologist, or maybe criminologist – those cattle had different names for themselves, but were all the same in essence: they strung platitudes together, couched in lecturers' jargon. Occasionally they were of use. Their platitude, put in new words, allowed you to see a familiar phenomenon in a new light.

This one as he recalled had been going on about solitude. The modern structures of society, intensely fragmented, with their ever-narrower appeal to small areas of specialized knowledge and limited responsibility . . . yes, sure. Creating numerous areas of solitude – yes, sure. Mankind went about thus inventing pretexts for obscure types of togetherness – right, mate. Hence the amazing proliferation of little groups. The secret societies, the fellow called them. People belong to a multiplicity of little gatherings. Breeders' club of boxer dogs, wine-label collectors, neighbourhood betterment-league.

Castang hadn't thought about it much. He supposed so. So what? He wasn't a joiner himself: the Friendly Society of Worn-out Police Agents was about his speed. Married moreover to a very resolute anti-joiner.

It was normal; it was even a basic ingredient in the fabric of social intercourse. You live in a tiny box, work in a tiny box: you go thus nowhere, see nobody. People no longer have close family links. The poor still do to some extent; going to see Auntie at weekends, dropping in at Granny's. But fewer and fewer are born, grow up in, stay their life in the same quarter. Social mobility.

Provincial towns there were still like Georges Simenon's Liège, where the patterns were so tight that men went to drink a cup of coffee in their mother's kitchen every morning on the way to work. Sat in the same bench of the same parish church at Mass every Sunday. The same table in the same pub. You knew everyone. Those you weren't related to by blood or marriage going back three generations, you had polished the bench at school with, you'd done your military service with. There was nothing that bound you all together like your distrust and dislike of outsiders.

Oh yes, some of it still held good. But such a mighty flood of Outsiders now came bursting all the old bonds that you had to seek new ways of finding togetherness. Other powerful forces fight against it, the most notorious of which is television. So join the canary-fanciers.

Harmless gossip-marts for the most part. Shoptalk about canaries blurred after a drink or two into a delightful exchange of inside information, which Chose had from Mrs Thingummy's son who works in telecommunications. 'You want to dial long-distance, right? For next to nothing, right? What you do is this, and same again all round, Jeanette. There are these ten figures, okay, before your real number. You're getting Chateauroux all right, only down the road but your call's gone to Barcelona and back: I've got one and it goes through Glasgow: now where is Glasgow? I'm playing these numbers on my lotto ticket this week.'

"Very funny people," said Fausta. "Extremely touchy and elitist, and of course a perfect mania for secrecy. Don't have anything to do with them. You won't get anything out of them anyhow. They sent in a report to Richard, practically with lead seals on it. I wasn't allowed to handle it of course: confidential file. There can't be anything much in it: I caught sight of his face while he was reading it. It's not anyhow being pursued, that side."
"How do you know?" A silly question since Fausta always knew everything.
"There was a long confabulation with the Proc. They may of course be pursuing it, but for reasons of their own. Their word was negative on the homicide but that you know already."
"I'd like to have sort of an unofficial chat."
"Well they're not in the phone book, you know. Everything is masked in obscurity. One doesn't even know how many there are – nor even what their salary scale is."
"Bound to be higher than ours."
"I suppose so," said Fausta sympathetically. "Here's anyway a number you can ring. I'll probably get into trouble just for giving you that."
It was a secret society. Normal enough, he supposed. They were after all supposed to be the experts on secret societies, and had acquired the mannerisms.
Grudgingly, a man who said his name was Boileau thought he might meet Castang in a pub for a beer. Sorry

140

but a quarter of an hour was all he could manage; okay?

It's a murky crowd, DST. Even the name, Direction de la Surveillance du Territoire, one of those pompous mouthfuls of pebbles to be found in the mouth of the President of the Republic, is meaningless. There's surveillance there all right – this after all was what interested Castang – but what of? The Territory, hm. Geological surveys no doubt: any uranium around here? Archaeological: much interested by fragments of pots.

It is possible of course to find out a little about them: what Castang knew already. France has always been a great place for Secret Societies, and at turbulent moments in this country's history up they pop, surrounded by a melodramatic aura. Older people whose memories go back before nineteen thirty-nine will recall the Croix de Feu and the Cagoulards (that's right, just like the Ku Klux Klan: sillier, if possible) and Colonel de la Roque. Throughout the duration of the Fourth Republic, numerous nonsensical conspiracies. At the time of de Gaulle's accession, Algérie Française – everyone remembers that! And the Organisation of the Secret Army: more colonels, and even several generals.

The present rulers of France are conspicuous for liking a quiet life. The General was estimable, even likeable, in his distaste for mediocrity, a fondness for barrackroom language, and an elfish impulse to set the cat among the pigeons. He even told the French the truth about themselves now and again, causing consternation.

We are modern now. The pigeons strut unflustered. Security has been tightened up no end. Nothing ever happens. France lies on a feather bed and says little prayers. Matthew, Mark, Luke 'n' John, bless the bed that I lie on. Were anything at all to happen, from the explosion of a nuclear power station to an apparition of the Virgin, it would be quickly wiped away with a soapy flannel. And illustrated on national television by little animated drawings: the average age of the French population is four, and backward at that.

In this atmosphere, DST flourishes. Nobody hears of it. It laughs heartily at the welter of publicity surrounding

American secret services, and does so in a whisper. It is blissful in its mediocrity. Oh, it's well enough in its way. He's well served, the President of the Republic. But what by?

Monsieur Boileau was another beaming fatface, freshly washed with a soapy flannel. He wanted to be helpful. Castang would really have preferred his being sour.

"But of course we're pleased to co-operate with the Police Judiciaire. What we're there for. Homicide naturally isn't a terrain on which we function – normally," chuckling. "As our report made clear – you haven't read it, naturally – nothing abnormal about this. Your Commissaire accepts this. You've got a lingering doubt – glad to reassure you." Four angels round my bed . . .

"Tell me about secret societies."

"I see. Thanks, no, I don't smoke. Yes, Marcel was a great joiner. One of his power bases. Join them all, and become a power in them all."

"You do much the same."

"Yes, yes. Can't join them all; bless my soul, one wouldn't have a minute to call one's own. Put it like this. There are innumerable groupuscules, to be sure, and they get together in cellars and talk all sorts of subversive nonsense no doubt. But to acquire leverage enough ever to do anything, mobilize anything, in a word to jell . . . Need money, right? Keep an eye on the finance, and the rest will look after itself. We can't prevent some discontented comrade stealing a stick of gelignite from a quarry and blowing up a television relay. But said comrade hasn't threepence to bless himself with, so we can generally lay hands on him if need be with no great pains. As for assassinating your Monsieur Marcel – there's a pattern in these things as you're aware. Look for money, or publicity, or both. If he'd been held to ransom now – there's a body of opinion that holds it's cheaper and easier than cracking banks. But no. You've the odd crackpot group that preaches violence. But what are they getting out of it here? Nothing. Pillar of the glee club, great man in the local football, no percentage in that. Might as well shoot any early-morning

jogger. Set your mind at ease. I'd love another beer but
you do understand, don't you?"

Castang went to see Monsieur Bianchi.

This old gentleman had been a cop for donkey's years,
probably since before the war, since he would by now have
been at mandatory retiring age. He had been retired a
year early by force majeure: a bullet in the lung. This had
actually stopped him smoking, a thing nobody had thought
possible by human agency. Being an honest cop he had
nothing to live on but his pension. But he occupied a house
built before 1948, and since he'd been living there since
the same date his rent was laughably low. My penthouse
he called it. A row of three attic rooms, eighth floor of a
big bourgeois house, the rest of which had long been given
over to luxurious living at great expense, on one of the
noisiest streets in the city. But up there he had light and
air, little noise, lots of space, perfect peace. One simply had
to climb eight flights of fire stairs, starting from a dark
corner by the courtyard, where there was a smell of dustbins. 'There's nothing wrong with my legs.' For his shopping basket, and his garbage bin, he had a cord on a pulley.
Served for coal too. 'I never did like the smell of oil.'

'What'll you do when you can no longer manage all this?'

'Then I'll die up here,' said Monsieur Bianchi happily.
'But I reckon, you know, it won't be yet awhile.' He had no
telephone, no electricity, and no gas. Vera was attached to
him. She couldn't get up there though. Too many stairs.
Castang himself, at the top, unstuck his shirt from his
back and took deep breaths of the antique dust on the landing. Not much light filtered through the skylights, grimed
with the patina of ages, and many strange objects of unguessable purpose stood about on the dust-coloured coconut matting. There was a knocker in the shape of a naked
girl: he rat-tatted with her brass behind.

Le père Bianchi had never looked better: a man at
peace with himself. The place was as dirty and comfortably untidy as you would expect. Odd patches were clean,
and an old pedal sewing-machine stood in a good light.
Castang arched an eybrow and the old man got his cop
look back on.

143

"Old ram," said Castang.

"Not a bit of it. Like a daughter to me. Mark you, I like watching her dressing. But it doesn't bother me any more. I enjoy her little female ways. We're company for one another. Like a cat. I've a cat too. She doesn't talk much, and that's very restful."

"She a student?"

"That's right. Old man's got to have something to love, you know. Cats are all right. A girl's better. How's your girl?"

"She's fine. She just had a baby."

"Good. That's what they're for. Mine don't, of course. Pill 'n' all. Got lots of boyfriends. They look at the dirty old man. I can tell by the way they look at me, whether they're any good."

"This is why I came to see you," said Castang, and explained.

Bianchi nodded.

"Sure. See it in everything. All those people with dogs. Phone-in radio programmes. Young fella amiable enough, but knows nothing about anything. Women tell him everything, all their private lives. Say it's daft. Does them good though. Look at the small ads. Every week a page full. 'Meetings'. Sure, lots of whores."

"Tenderness assured for small personal contribution. Discretion assured."

"You're reading them too fast. Me, I've got the time."

"Couple looks for other couple, or tactful young girl for threesome. It's only sex."

"Sure it's only sex: what the hell else do you expect? Talking about love all the time and wondering what the hell that is. Sex is all they know how to do. Bloody poor substitute for the other, though. You don't know how lucky you are. You got a girl. You don't know how lucky I am. I got a girl. What most people got is a lifesize doll." Castang nodded. "You know otherwise, you couldn't do this stinking job."

"There's no way out of it. Get into your boots and up and down, up and down. That girl of yours – what'll you do when she's gone?"

144

"Let her go. What you want me to do – have her stuffed? What's yours, a boy or a girl?"

"Girl."

"Lucky you. Just think of all those daddas who don't know how to cope. Smash the baby on the floor. Want to stay for a drink?"

"No, I've got to run. Come and see Vera."

"Sure."

"As one nun to another, you'll get on well together."

"Sure." Castang knew he wouldn't come.

"See you." The old boy had gone pottering over to a table full of junk, hunting for something.

"Richard, you know – hold on a sec, I've something to show you – he'd never keep going. There's more to people's private life – here, catch hold. F'your little girl. Sugar almonds, like." Something in a small twist of dirty tissue-paper, like a pinch of snuff, but oddly heavy.

"His wife came to see Vera."

"Remarkable woman," said Bianchi. "All right boy; keep y'boots in shape."

Out on the street Castang remembered the twist of paper. He'd thought a medal or something, a Saint Christopher or a Star of the Sea. But it was quite materialistic. Vera was enough of a star for Monsieur Bianchi. Two gold napoleons. He stood staring up at the building. A student girl cannoned into him and said, "Mind your bum, stupid chum." Well – even a bump in the street is better than no human contact at all. Quite right, Bianchi. Sex is not to be despised. Given a scrap of sex, a scrap of money, even a cop could face the future. Forty gold francs for Lydia. Incidentally, over seven hundred in today's small change. Worth a lot more than that though.

Monsieur Bianchi had agreed that he was not making a fool of himself.

"Follering people about an' taking little pictures . . ." He himself had been the best hand at it in the department. "Won't tell you much about them. But it's that old gag about the planets. Observe them. One or more get a little tiny bit out of position, means there's something unseen, unknown, around the shop."

145

22. Exchange and Mart

"Now where the hell did you get to last night?" Lucciani had only just come on and had still not had time to write his report up. But this was the only moment for getting them all together and Castang was holding a round table. He had to shove the accelerator down. Richard was none too pleased about Noelle, who had been dragged back into quite sound physiological shape, but was like Queen Elizabeth on her cushions: face to the wall and say nothing. Richard like Monsieur Bianchi had reached an obvious cop conclusion; this was a planet out of position. He'd used the phrase 'fucking fishy' which in a man not given to casual obscenities was forcible.

"Relatively restrained circle, there's been five of you on it. Now there's one more of you and one less of them. Now get your foot down on it. There's more to it than this," flicking at Liliane's neat pile of typescript about a week's blameless behaviour of a dozen blameless and boring lives.

"Well you see," Lucciani shuffling and mumbling, not very sure how this would be received, "a partouze, actually."

"A what?" Tone of incredulity. Castang was one of these virtuous cops, houseproud and priggish. Group sex parties are not counted among normal police activities, despite all the jokes about Vice Squads. Still, one could say for old Castang, he did have humour, and so thank God would Richard think it funny: at least he hoped so; they'd better.

"Well I knew you'd be back today, and would start moaning about all this got-up-and-went-to-bed stuff, which is all we get, hanging about, so I decided to get closer."

"A partouze! We're seeing life." The whole table was enjoying itself – Castang with a finger in his ear, pretending he'd wax stuck in it. Orthez guffawing and scratching his crutch.

"Get any good pictures?" Liliane humorously tolerant and less like Reverend Mother than usual despite the armour-plated bosom. Maryvonne thoughtful, wondering what she'd have done if invited. Even Davignon, all high intellectual forehead and hornrims, had a grin twitching at his severe mouth.

"For once you've an attentive audience."

"Well, I've been stuck with this Thierry . . . goes out every day; doesn't do anything much. Frigs about in the National Library, always reading up this occultism and eastern religions and stuff; you know, The Way. Telling fortunes out the I Ching 'n' all that. Pally there with the attendant, the weaselly one with the old car."

"Who belongs," said Orthez, "to the Veteran Car Club, and they go to the clubhouse out at the place where they've an Advanced Driving School out on the old motorbike circuit."

"Yes, that's the one. Thierry's got one of these old hotted up Renault Tens with a Gordini motor, and they're always busy making it go, which it don't, half the time."

"Get on with it."

"Another place they go is that café in the old town behind the bishop's palace, the Vienna Woods."

"Where they play billiards."

"Right, and they've an English pool table too, and there's a fellow there sometimes who's real hot. So as I said I was sick of sitting there dumb so I got into conversation, and after havering about they decided to go down the airport. Not the commercial port but the old field beyond Saint-Just where they have the parachute club. The café there is a hangout for the free-fall types. I did it myself a bit till it got too dear. So I know a couple of them, and it fitted in well, and I thought I might see something. One of those instructors, ex-marine type, found there were six or seven of us and said how about hotting the party up, get some girls."

"Is that the one with the old Mercedes? SL 190." Orthez' interests.

"Right. There's another, a mechanic with a gull-wing 300 who gets out the car club but that's not the same."

147

"We'll learn to distinguish," said Castang dryly. "You were just organizing the girls."

"That's the funny thing: I thought it would be a lot of scruffy sluts and I wasn't keen to have a dose of clap as a souvenir. Anyhow the fellow phones and I wasn't close enough to get the number but he talks to someone called Jackie. The upshot of which is hang on and I'll ring back. Which happens two beers later: we pile in the car when the word is given and we go into the town, and those big old houses off the Boulevard Wilson: I've the number of course in case it ever does us any good. Second-floor flat, big like all those, and it's not a whory setup; three of these dames live there and they're secretarial types, quite hoity-toity and Now boys don't make so much noise, and nothing to drink. In their thirties at least and two at least are or were married women but not les or anything . . ."

"What's anything? So there are you six big husky studs and there's only three girls."

"Three or four more came. One, no two, young crumpets but I didn't get them; I got . . ."

"Spare us; just put the essential on paper and Fausta can curl her lip. I take it you got no pictures."

"I wasn't set up for it but they weren't having any. A fellow said how about the Polaroid then, but the girls weren't having that. No no, Nanette, not a chance."

"No blackmail material."

"I suppose that's it but I was surprised. I mean nobody asked me for the password, nobody checked me out. I could have been the damn Vice Squad for all they knew."

"You were just a spare stud," said Castang, at his driest. "Why should anybody check you out? Nothing illegal about a partouze, as long as nobody's under age and you're a consenting adult or so I imagine. Very well, go and reduce the exciting performance to police prose."

The assembly fell silent. A few sideways glances were exchanged.

"Anybody got a comment?" said Castang in a Richard voice. "Orthez, you're the expert on the fast-car brigade. Hot rodding," trying not to sound sarcastic. Orthez had often been the butt for mockery. "No, I'm serious. This doesn't sound serious, Lord knows. But we'll have to find out, and you're in line."

"I've heard rumours – as who hasn't. Nobody ever pro-positioned me; I'm not good-looking enough," a slap at Lucciani's delicate complexion. "It's known I'm a cop. I mean those of us who have a serious interest in mechanics, we know one another. Out there at the anti-slip school they split up into cliques. But there's always a bit of overlap. Like I've a technical interest, I've done a bit of hill trials and stuff. I don't know the formula-three crowd or the Harley-Davidson types, or to nod to, but they'd know who I was. Stuff like this, you hear of obliquely. A silence would fall when I was around. Nothing much illegal, as you say, but I'm a cop after all, and you never know, huh? And if I were to start asking questions, people would wonder . . ."

"And clam up. And this aeroclub?"

"I've been there. It's the same world to some extent. I mean, there's nothing surprising about all this, is there?" They all nodded. "But only as regards the fringe, the hangers-on. I mean, motors and that, it's an expensive hobby. So are planes, or parachuting. You don't find many who have the money for both, or not seriously. You see?"

Castang did see. Hangers-on; apt enough description of Thierry. It was hard to take any of this seriously.

"Try prodding around this aeroclub. And that café where they play pool. Don't get blown. Lucciani will have to be careful from now on. See if you get a line on this Jackie. Davignon?"

"A comment? – I've none. It's like Orthez says, you find this sort of thing everywhere, inside cliques. A noisy crowd like that, nothing much at stake, sensation-seekers, no real responsibilities, that's where you find it most publi-cized. I don't want to sound denigrating but you know, where anybody can get in. A crowd like I've been looking at, Bertrand and the rubber-goods executives, Magali and her brigade which are just like all suburban housewives only they're richer – you'd need a passport there all right."

"You mean they play, but they like to know who they play with."

"Sure. You don't get it out in the open like that. It's no

149

real blackmail material, right: you'd say nowadays who's going to get excited about a bit of suburban adultery? But plenty of bosses still are very puritanical. This place of Bertrand's – one of the old family firms, very Protestant: you'll see that, if you read the dossier."

"I haven't had time yet."

"I know; that's why I'm telling you. Not 'what would the neighbours say' but 'it wouldn't do the firm's image any good'. A gang like that, likes to get off on convention, go to be recycled in Paris – somewhere preferably where the firm is paying," dryly. "Let their hair down among themselves – feel confident, then."

"You've been on them long enough anyhow; even from far back your silhouette will be getting familiar. Change over with Maryvonne. Nothing has come of this estranged wife of Didier's, or the secretary – that's the kind of milieu you'd expect – am I right, Liliane?" Big square face, heavy muscular shoulders; she hadn't had much to say. Group sex parties – not much up her street! She had been doodling on a piece of paper.

"I live by myself," she said. "The only group I see much of is the ones who sing. We do things like plain chant. Others do polyphonic, some of us sing in the Bach Choir, or Etienne Marcel's gleeclub thing, operetta and stuff. As Orthez said, the circles intersect. He's right too of course when he says that serious people don't fool with sex parties – with us it's not money; singing doesn't cost much in material. But a mentality: if you're serious about one thing, you are so about others. But you find fringes everywhere, people who can't take responsibility or don't want it: Thierry, like you say. I don't know how to say this . . ."

She pushed across the piece of paper. One doodle was like the Olympic flag; intersecting circles, with different sorts of shading and cross-hatching. Another was of circles that met without intersecting.

"Tangential?" suggested Castang.

"That's the word. The fringe groups of an activity – they form a clique. It's the being unserious that holds them together. That's where you get the gossiping and backbiting, the sort of – lack of self-respect. The ones who are a bit neurotic, or have a screw loose. And you often find they have a leader. Who isn't neurotic at all. But is ready to exploit those who are ..."

"Go on," said Castang, sufficiently impressed by her reasoning to be listening carefully.

"Well, if I'm not talking cock. That sort of person is where circles touch. Like – look at small ads," sounding now like Monsieur Bianchi. "The silly-sexy, you know, broad-minded couple, anxious to meet those with similar interests – you'll always find people exploiting that. Phony marriage bureaux and pederast bars. Look, I've – with Maryvonne here – been looking at that family while you were away. Etienne Marcel I knew a bit about – the music you know – well, he was terribly serious about all he did. Municipal fiddles and kickbacks, I suppose you can't be a councillor and an adjunct mayor without getting involved somehow with a lot of shady people. That's Richard's area. But in his side interests – no, serious and hardworking. And you know Noelle enough . . . But moving on the fringes of these worlds . . . Didier was a sort of fringe-person. I'm being hopelessly vague."

"We've got nothing. Got to connect it up any place we can. The judge would hold up her hands, we'd be laughed out of court. Know nothing, so fabricate something. But something's there."

"And this Jackie. Lucciani didn't notice, but the people one phones up to organize girls . . . The small-ads again. There's an exchange and mart in people, as well as in second-hand cars. Or look at the way dope gets handled. Junk comes with other junk – the fellow who knows how to get a fur coat, real cheap. But it's too vague to take seriously, I suppose," shrugging. "What Richard would say . . ."

"I don't know . . . Maryvonne, you've been very quiet."

"I couldn't make much out of Noelle. Or the pub. The brothers. These are the real people, aren't they, the classic 'kleine Leute'. They work, more or less as little as they can, in ordinary jobs, and they club together, and they play the horses, and the lotto, and they'd gamble on the football forecast if we had one, or play bingo. And somebody's got to organize that, and make money out of it, and Marcel did, and Noelle does. Didier's affairs – a lot of little tax frauds. I tried Massip but he doesn't want to know and who blames him. I put the papers into a file. That secretary very tight of mouth of course – a cow that woman. Frightened of me naturally. And Clothilde . . . she's another fringe person."

"You sound as though you don't like her."

"Like her? – what's that got to do with it? No I don't like her, or from what I know of her, which is little. There's not been much I could get into a report. But people don't like her much. She's very sweet, and she's funny, and amusing, and she has this act of being always fiddled. I think she pulled the wool over your eyes. I'm sorry."

"No, go on."

"Well, I'm a woman. I find her false, and sly. And on the make. But I haven't got close to her at all, naturally. The light surveillance act is necessarily superficial. Get close enough to become interested, and you're blown. You are only there to log movements, note meetings, observe a general manner."

"Remember this is a report I haven't read yet."

"It's not worth reading and so said Liliane. The riding-club. She's a bit marginal there, as you can understand, among the high bourgeoisie."

"Divorced woman. Kept woman. Living marginally."

"Right. And she works part time in a dress shop, so of course some of them are her customers. And she does secretarial work at one of those lose-weight places. And she does fill-in things in a hotel, reception or bar or taking orders, at week-ends. The horse is very expensive."

"She didn't take money, from Marcel."

"No, but the rent, of that little house. Which is quite high."

"We'll look a little further into Clothilde. Openly. She was after all in an equivocal position."

"Richard went, you know. Just as a pounce."

"Ah yes. To see if she had any papers or stuff of Marcel's. It was an idea he had."

"She did too. Said brightly she'd never thought of mentioning it to you: it hadn't occurred to her as being of importance. But it was only stuff about the house. It was his house, you see. He kept that quiet. The registration was a bit phony."

"Because of her? Or because of tax? Bit of both, I suppose. Mm, just a bit of departmental arranging. Or not really criminal – just fringe. Nothing more?"

"No. She had a wide acquaintanceship. You wouldn't say she had any really close friends much. People drop in on her. Men and women. Nothing to point anywhere, one way or another."

"Mm," said Castang.

He rushed home, too late for the local shops which had all closed. Had to go to a huge supermarket that stayed open. A bore. But 'the family' couldn't live on tins. There was nothing much out of the way for him, about this. When Vera was paralysed he'd done all the shopping.

23. Clothilde

The weather was still the same, which was never the same two half-hours running. The sun came out and blazed hotly; a heat intolerable because of humidity. The most inoffensive meadow became a steaming great jungle full of biting insects. The sun went in, and another cloudburst caught you in your shirt, left you sodden and shivering.

It played nasty jokes, like snatching your hat off and emptying a bucket of stinging hail upon your ears.

Even in the city everything that was green and grew, grew too much and too fast. Crowds of flowering shoots poked menacing fingers in your mouth; riots of vulgar foliage slapped you in the eye. It had a lusty smell, like a girl gymnast just off the floor. So, as a trainee posted to crowd control, not yet in the Police Judiciaire, had he first seen Vera, pungent from her ground exercise, pulse hammering in the muscled throat. He'd been standing by

153

the barrier watching – a gymnast himself in a small, police-sportsclub way. He'd said a joking word to her in his funny, broken German.

Wind came in violent gusts, snapping off the fragile, rain-heavy young branches and scattering them in the street. The trees didn't mind. They were growing so much and so fast. Even in the concrete desert they could afford to show arrogance. In prim suburban streets robust and rustic trunks of wood came and leaned on fences, laughing at the scrawny little trees cowering inside.

She hadn't understood, and smiled nervously. That was on the first day. A week later, at the end of the competition, the moment when tensions were relaxed and even the watchfulness of women trainers straying (the children allowed to stuff themselves with indigestible food, and even drink a glass of champagne) she had appeared, hair neatly combed, clutching a pathetic overnight bag. Age nineteen. Gawd, like something out of the Constant Nymph. "I'm running away" she said calmly, much too calmly. A lot of trouble she'd brought with her. Ten years back. A lot, and very little.

The Czechs started by making a great fuss, and then suddenly changed tack, laughed it off. No loss. Lousy gymnast anyhow. Only brought as substitute for a good one. Disruptive, disobedient girl. Nasty little bourgeois whore.

He'd had a fearful black eye. "You weren't put there to seduce little iron-curtain girls" screamed his commissaire. Seduce! If they could have seen her . . . arms and legs tight-crossed, glaring at him. Nothing had ever been more difficult to get into bed. What a bashing the child had taken. He'd taken one too. Lucky for him he'd passed out from police-school already, and with a high mark. He hadn't been punished finally. Been sent here, and not to Paris. This was his home, now. He didn't regret Paris. Vera didn't regret Bratislava. Scarred, yes, but resilient.

They'd watched the last gymnastics championship together on the television, perfectly detached and professional. Unselfconscious hard little behinds. Tanned thighs barred with chalk powder. The dignity of these children . . .

154

"The Hungarians are excellent."

"The Russians aren't that much, really. Except lovely Nelli."

"She's worth the other five. Ha." Curt laugh from Vera. "Comaneci has bloody well insisted that she was going to wear underpants."

A drink at the end. "Kim should have had all the gold medals."

"Including a few given to the men. So – to Nelli?"

"Yes, I'm all for married gymnasts myself. Their rhythms are better." The wind took his hat off as he got out of the car. He was tired. There was lead in the boots. The bushes on either side of Clothilde's little gate leaned over and brushed against him. His hair needed clipping too.

She let him in looking much the same as last time; a lot of silk scarf and jumper, well-cut skirt swinging on those long segments. She got clothes cheap, of course, from that dress-shop. Even so, she had plenty of money to spend. Well, a few part-time jobs, not declared to the tax office or the social security – she'd be making more than he did.

"I thought I was finished with the police. After Mr Thing was here, and turned the desk upside down."

"One is never altogether finished with the police, you see, as long as a homicide investigation continues."

"So I see. I begin to feel quite guilty. What happens, when you don't catch anybody?"

"These cases aren't necessarily classified. They can go on for years. They may lie dormant. Waiting for a little fact, trivial-seeming."

"How many years?"

"There's a prescription. After a certain number, a criminal act is deemed in law to have become extinguished. Otherwise there would be cases stretching back to the years after the war."

"And during the war?"

"No – the Germans destroyed all the criminal files when they left. Since then – it's all there in the archive. Paper, paper. It's what most of our work consists of."

"So that I'm going down in the archive?"

"As a witness, yes. Not in the archive. You're part of a very active file," pleasantly.

"This is a sobering thought. I'd like to know why. I had decided you'd understood – that my connection with Etienne was at best – well, narrow. And that you had gathered all the information relevant to it, on your last visit."

"What did Monsieur Richard say? "

"Is that his name, who was here? "

"Yes, he's the Divisional Commissaire. My chief."

"He asked quite politely whether Etienne had left papers here, and might he look. Rummage, was his word. He did, too. Was that just a pretext? He came really to take a good look at me? "

"He didn't say, or not to me."

"At least he didn't make any indecent proposals, as you did, even as a sort of nasty joke."

"Yes, that was unfair. I did apologise. I will again."

"I've put it out of my mind. Well, what is it you're poking at now? "

"As you say, your connection is narrow. Tangential was a word used, in discussion. Fringe, was another, as I recall. There are other figures like yourself, standing as it were on the rim of Monsieur Marcel's circle."

"I haven't much interest in them, whoever they are, since I don't know them. I'm interested in what importance, or significance, I can possibly have."

"You had concluded there was none?"

"Concluded – I don't know what I concluded. It's a final sort of word. I'd assumed – you said something about a judge of instruction, she might ask to see me. I'd heard nothing, I suppose, yes, I concluded that the matter was finished with. You promised me discretion, if I was frank with you. I'm not all that ashamed about my relations with Etienne, but I don't exactly go flaunting them from the housetop."

"I've come to call on you in mid-afternoon, anonymous in an unmarked car. Nothing indiscreet in that, is there? Friends and acquaintances do drop in? It wouldn't arouse gossip? Or you wouldn't care that much if it did?"

"Of course not – I wonder simply why you choose so to spend your time. And mine."

"But I'll tell you perfectly frankly. We speak of a circle, as a loose image for friends and relations. People like Etienne Marcel have several. Some business, others personal. Figures like yourself, as we agree peripheral, they have their own circle. These groups often interlock. In this way, a man does not know fifty or a hundred people. He knows ten thousand. One of those ten thousand killed Etienne Marcel."

"I'm afraid I'm completely confused, and that I haven't followed at all."

"Take yourself. You'd say your circle of acquaintance was small. Then start including the people whom you know at work. Customers, say, at the shop, or guests at the restaurant. Whose names you know, with whom you'd exchange a few friendly words."

"You seem to know a good deal about my rather boring doings. Again, I had no idea I was such an object of interest."

"That's commonplace routine. Exactly the same if you want to do business with, say, an insurance company. They like to gather a bit of information – stroll round the neighbourhood, does this lady seem a trustworthy sort of person? Banks do it, if you ask for an overdraft. Nothing secret or indecently prying, really. We do the same. It's to be expected. Your phone isn't tapped."

"I should certainly hope not: I shouldn't hesitate to complain if I thought it were."

"The purpose of my coming was nothing of any great consequence. To ask, perhaps, whether in your circle – we're not talking about Etienne now – in the village and around the town, you'd hear first and last a lot of casual personal gossip. Mm?"

"Any woman working in such places, since you seem to know all about them, is bound to hear a lot of gossip. If of course you listen to it, which I don't much. Much of it's catty."

"Like who's sleeping with who and so forth?" lazily.

"Was I right the first time, and the police are really only interested in sex?"

"I don't remember what I said, then. A joke, possibly. I'll say now more seriously that the police are interested in human relationships. Sex is a fairly frequent manifestation. And we're interested in solitude, a thing which makes people join little clubs and groups and clans."

"Uh?" sounding puzzled.

"A lot of lonely and bored people take up exciting-sounding pastimes. Key parties and stuff. Particularly when they haven't children. Ever hear gossip of that sort?"

She seemed startled.

"I – no. Dear heaven, no. Sounds," with humour and a touch of malice "as though you'd been reading 'True Detective'. Seriously, there's not really much of that, is there? I mean these stories – made up, I'd have thought, for the sort of man that collects girly pictures."

"Some of them."

"I feel that in your eyes I'm a sort of call-girl. Which, dear Inspector, I ain't. I have a living to earn, yes. I hardly think you'd be so old-fashioned and provincial as to claim I 'wasn't respectable' because of a discreet liaison in my private life and a part-time job. I've read these stories, as one does at the hairdresser's, just as one reads about Amsterdam, or the Bois de Boulogne, and these places I suppose attract the timid and the feeble. But because you're brought into contact with a lot of people like that you mustn't imagine too far."

He said nothing, which seemed to disconcert her.

"I suppose I'm very innocent but I swear I don't know how to take you." Half-laugh; humorous despair in a wrist movement with the big strong hands. "When you were here last I got the idea, clumsily I suppose and over-hastily, that you were the sort who abuses official powers. Since I was in a vulnerable position, without even the protection Etienne could have given me, I was frightened. It doesn't do – I know that much – to get on the wrong side of the police."

He still said nothing. She looked at him with her face

twitching; collected herself by going to take a cigarette from the box.

"I think you're playing with my fears in a rather odious way."

"Don't exaggerate," he said, getting up and looking for his hat. "I think you're well able to look after yourself. I came for no other purpose than I said, to ask whether your acquaintanceship included any other member of Monsieur Marcel's family or friends."

"I thought it was the second time I'd said no to that."

"Furthermore you can relax. The examining magistrate has shown no great interest in your private affairs, has no desire to pester you, and it's likely will content herself with asking you for a formal statement concerning your relationship and its extent. There'll be nothing odious about that. These visits from the Commissaire and myself have been verifications of what we have learned elsewhere. We're quite satisfied."

"Had you already thought – did you get told – that Etienne and I went out to key parties or whatever these awful games are called? Hadn't you believed me? I told you – I tell you again – Etienne was terribly discreet. We never went out together. I never met his friends or his family. I know his wife, at the riding club, just enough to say hello to. She probably scarcely knows my name. I told you all this. She's a business woman. She has no animus against me, nor I against her. It was completely separate."

"Please don't work yourself up. No doubt has been cast on what you told me."

"Is it true she tried to commit suicide? . . . Poor woman. But it's not my fault – I swear it."

"It's among the things that, you understand, bother us."

"I suppose you've asked them at the riding club."

"No more than was necessary. And believe me, they know how to be discreet too. They have to be, you realize. If they started spreading gossip about their customers they'd soon be out of business."

"And you'll leave me alone? You won't spread gossip about me? You promise?"

"We have better things to do, you know."

"I mean persecuting people about their private lives."

"Exactly. Infringements of the criminal code are enough to keep our plate full, I promise you."

"Popping in with nasty insinuations. Or twisting my arm about 'living with' a man or something."

"This isn't Libya you know," grinning. "You aren't in danger of being stoned or whatever. We've neither the time nor the inclination. Goodbye then, Madame."

Altogether too much of a hypocrite? wondered Castang. No more than at all times. It's a government-approved additive, hypocrisy. Passed by the U.S. Department of Agriculture. Nothing that causes any ill-effect in white mice. But to get back home will be good. I only wish I didn't have to go out again.

If Vera says she won't have it – then I won't. And the hell with it. I have, after all, three people tonight at my disposal.

He had to go to the hospital, to see what shape Noelle was in. The reception here, for the Police Judiciaire, was chilly.

"Doctor Beauvois wants to see you." An elusive pimpernel, but run to earth at last. Very unforthcoming.

"I'm not going to let you see her, you know. And I'll take full responsibility for that. Neither physically nor psychologically is she in any shape for being nagged at. I won't compromise on that, and I'll tell the Judge of Instruction as much, or anybody else. A week, at least. If then. Her condition is no longer critical but it is dangerous. I'm not having my patient put at risk and that's flat."

"You'll discuss it though. Do me this credit. It was myself that followed her, found her, brought her in. And gave the details to the Emergency Receiving Officer. Okay? Ten minutes of your time?" The medical person rifled through his papers, glanced suspiciously up at this police person.

"You're Monsieur Castang? Hm. All right. I'm not sure how much credit you should have. Apart from rescuing her from this state it seems to me likely that you put her into it. Still, I'll give you the ten minutes."

160

"Description of her condition?"

"Weak, profoundly exhausted, danger of pulmonary infection, apathy: she's under sedation. Psychologically of course no diagnosis has yet been possible. Profound depression and anxiety. Apart from all else you could place no reliances on anything she said."

"What if anything has she said?"

"Covered under professional confidence. No soap. Nothing, I'll tell you, fit for you to hear."

"Does she speak of her husband, her family, of other persons – who is uppermost in her mind? No harm in that." But the face was unyielding.

"Good; shock, and loss of blood, and a toxic condition, okay, I understand the gravity. But perturbed, in a real psychiatric sense?"

"A suicide attempt, dear sir, is itself a sign of gravely impaired equilibrium, even when faked or feigned. Is the expression 'cry for help' either too simple or too sentimental for you? I have no means yet of knowing what brought on this condition, whether it be chronic or deepseated. Before risking an opinion I would take a colleague into consultation. I wish to see her first healed, reassured, rested. Meaning I'll keep her well away from the likes of you," looking at his watch, "and those will be the instructions I'll give to all the personnel."

Castang was too used to the hostility of medical persons to be bothered. Richard would shrug. If Madame le Juge, armed with majesty of the law, sought a confrontation with the quacks, she was welcome to go ahead.

"One question then. As far as you can judge from what you've seen and heard, do you feel able to say this: an attempt like this is an effort to escape from a position felt to be intolerable?"

"Platitude. Truism. Not too fine a point on it, cliché."

"A situation that is painful? Or a threat, a definite menace, even if undefined?" Ferocious frown.

"You're muddling terms you don't understand. The wish to escape, to flee, is precipitated by fear. Use layman's terms like shame, or disgust, or inability to cope, and you'll get nowhere. Insecurities, anxieties: it's the child that hides under the bedclothes."

"We're talking about a basically tough person. Hardy, independent, strong-willed, highly self-reliant."

"There's no such thing as a basically tough person. All that you describe may be compensation factors, developed to defend a personality. This is all futile. You people see things in terms of guilt or innocence, and we're not in court. No diagnosis can be arrived at without clinical observation, and what your judge can do is name experts, to conduct or confirm the same. Attempt to invalidate if he so desires; somebody generally does."

"A state like this, just as a hypothesis that could be helpful, in general terms, would easily be brought on by knowledge of a crime? I don't say participation. Perhaps a certain sense of responsibility? One could have forewarned or one could have prevented, say for example."

The medical person adopted a humorous air.

"Such a state, we could say equally accurately and with even less fear of contradiction, might be brought on just by having you people under one's feet. I'd better run before I start thinking about an overdose of barbiturates. Time's up, mon vieux, and I'm a busy man."

"Incidentally, was there any other drug besides aspirin?"

"No. If you must come back at all, come back in a fortnight."

He'd have to do the best he could, with Thérèse.

24. Simon Tappertit

Dickens was a great help to Vera. Already back in school days Dickens had been a sociological text as well as Eng. Lit. The capitalist society was like this and still is. Going on a bit, the dogged desire to learn English. Worse than Russian, by a long way. As the Pope says, 'we all understand Russian even if none of us speak it'. But English: damn it, why can't we all talk Latin?

Going on a bit more, he's so good. Hm, said Castang, who had tried. The thing about Dickens to his eyes was learning how to skip. Come to that, he felt quite sure that skipping is the secret of all Lit. And as for Sociology . . .

Dickens had his uses. Like Mr Jaggers, who washed criminal cases off his hands with 'scented soap': Castang's habit of taking a shower when he got home was known as Having a Jaggers.

There was a noisy smell of fried fish. He liked loud fierce things to eat, and when he did the shopping brought vulgar stuff Vera did not much like, but ate uncomplainingly. His nose had been caught by 'angry whitings' – so called because they are traditionally cooked biting their own tails – just out of the pot and making their anger felt, said Vera, through the whole street. A vague idea that this would make cooking the supper less trouble. As often happens the opposite was the truth, since whiting are full of bones. He pulled them to pieces happily, added some leftover rice, grated carrots, and lots of sliced spring onion, which would make a delicious salad, he said, tasting and adding more vinegar.

"I'm not quite sure whether the child will enjoy this," said Vera, shuddering slightly. He got cross if she didn't eat. It was a reflection on his cooking. She had several glasses of milk. He had a beer, sighed with satisfaction, looked at her plate and said, "If you're not going to eat any more I'll finish that," belching slightly.

"You seem pretty well organized," running cold water on the plate. "Would you think it awful if I went out again?"

"You mean work? No, I don't mind, if it'll help."

"I don't know whether it will or not. This thing is all loose ends. That's not quite right. Like old-fashioned knitting wool." Nowadays one buys knitting wool in nice softly-wound balls. Before, one got skeins, and had to wind the wool off, preferably with somebody else to hold the skein. If you got the right end it wound off quick and easily. Getting the wrong end of a tangled skein could be an infuriating performance. Especially if you were in a hurry. Vera saw perfectly. Because of her, he was in a hurry. And because of her he didn't want to be in a hurry. But was getting hurried, by Colette Delavigne, and the Mayor, and a lot more tiresome people.

"I wouldn't be late or anything."

"Day or night is alike to me. The tiny one sleeps, and when it wakes up it's hungry. Then it falls asleep in the middle of its tit, and I fall asleep, and we all muddle happily along together." And you give it a clean nappy, and it loves that, and pisses in it instantly – this is all too like the wrong end of the skein. But women have patience.

"But unwind first," added Vera.

"No, I'm early. I'm not in a hurry. I'm going to have a cigar. And a cup of coffee. These people are a puzzle. I don't know what to make of them. Like this idiotic Thierry." He enlightened her about a few of Thierry's fantasies.

"Sounds all rather innocent. I mean, in a homicide."

"It is, and it isn't."

"Rather like Simon Tappertit. You wouldn't know him; he's in an early Dickens book and frankly, most of it's unreadable. But in the middle of a lot of bilge you tumble up against something good. He's an apprentice, and quite ineffectual, a poor object, but of course he thinks himself wonderful. He sneaks out at night; he's a locksmith so he can make keys to all the doors. When out he's the chief of a ludicrous gang and swaggers about breathing fire but of course they never do anything at all. Until he meets up with some characters planning a riot, who intoxicate him with violent talk. And then, of course like all vain and ineffectual people he suddenly becomes dangerous."

"What sort of a riot?" asked Castang, curiously.

"A religious one. There's a completely dotty person, a kind of gloomy fanatic, who mumbles on about Catholics gaining political power, and being generally a menace, and who excites the mob into believing there's a conspiracy to overthrow the government. They racket about screaming 'No Popery'. The English quite often did this. The

164

writer Defoe says that anybody would yell No Popery at the top of their voice without knowing, he remarks drily, whether Popery was a man or a horse."

Castang laughed and said, "It still goes on. And what happened then?"

"I forget really. The mob starts breaking things and burns a few houses, and then hysteria sets in. They all get drunk and begin killing people, get quite out of hand, but then reaction sets in and it all collapses. It lasted I think about two days. It's a historic event – I think he describes it all quite accurately but adds fictional glosses. Tappertit is the kind of grotesque comic figure he couldn't resist. I think it's exact; I mean riots always do attract pathological figures. One is the public hangman: the rest are just pathetic."

"And what happens to Simon Thing?"

"I don't recall exactly. I think Dickens couldn't bear for anything too horrible to befall him. He's punished for his vanity by breaking his leg, or getting all his hair burned off. You seem interested."

"I don't know whether I am or not." He was looking out of the window. As often at the end of a turbulent day the wind had dropped and the sun had come out, and had gone down over the roofs on the other side of the canal with a big dramatic cloudscape lit still from the afterglow. Romantic scenery, such as fills the engravings of Gustave Doré, which Vera was fond of. There is bad good art, and there is also good bad art. Dickens was often both, and so was police work. He finished his cigar and put his gun belt back on. Vera was sewing placidly, mending a jacket of his that had had a pocket ripped out a month ago, arresting somebody. The arrest had been a bit of a brawl. It meant, for her, several hours of minute, difficult, totally unpaid work of much ingenuity to make an invisible mend. Most people would have thrown the jacket away, even though it was an expensive one, and nearly new.

The baby was asleep in a basket. He opened the window to air the room, and get the cigar-smoke out.

"Is there a villain?" he asked.

"There's always a villain. Black melodramatic ones with

165

sinister pale faces. There's one in *Little Dorrit* so dreadful that everybody gets the shudders just looking at him. He's French, of course."

"I thought Dickens liked us, rather."

"So he did. Lived here a lot, and goes on a good deal about how much better things are done here than in barbarous England. But for an English audience a really foul villain, painted extra black because in fact he's singularly unconvincing, simply had to be French, you see."

"One of my troubles is that I can't find any villain. I should have a sinister Englishman, but there aren't any around."

Taking the step past 'surveillance' and building a watch around a person is not as simple as it seems on television. It is expensive; it is time-consuming; it needs a lot of personnel – all this means that it must be approved by higher authority, which takes quite a lot of convincing. To be any use at all it must also be quite ingenious. A population saturated with cheap cop-and-robber serials becomes fussy: that fellow who's forever reading the morning paper in the lobby is going to be tapped on the shoulder and have a lollipop handed him. The mailman, the chap with the toolbag – they go on hanging about waiting to use the telephone and complaints will be made.

The commonest device used by real police is to pretend to be exactly what they are: cops. After all, the police do inquire into things. A cop who goes about opening other people's cupboard doors, when asked what he thinks he's playing at, can say 'Looking for corpses' and be found sufficiently convincing.

The classic 'open watch' is nothing but a variation on this technique, and consists of following someone in a heavy-handed way, to see what he will do. If he goes to trouble in order to shake you off, you let yourself get shaken: what he will do subsequently is evidently more interesting. It stands to reason that you have a more discreet follower in reserve. Castang, known to all the family as the officer investigating Marcel's death, was the natural choice as decoy.

The flying-field 'club-house', however grandly named, was nothing more than a café like any other village pub; a low long building originally a cottage, with a sort of shed tacked on at one side, handily near the equally pompous 'Air Traffic Control' office. Facing the flying-field was a terrace sheltered by privet hedges, much haunted in fine weather by wives and girl-friends: part of this had been glassed-in, covered with a galvanized roof, and served for meetings or reunions as well as for playing cards and drinking beer when weather conditions were bad. It was a pleasant, unpretentious place with the typical atmosphere of amateurish enthusiasm, decorated with badges, banners, and the odd cup or medal won in competition. Aero clubs are the same whenever there is an old grass field long out-dated for military or commercial use but proudly showing its origins in the heroic stick-and-string days. A little con-trol tower and meteorological office, a group of hangars with service and maintenance areas, the local air-taxi and -charter firm. A helicopter or so for hire, a couple of old biplanes kept for stunting, and generally a few treasured wartime souvenirs, Spitfire, Focke-Wulf or Cobra kept carefully painted up and decorated with squadron mark-ings. There is nothing from the jet age: the field is too small. At other corners you will probably find the local glider enthusiasts, and almost always a biggish hangar for the storage and folding of parachutes.

You will find this set-up near any largish town. Secret societies of the Tappertit-type (his was called 'The United Bulldogs') abound there, each with its inner circle, private jargon, and special recognition signals. The balloon-freaks (the great status-symbol is to have been to Albuquerque) and the hang-glider fiends: high-jump and free-fall types who make artistic patterns in formation way up there in the blue. All perfectly charming, until the moment when they become grindingly boring.

The weather had been too uncertain these last days for any really serious work, and there was not too much of a crowd. Castang went up to the bar and ordered a beer. When he got it he flashed an official card with a show of slightly clumsy discretion.

"Robillard," he said portentously. "Inspection de Douanes."

"Huh?" said the barman. "Douane?"

"Not so loud you silly twit. Service de Suppression de Fraudes." Having just made it up he was quite pleased with the rotund cadence. He wasn't certain it actually existed. Somewhere surely it must. Well, if it didn't, it did now.

25. Police Work

"I've no objection," said Richard, "as long as I don't have to justify it all to the Controleur. The real Customs-and-Excise inspectorate will of course be vexed, but it won't be the first time. The thing is, enough local businessmen keep planes there to constitute a fairly powerful lobby; enough I may say to squash all the complaints from neighbouring suburbs about noise. You've stirred up quite a lot of shit and what exactly have you got?"

"I took that boy from IJ with the super Japanese; we'll see how much good they are when the lab has finished processing them."

"Hm; stills, you know . . ."

"And Lucciani with his movie camera – I kept him in the car of course. His infra-red thing; the lighting's not famous. But he has some clear footage of the chap walking. Now if we got a dubious identification of a face; it might strengthen if a witness saw something in a gesture, a movement."

"Thin! Better, I agree, than nothing. Fausta, can I have the original Marcel file, if you please, the ground inquiry? That young woman, we'll have to have her here. And the taxidriver. Mm, she's had the honesty to say all along that she was so startled and flustered that she didn't believe she'd ever make an identification. Mm, tallish, brownish, hair short."

"One thing I like," said Castang, "is that a fellow came up to the man and said Hello, I see you've shaved the beard then: wasn't it getting you enough crumpet? If he shaved it just before, it could be a pointer that he wanted to change his appearance. Still far too thin, I know, but I need more time. Got this cat on the hop a bit, and where will he hop to?"

"How much did you shake him?"

"Good, he's a parachute instructor, always around, knows everyone. I had a bunch of old tat photos for him to recognize. He made a dab at one, who in fact is safely in the Centrale at Melun, up for five years on armed robbery. That could happen to anyone. But I'd slipped in one of Lucciani. No no, never seen him before – having spent the evening together just twenty-four hours before."

"The idiot partouze – discreet about that."

"Is a fraud inspector interested in a bit of booze and girls? He doesn't want his associates looked at. Good, I've Davignon sitting on him. It's in my report; he went off to that pool-table place, the Vienna Woods. Thierry wasn't there; early night last night and needed. Neither that library fellow, the Bouvet."

"You like him do you, for the driver?"

"Too tenuous at present. Longish hair, could be anyone. But they wanted a hot driver, and this fellow is, or so Orthez claims. By the way, he got nowhere on Jackie. Unless – Lucciani heard mention of someone who's a super billiards player. Orthez identified him with no great trouble: he's a Monsieur Maresq, a bourgeois, a grower owns some vineyards up in the hills. Not often seen – once a fortnight maybe keeping his hand in at the table."

"What interest?"

"None – the barman there refers to him as 'Monsieur Jacques'."

"You may as well follow it up since we've so little. It's barely possible you may have found a crack. You've nothing for a *prima facie,* even if the eyewitness thinks there's a resemblance, any lawyer could knock it down. And where on earth is your motive in all this?" Lawyers do the same. Talking to one another about clients they may be

169

appearing for they say 'You, I don't think much of this alibi of yours' chummily outside the courtroom.

"I haven't got any motive. I've screws enough loose I'm wondering whether I really need any. It is, possibly, who I've been associating with."

"Tell me," said Richard irritably, "that even if it's a pinch it's a psycho case."

"No I'm not saying that," crossly. "I don't know why I should be expected to say anything on the base of ten minutes acquaintance."

"Quite right, let's not nag at one another."

"Not conspicuous for brains, certainly. One of those vague, good-humoured, slightly apey faces, hail-fellow with everyone. Too much talk, too many smiles, too much movement. Influenceable and excitable. That's all I'd risk, this far. I just wonder what ideas he gets, there high, high in the sky."

"You mean illuminated?" The word, vaguely suggestive of St Francis of Assisi, does duty in French for a wide miscellany of pious fanatics.

"Conceivably. We had a bit of chat. He had to be easy and forthcoming: that's his act with everyone. I soft-soaped as usual; that's an interesting job you've got. He was a professional soldier, marine paratrooper down at Tarbes or wherever."

"Ah. Military training – would know how to hold a gun. Might even think of wiping the cartridges clean – a point that's always worried me. Mm. Your man's looking a little better."

"What I thought," said Castang, "a para regiment, even after his discharge there'd be a dossier. And a medical record. Might help us a bit in a diagnosis."

"Army doctors!" said Richard with a snort. "You've the piles, have you laddy? – swift dose of syrup of figs will set you right. Next. And you're seeing visions are you – double the dose."

"Seriously – don't they have a psychiatric exam, now, as standard?"

"Fausta! Letter to Commanding Officer, Military District of Pau or where Castang tells you. Please furnish details of dossier on discharged soldier Chose, under rogatory commission zingzing, reply please greatest urgency all relevant bumf."

"Telex?" asked the lady, writing swift shorthand. "Okay."

Richard was back at page one of the dossier.

"The assassin did not speak, but called out 'Etienne' in a funny voice – not enough, that, for a voice-pattern. No finger or footprints, the poorest of physical descriptions – photos won't take us far. You're on the thinnest of grounds. As the Mayor got so fond of saying – a meaningless arbitrary killing. And you pick someone meaningless and arbitrary."

"Let it cook some more. In there anybody, on the fringe of this band of Thierry's, able to extract any profit from the situation? The theory is Liliane's and I like it," suppressing mention of Monsieur Bianchi. Leave the assassination aside altogether.

"Profit how?"

"I don't know. Say Marcel is dead and Thierry's mixed up in that somewhere, however obliquely. It could become grounds for pressure, if not actually blackmail. Too many funny things happening in that family. Didier – dead. Noelle attempts suicide. And the daughter – Magali. I gave it no weight at the time: now I'm wondering. She was wound up, nervous, sweaty. Mentioned, even, the possibility of a blackmail pattern, as though she saw something on the horizon."

"Don't fall in love and get carried away," said Richard, dry. "You've a suspect, and that's a very fine thing to have." The warning was unspoken: Castang didn't need it spoken. Harried by overzealous prosecutors, a cop will go far to make a good arrest. Far can mean too far. It hasn't just 'been known'; it's a commonplace. A cop in love with a hypothesis . . . the suppressions and distortions start coming unconsciously. "Go work on it," said Richard chillingly.

You learn early not to put faith in witnesses of things which took place in a flash, even when they are not shown

171

to have had their back turned throughout the entire episode. Some change their stories daily. Some, perhaps more, become increasingly rigid. Concerning something that happened three weeks before, as now, the distancing in time will not have brought perspective to the violent foreshortened moment of drama. It is still painted in the bright hard colours of terror, and ashamed of their terror they will not admit to it. It was that way, and nothing changes their mind. Like a bad cop, they are in love with their story.

Young Madame Thing, within the dreary portals of the Banque de France, could have been forgiven either immovable obstinacy or even the total amnesia which often overtakes witnesses to a blood crime; not only those who were told by the mafia to cultivate a faulty memory. This august financial establishment dislikes cops, loathes dramas, and takes a dim view too of junior, especially female, employees being a witness to anything at all but what they have been told.

Castang, after hesitation, got stood in one of the soundproof boxes where only one of the world's two principal subjects of interest is habitually discussed. Love, and ten per cent: guess which. He was given leisure to reflect on things like mortgages, which no bank is inclined to grant to cops. Too much mort for their liking, and not enough gage. Finally the young, pretty, composed woman who had seen Etienne Marcel shot was ushered in by an official who glanced pointedly at his watch.

"Let's sit down. I wouldn't disturb you, bar a thing which might turn out to be important. Will you just look at these few photographs, and try to tell me whether any of them are at all like the man you saw."

She took her time.

"This one, I think, and perhaps this one." She was consistent at least. Tallish, brownish, shortish hair. How it grew, what kind of texture, was it parted – all crushed under 'one of those little hats'.

Neither photo was his bird. But after hesitating she came back to it and said slowly, "Possibly this one too."

"Very well. Now try and see what it is that prods your

memory. They are all roughly the same type and colouring, so . . . perhaps features?

"Or a stance; an attitude?"

"I don't remember the features, not distinctly. Rounded – not sharp features. Perhaps something in the build. I don't know about stance. Hard to tell, in a photo."

"I'm going to ask you to pass by this evening, when you get off. Will you do that? It won't take above ten minutes. I'll ask you to look at a few feet of movie."

"All right," reluctantly, "if you think . . . I don't know whether . . . I mean, I saw so little." He wasn't going to say 'sign of a good witness'.

"You'll only be asked 'is that like'. If you can't confirm, but can't deny, that's reasonable. Don't try to strain your interpretation. But you must accept your responsibilities. You saw an assassin; it can't be repeated often enough."

"Yes. I'll try."

"Till six, then."

The taxi-driver was 'on the rank' in the Cours la Reine. Castang got into the cab with him, wondering afresh why taxi-drivers hate fresh air.

"No good, chum. I saw a fella, half-walking, half-running, jump in a car. T'other chap driving. Never saw faces, not to recognize, not what you'd say profile. They didn't stay still to take pictures of them."

"Think you could do better with some movie, like a man walking across a parking lot?"

"Couldn't say. Might. I doubt it. If I did, even – I don't want to get fingered by no terrorists. Get a bomb wired to my ignition and Bam – thanks very much."

"There aren't any terrorists," said Castang. "Okay, six or a bit after."

The other reports weren't up to much. Clothilde had helped out at a wedding party, and that night with another, family kind of gathering – a boy celebrating the passage of a difficult entry-exam. Nothing there. Magali and Bertrand, like Thierry, had had a quiet evening at home. Noelle's restaurant, and the Three Crowns brasserie, were functioning normally enough, or as best they could, as the case might be. Maryvonne had worked hard on possible

173

letters and phone messages, and got nowhere with it. A dogsbody looked up Monsieur Jacques Maresq. That's right, local wine-shipper in quite a high-class way, grower in a small but aristocratic way: well off: lived in an unpretentious but elegant country house locally known as 'the château'. In his fifties. Widowed, or divorced. Office in the town staffed by an agent. Moved around a lot, travelled a lot: the business ran on wheels. A good life, what. Like many another prosperous businessman, had an aeroplane.

The detail was of sufficient interest to make Castang want to know more. Without much trouble he ran to earth a man who knew Monsieur Maresq fairly well: the gentleman was, simply enough, fairly well known.

"Not an awful lot to tell, probably, that you don't know already. He's got some very good stuff, knows his job, looks after it. Stepped of course into a very good business: Delestang was famous a hundred years ago and more. He married the old man's daughter. Old Mother Delestang died a couple of years back and since then he's done what he wanted. The wife had some obscure illness, aplastic anaemia or something. What? Well, summertime they have to work like hell, from now till the vintage you're watching your grapes virtually every day. He works very hard when he has to. In the winter they can take it easy. Place on the Côte d'Azur, nice trips to markets. Tokyo, New York, you know. Sure he's got a plane, whip down to Nice or up to Paris, nothing odd about that. Competent pilot. Bit of a playboy in off hours, likes to throw a party, for the vintage or whatever. Women – oh, I dare say. Nothing serious. Gambles a bit – likes to enjoy himself, huh?"

"Fast cars?"

"Oh, only the usual – BMW or Mercedes."

"Reputation?"

"Commercially excellent. Private – nothing against him I ever heard. Why?"

"Nothing at all, probably. Wizard billiards player, is that right?"

"Oh yes, I've heard about that. Pool table up in the

château: I've been there occasionally, but not in recent years: I knew the old lady quite well."

It didn't really sound as though the 'Monsieur Jacques', occasional visitor to show off his skill with little balls, could seriously have much connection with the 'Jackie' who arranges partouzes. Fellow lived way out in the hills, anyhow.

He was right or he was wrong and if he was wrong then heavy witticisms about barking up the wrong drainpipe, such as Lasserre would not spare him, would look like profound thought compared with his own substitutes for ideas. Richard had let him down gently . . . If he was right all these threads led somehow back to Thierry.

Castang took a piece of paper. What was known – Known – about Thierry?

Workshy. There was no way of persuading Master Thierry into a permanent job. Suggest such a thing, and he got hay-fever. Psychosomatic: Proust's asthma. Monsieur Proust had been working away there in his head, and hard, all the time he seemed to be doing nothing but go to parties. Hm: maybe Thierry is an unsuspected genius, but it's against probability. Meanwhile – over thirty and his gravest affliction is laziness. A perpetual student, and is that just laziness, or chronic immaturity too?

Means of support. Pa and Ma, plus scratching up ten per cent here and there on go-between trivialities. Says he's not interested in money. Manages to keep himself in comfort, and whisky. Sponges off Thérèse, and the old folk too. Off anybody, in fact, susceptible to charm – or his jokes. Still, unless he's on a famous big retainer from the C.I.A., he can hardly pay for his amusements.

Now that Etienne is dead there's a source of income the less. Everybody argued that Thierry, at least, had the poorest possible motive for seeing Dad dead. Has he now come into any kind of an inheritance? Richard, or Massip, had thrashed all the finance out with the notary, and Etienne, apart from the house, didn't have a lot to leave. Or not in Noelle's lifetime.

He hadn't thought of this before. An interest in Noelle's death? Mm, some house property: the restaurant – sort of

175

business whose 'goodwill' is worth very little. The pub the same: half the income would disappear with Etienne's death, and more again with Noelle's, i.e. with the death of both his parents Master Thierry would lose as much as he gained, save in the very short term.

Interests: occupations, amusements. Slop. 'The Way', occultism and eastern religions: over ninety per cent intellectual laziness, on the average. Cars, motorbikes and parachutes: machismo stuff, to impress the girls. Tends to impress the kind of girl that's rather too easily impressed. Work at these things hard enough to achieve competition quality, you deserve respect. Play at them, you're nothing.

Conclusion, as far as there's any – Thierry's one of these people who seem to have no centre, who don't cohere. Brains enough, talents enough. What do they want? and where are they going? They have little notion themselves. They dabble at arts; write a bit, draw a bit, criticize a lot. Make themselves phony reputations as experts in something esoteric. A bit of journalism, a bit of agencing, a bit of 'designing'. When plausible and bright – as he is – they can make a living out of it. If they have to. A generation or so ago they were mostly angling to marry wealthy American widows. Pretty stony ground that, nowadays. What were Thierry's real ambitions? Did anyone have any real idea?

26. Magali

Driving home he stopped at the butcher, leaving the car in double file. He came out to a traffic warden gloating over his crimes, and told her blandly that he was on duty, his packet of steak bulging in his pocket and looking like a gun, perhaps. The lady and himself had words: she said she didn't believe his excuse, would have it verified, and if he was lying the retribution would be dire. He told her pleasantly to take her complaint and . . . send it to the Nigerian Embassy. He was rather rude, but people who are forever in the right are annoying.

Feeling saintly, he did boring chores at the supermarket. Babies being nearly as profitable a market as dogs (fewer, but more expensive) there was too much choice on the shelf. There was super-absorbent, and there was hyper-absorbent: he looked in vain for something that was absorbent. Technology has overtaken the disposable diaper, now double the price of the throwaway nappy, which is just cellulose, and low.

Vera was fully dressed, whizzing about actively, and there was a superb smell of slightly-burned cake.

"I have a very Antique marriage," she said primly.

"I Disagree."

"Not very Victorian?"

"Go back and read the Married Women's Property Act."

"I have no interest whatsoever in anybody's Property."

"Yes, it says about her bank account, but there's no mention of her fan. A woman was what your Mr Wemmick called portable property."

"Nowadays disposable, like these things. Yay," opening the packet "smelling of lavender yet."

"You know what the Bishop said about his London Club? That it was where the Women ceased from troubling."

"Ah. I can well believe it. You know what the same bishop said to the actress?"

"Yes indeed."

"That's a good hard fuck," wrathfully, "does his pulpit voice so much good. Let's have twelve dozen oysters and try the same again. What's this? Oh steak, goody, I'm starving. I'd like to meet that bishop," thoughtful.

"You see?" busy with the coffee-grinder, "you aren't fifty years behind. Think it quite likely though you're ten years in front."

"I've never been anything else," said Vera. "Come here, lovey, and smell of lavender." He got back to the office much refreshed.

177

Lucciani, with his little tins of cement and stuff, was busy threading up movie. Richard, hands in pockets, had a sniff upon his face. The young lady from the Banque de France was shown in, and viewed the cine-film with interest.

"Like," she said. "Certainly it's like."

"Very like?"

"I can't say, you know, honestly. I mean, this is night, and the clothes are different, and with this lighting the features are sort of flat, I mean, it's a terrible responsibility. You can't expect me to say yes when I'm not sure."

"Certainly not."

"Like a football match," said the taxi-driver cheerfully. "Pissy reception on this set. Off side there, you."

"This bit, here – like?"

"Run it again . . . First time I thought yes, second time I thought no. How's it you get this – with infra-red? I only caught a glimpse, you know. Might do better by daylight."

"We'll try. Lucciani! "

"I've got some – but in parachute overalls with packs on – bright orange! "

"Yes, must have ordinary street clothes."

"He goes about all day in a track suit . . ."

"You'll have to tighten this up a lot further," said Richard, "to have anything for a judge."

"I believe you," said Castang.

He went to see the technicians, who were fitting a radio-telephone into Vera's car and putting on a bit of disguise, like fog-lamps that didn't light. Getting enough cars out of Lasserre was like drawing teeth. They were even using Liliane's little Fiat, which was now a new colour.

"You're sticking to Bertrand?" he asked her.

"Yes. I better buck up too; he'll be home from the office by now."

"Maryvonne will take the Simca: I'll stay with this thing. Make sure we're tuned to the same wavelength."

"If we find we're wasting our time . . ." said Liliane gloomily.

The fact was that he'd been struck by Liliane's last re-

178

port, which Fausta had passed him with a note from Richard saying 'Castang' in red ballpoint.

'I've only been on this 2-3 days, and that's about enough or they'll start saying who's-this-female? I can change my face and my clothes, but not the way I put my feet down when I walk.

'Quite definitely, both are acting preternaturally alert. And I don't put this down to Davignon or anyone else of ours. They are staring about, both independently, as though expecting to see somebody. B's style of driving the car, habitually relaxed, has changed: more jerky and hurried. M. likewise: e.g. on a perfectly easy piece of road (traffic light) suddenly swerved over to midway line & nearly touched oncoming car which cursed her.

'Nor can I agree with Castang's definition of a harmonious family. I find her shrill and abrupt with her children, silent and sullen with her husband. B. appears gloomy and preoccupied. I don't want to make much of this: too easy to exaggerate. Meaning I don't want to start reading things into everything.

'Suggest put Davignon back on this, + Castang self if possible: this seems to me a break in pattern important enough to merit verifying where possible. Example: they are logged as going out together habitually: as far as my observation goes they seem to seek pretexts for shunning one another. B. has not been at home in evenings above one day this week, when M. spent evening with neighbourhood wife (see log) not known to us as anything but casual (supermarket-gossip) acquaintance.

'Feel this should be brought to your notice.'

As it had.

Indeed before they had reached that desirable residential district Liliane's voice came harsh on the intercom.

"There he goes again. I'm picking him up then – the Fiat's new to him – and phone when he's fixed. She's still at home, putting the children to bed."

Castang reached the end of the street, parked on the pavement as though he belonged there.

"I'm up the other end," said Maryvonne's voice. "If she's going out this is generally the time the babysitter

179

turns up. Fair hair and a woolly cap, mostly, on a Peugeot moped. Will you look, or shall I?"

"I'll walk the dog," said Castang, getting out with a leash looped over his wrist. Magali's Mini had not been put away, but was standing backed up to the garage door. The overhead light was out in the children's room. Light was on in Magali's bathroom. He strolled up as far as the Simca and got amorously in beside Maryvonne.

"Looks like a dud," said Liliane's voice in the handset. "Bridge again."

"If I recall the log it's not his day for bridge."

"Exactly."

"Was there last night," muttered Maryvonne.

"Yes, that's odd. Tell you what, Liliane, log the parked cars. Most of them will be the habitual bridge maniacs, right?"

"Familiar stuff: Davignon has them all logged."

"So a new one might be of interest."

"Okay. I can see that old Citroën of the Proc's from here."

"If the Proc gets kidnapped by terrorists," muttered Maryvonne frivolously, "she'll come in handy there."

"I never even knew the old fucker played bridge. All right, radio silence please." Even if the boy back in the office had sense enough not to log the *obiter dicta*.

Castang stayed ten minutes, got out to walk his dog back again, swinging his leash and stopping to admire forsythia bushes. The bathroom light was out. No gleam showed through the living-room curtains, but they were velvet. Still . . . No sign of a baby sitter. If she were going to settle down, you'd expect her to do so now. He reached his car, which smelt faintly, attractively, of Vera, despite technicians.

"Negative. But she hasn't put the car away. We'll hold it awhile." Two or three people, who had also left their cars out, were slamming doors and starting motors noisily. Too late for theatre or cinema, but not too late for socializing.

"Alert," said Maryvonne suddenly.

"I'll take her then. Relay me when I give you word.

Okay." The little Mini stopped on the street, and Magali, in slacks and a jacket – it was still cool at night – got out to shut the gate. "Informally dressed. Left the children alone. May be just popping over to a friend." But at the crossing of the main road the Mini did not turn towards the town.

"Heading out downstream – no, turning for the ring road." There was nothing much along here – industrial quarter. "Left turn again. Move up on me, Maryvonne; she's picking up speed. All right, got you. Dropping off – now." If, as Liliane thought, Magali had really an alert eye for a little lamb tagging in her wake, they would not risk the same car for more than a few minutes.

"She can't be going back into town; makes no sense. Unless she's checking whether she's really got a follower."

"Backing up behind you."

"Hold off – red light . . . Half right. Go easy . . . Looks like she's heading up the hill."

"Yes. I see it now. Just dodging city traffic." They hadn't doubled but made a wideish loop. It wasn't easy either to adapt to the ragged, irregular style of Magali's driving.

"She does that sort of tango step again, don't hang back, Maryvonne; looks too queer. Keep your rhythm and pass her fast, and put on a hat or something."

"I've dark glasses."

"Then take them off, idiot."

"All right now. On the main road she's holding more of a rhythm."

"Make an ostentatious left turn at a well lit crossroad. I'm about two back, and one's turning off right. See him? Okay, now." The Mini's distinctive rear end went trundling on. Castang had taken his hat off. On dark sections the dazzle of the lamps behind is enough to mask a driver, but at brightly lit intersections a silhouette is cut sharp.

They were well out of the town and beginning to pick up the hill villages of the wine land. The steady flow of traffic into town thinned; that going out stayed steady: it was a nice night to go out for a drink some place. Nothing very interesting to watch on the box. Following someone the night of a football final is harder work.

181

Magali did not go on teasing them for long. Twenty kilometres out, in a little market town popular with commuters – gone from three thousand inhabitants to nearer six in the last five years – she slowed, stopped, and parked outside the Hotel du Cerf. Castang, who had overshot firmly, went on and got caught in narrow one-way streets coming back, but Maryvonne was over the other side of the square: the Mini stood empty.

"Odds she's in the pub. You might just visit the Ladies there, Maryvonne."

"I could do with one anyhow." He parked to be facing back the way they had come, and waited.

"Yes, she's in the big room. Got into a corner by herself. Not eating or anything. Looks like waiting for someone."

"Then I'll join you, if she's anchored for a bit." He was not anxious to go into the bar, however dimly lit. Magali might think meeting him in the Hotel du Cerf was rather a coincidence. An amorous couple in a Simca did no harm to anyone, and is incurious by definition.

"You know anybody on the log, lives not too far from here?"

"I know somebody on the file who lives quite close, and has a boyfriend up the road runs a little timber business, and that's Salome."

"Ah yes. Didier's ex-wife. That might explain something."

"She and Magali were quite close once, but not for some time now, so is it a little unexpected?"

"Who to – us or them?"

"Yes, we haven't been taken into their confidence."

"What does she look like?"

"Kind of Venetian red. Pretty colouring, and moreover it's real."

Castang smiled. The strawberry blonde alongside him would know.

A car came, and tucked in just ahead of them. Maryvonne suddenly became acutely amorous, tucking her head into his neck. Castang swivelled an eye. A blonde, all right, but a silver-wig.

"She dyed it or what?"

"No, that's not her." Excited.

"What you excited about?"

"Someone who'd recognize me. The electrum blonde, ravishing if slightly faded, is Chantal. Didier's secretary."

"Ho."

"As you say, ho." This was indeed annoying, that both of them risked recognition, while Liliane, who was suitably anoymous, was stuck back there with the bridge players. Castang decided that having made a rendezvous this discreet the ladies were not likely to be staring round the room, and risked a visit to the lavatory. The dark and the fair head were together in earnest conversation. Whatever they had to say was certainly interesting. He scuttled back and found Maryvonne in a head-scarf consulting a road-map.

"Yes," she said. "She just passed you." He'd been full of the other two. Well . . .

"They can play bridge, and I'll be dummy."

"Who of the three to follow?"

"Find somewhere else to park, for a start, and then we follow our brains . . . Salome lives near here, you tell me, so will probably go home. As for Magali, she went out on short notice, since there was no babysitter. Any conclusions?"

"That it wasn't arranged beforehand? – she got a phone call, perhaps. Or she doesn't want her husband to know?"

"And she meets these others in a café. A business-like sort of meeting. She'll be going straight home, by all the signs. Tag her, but from far back; I'd rather you lost her than risk being seen. Whatever's cooking up here I don't want her suspicious. The silver-wig lady you leave to me. Busy little thing she seems to be."

These precautions turned out to be unnecessary. The ladies stayed a half hour, and nobody came to join them. They left together, without afterthoughts or backward glances. The two cars went back to the town. Not exactly in convoy, but only because the Mini was for a second obstinate about starting. Magali, as expected, drove straight home. Silverwig led him to a studio flat, rather expensive he thought, for a secretarial type. She might have noticed she was being followed, over the final stages, but a woman in a car alone, at night, is not unduly surprised at prowling tomcats. She jumped out quickly and was up the steps in a flash. He picked up his handset.

"Is this where she lives?"

"Yes, that's right. You want me to join you?"

"I don't think so; we'll call it a day. You agree, Liliane?"

"I do indeed. You two have at least had a ride in the country. While I've been sitting playing bridge. Is there anything more boring than bridge?"

"It keeps your mind off things," said Castang.

27. Law of Simultaneity

"I'm in the dark," said Castang. "There's a link between this woman of Didier's and Magali, and I've no idea what it may mean."

Richard said nothing.

"The ex-wife too. She and Magali by all accounts were friendly but not especially close. She knew the secretary of course. We may suppose they didn't have much to say to one another. The marriage broke up, we are told, because he would frig about with other women including the office help. What is one to make of these confidences in pubs?"

Richard was gazing dreamily at the ceiling.

"What does the good Doctor Jung say about a law of simultaneity?"

'I've no idea." A lot of help that was! "Who d'you think I am then – Doctor Kildare?"

Richard didn't have his mind on things this morning, he thought. Been out late last night. They'd had a bit of a drama. A fellow had shot up his wife (estranged) and snatched his child (small), and had then gone raging off after the wife's lover, with a twenty-two rifle. There'd been a chase. The fellow had gone mataglap, barricaded himself in the neighbours' flat with the neighbours at gunpoint, and dared the cops to Come and Get him. Richard had dealt with the matter: it was all in the paper this morning. But it had taken half the night. He looked as usual but was going off into trances.

Liliane came in, in something of a bustle; heavy Polish feet.

"I wanted to catch you. Castang, look. I had the duty guard, who had nothing else to do, check all those car registrations. That bridge circle after all is a pretty exclusive affair. High bourgeoisie. The house belongs to them and they pay a high subscription, and not just anybody gets in. Well, who do we turn up? – none other than this chap you were asking about," looking at a piece of paper. "Monsieur Jacques Maresq." He seemed to be sharing Richard's apathy. Not that he'd been late last night. The baby had howled a good deal though. He didn't feel bright.

"I suppose bridge is a commonplace sort of pastime. In those circles. What d'you want to make of it?"

"Oh, wake up, do. Bertrand Jouve – it wasn't his night for playing bridge."

"Maybe there was a special match or something. I can't see that it establishes any connection."

"Look, you find a link, last night, unexpected. Here, dating from the same moment, here is another. Equally unexpected."

"Law of simultaneity," said Richard. Castang looked from the one to the other, mouth open.

What got him off the hook was Fausta – not for the first time – making an opportune entrance.

"Telex," she said sunnily. "For the attention of Mr Castang, here present, partly at least."

"What telex?"

"Everybody was going on at me like anything yesterday about the Military District." Castang snatched at the flimsy.

'Furtherance your demand details service Roger Lallemand . . .' A tangle of figures and dates and military jargon

185

in telegraphese. 'Bad conduct discharge annulled. Discharge medical grounds recommended ... confirmed order Officer Commanding Military District no ...' Oh. A snotty ending. 'Written records deemed confidential ... personal dossier ... only communicated on receipt of written order made by competent tribunal.' Ha. Madame Colette Delavigne would have to explain something about the powers of an examining magistrate to the Officer Commanding.

"Sorry, Liliane. Yes, of course: there must be more to this. Look, girl, I've an urgent thing here; I'll be back to you in an hour." He went to his office. Roger Lallemand, Marine Parachute Regiment number – discharge recommended on psychiatric grounds; get me a girl quick in the communications office.

"The military district, I want the staff headquarters of this particular regiment, reference their telex of last night, I want the chief medical officer, person to person and I'm here at my desk."

A long-distance telephone call to South-Western France, down there in the country of Gascons, rugby-players and parachute regiments (all thick on the ground in that part of the world) is no problem now that France is Modern. A voice in no time as clear as that of Ma Bell herself. But military bureaucracy, obstructions, evasions. The gentleman recalled the personage vaguely. It was a year ago and more.

"Police Judiciaire. I repeat, you've a telegraphed mandate for interrogation from Judge Delavigne, possible bearing I repeat on a murder investigation. That's right; you're talking to the investigating officer. Pull the file and ring me back, priority message, PJ regional service."

Obstruction lessened: the voice reappeared, became warmer, shed some light. Roger Lallemand had not been a very good soldier, in fact rather bad. 'Oh, physically fit, and apt, hm, for service. But this is a demanding service, Inspector. Unstable. Violence, yes, well, nothing in the sense you mean it to mean, um, but a grudge against authority, affectivity problems yes.'

Castang hastily dragged his man back from the yawning chasm of shrink jargon. 'Unstable, yes, hyper-excitable

186

yes, disciplinary troubles yes. On expiration of original engagement recommended by his commander for non-renewal. Not a BCD, no, because well, paratroops can be turbulent and still be good, but a fellow who threatens fellows with weapons, one can't have that. No. Brief, unsuitable for military operations at combat level, what? Fellow had appealed against this. Wanted to be a paratrooper, a real man, you see the significance, Inspector? So it had gone to the arbitration board, on which sits of course a military psychiatrist, and they'd decided against, and that was that. The findings of that board – ah, that's a confidential document, Inspector. No no, I can give no details, in any case, if you hadn't realized, I'm not a psychiatrist, man, I'm a psychologist.'

Damn all shrinks.

Rushing out of his office, Castang fell, according to the law of simultaneity, over another shrink, this one a police shrink who had been called to give an opinion about the homicidal husband of last night, who despite having been cooled ever since in the PJ detention-unit was still in a deplorably excitable state.

"I want you," said Castang. "Give me five minutes."

"Now look, Castang, I truly can't say anything about that suicide of yours. She's under care, and I haven't seen her. I haven't been called into consultation, and even if I'd the right to challenge the opinion of a colleague –"

"It isn't anything to do with that at all."

"Oh! Oh, well then," made meek by a sense of anticlimax, "what is it?" getting inveigled into the office.

"I put to you a hypothetical case . . ." Better said a rambling kind of description, of a party who might, Castang rather thought . . .

"Really Castang you do ask the damnedest questions" testily. "By your own admission your observations of this person are of the slightest: you have the cheek to come to me with this jumblesale of hearsay . . ."

"Look, I'm only asking whether it would be feasible, a person like that, to incite, to stimulate, to excite into . . ."

"Castang, what's the difference between an impressionist painter and an expressionist?"

187

"Huh? How should I know?"

"Then stop using jargon you don't know the meaning of."

"If you tease a dog into biting somebody are you inciting or exciting it? Does it matter? Shit, I'm asking whose fault it is."

"Reduce your hypothesis to the simplest elements, eliminate all personal elements, I'll try and give you a very simplistic answer."

"Take somebody with anarchist tendencies: warm in the heart, weak in the head. Ambivalent attitude to authority, I mean a need for firm orders in a strong rigid framework, and a rebelliousness, a need to flout. Physically strong and well co-ordinated, trained in handling weapons. But nervous, dreamy, excitable. Influenceable. A need I think to be liked, to be popular. I'd say surely idealistic, romantic. Affective problems I've no doubt. Immature."

"You don't need me for that. There are innumerable case histories described in the literature. The majority, probably, of political assassinations . . ."

"That's right."

"What I cannot do is attempt any attribution of responsibilities."

"Oh, quite. He's none too bright," as an afterthought.

"Sounds simple to me, my dear boy. If you've got any material evidence sufficient to justify, arrest him. I can then, possibly, give an opinion upon his state of mind at that moment. What it was at the moment when he was alleged to have committed a criminal act is another plate of stew altogether."

"Well thanks just the same."

Hunting about, he found a horrible Dutch cigar, pale grey in colour and of a dusty complexion as though constructed out of fluff from underneath an army bed. It tasted the way it looked: not an aid to thought. He picked his phone up.

"Get me Madame Delavigne at the Palais."

"What Palais?" The switchboard girl wasn't too bright this morning either.

188

"The Palace of Justice – please," patiently. He made a little list of palaces while waiting. The Elysée, the Palais-Bourbon, the Grand Palais, the Petit Palais, Chaillot, the Luxembourg ... "Hello."

"Yes, Inspector?"

"I'd like to see you on a matter of urgency."

"In an hour's time, Inspector," fairly frigidly. Ring up your dentist and cry eagerly that you've a tooth that's giving you hell, and he'll ask in the same chilly tone why you didn't come months ago.

The Bridge Circle was a town house of the period when it was fashionable to have residences imitating country houses, of manorial aspect, in gardens with laurel bushes and a cedar tree. Of earlier date, and much more prepossessing, than the house in the Rue des Carmélites; kept nicely painted, with a chaste brass plate. Much furniture of the time, plush and mahogany, carved and gilded candelabra and mirror-frames carefully dusted and polished: two Spanish maids doubling as waitresses, a concierge and his wife (who can cook) and in a flat above, a steward, or secretary, or whatever he calls himself. Not at all enthusiastic about the Police Judiciaire.

"You're aware that the Procureur de la République is one of our members?" bleakly, as a warning to behave.

"I'm aware. Equally, you're aware that a PJ officer has powers of interrogation, and also of coercion? That the public is obliged to reply, in aid or furtherance of an enquiry? Discretion, where not covered by a legally defined professional secret, cannot I'm afraid be invoked."

"I'm aware," bowing very slightly and not asking the police to sit down.

"Monsieur Jouve is a member. Monsieur Jacques Maresq is also a member? Or a guest?"

"A country member. Occasional."

"You can confirm that both were present last night?"

"I believe I can recall seeing them both."

"A special occasion of any sort? Perhaps a competition, or a committee meeting?"

"An ordinary evening."

"I ask since Monsieur Jouve as I believe has a regular evening, and as you tell me Monsieur Maresq is an occasional visitor."

"There is nothing untoward. Members come at their pleasure."

"People habitually play with the same partners?"

"Some do, some don't."

"Did these two gentlemen in fact play together?"

"I believe I can say they did not."

"Are they friendly?"

"All members are friendly. I'm afraid I have no information about the stage of warmth of any personal acquaintanceship. We have a rule of informality."

"My question is this. Were these two gentlemen at any time last night seen in conversation together?" The man did his act, pursing lips, putting fingertips together.

"You are doubtless unaware, Inspector, of our arrangements, but apart from the card rooms there is a library, a small bar and buffet, smallish rooms for various purposes, the cloakrooms. I circulate, to be sure. You may say that my duties imply having, as it were, an eye and an ear everywhere. It would be a mistake to imply that I allowed either to be intrusive."

"I'd like to see the premises if I may, and I'd like to put a few questions to the staff."

All very correct, and decidedly 'routine', and, very often, pretty inconclusive. In the event he got what he was looking for. The establishment catered well for the creature comforts. There was a very pleasant little cellar. Certain of these wines had been supplied by Monsieur Maresq; what could be more natural? A motherly Spanish lady had had her attention called to the condition of one of these bottles, by Monsieur. She had in consequence noticed him. Monsieur Jouve did not drink when playing. It was easy to recall, thus, serving two glasses of sherry in the little room next to the committee-room, at around ten in the evening. The two gentlemen were sitting thus quietly together. No raised voice, no sign of trouble or nervousness. The talk had dropped, as was normal, when she brought her tray. Monsieur Jouve signed the chit: here was the chit. She did not in any case listen to the talk of members, Monsieur.

"That is very clear and I'll trouble you no further. It is possible, simply, that you may be called on to confirm this."

"But there is the chit."

"Yes, and the other gentleman was Monsieur Maresq: there is no possibility of an error."

"There is no possibility. The gentleman had spoken sharply, that the label was dirty, and torn. Monsieur the Secretary knows well, that my service is not slovenly."

"There is no criticism of your work, Madame."

It was not, of course, evidence of anything. Two members of a bridge club having a glass of sherry, discussing the present price of Michelins, on the stock exchange.

28. The Mandates of the Magistrate

Having taken particular pains to be just a little late at the Palace of Justice he was quite happy to be kept waiting no more than a quarter of an hour. She listened to his argument with no very great enthusiasm. Her manner could be called polite.

"So you've got these three, or possibly more, malcontents, talking a lot and bragging – but from there to plotting and carrying out an assassination, there's a wide gap."

"I'd say – I feel sure there's a directive force, organizing and impelling. Taking a good deal of pains to stay uninvolved, and indeed unattackable. We're working on it, and perhaps we can forge links, but we can't get him on anything. This is exactly the problem. Take these three in, and we've probably got three psycho cases, and where are we then?"

"I'm not by any means convinced that I could issue a mandate for arrest – what have you got? – two lukewarm eyewitnesses."

"Photographs, and movie – very poor guides to an identification. If I can take this fellow for a start, dress him up in the clothes as described, have an identity parade . . ."

"Double-edged. If then your witnesses fail to recognize him, I've got no good grounds for holding on to him, your famous evil genius in the background has been tipped off, and what then? What about the others?"

"If I arrest all three there'll be an uproar of publicity. And the family will be up in arms too. Thierry . . . Upset the cart if you lay hold of the horse, and if you touch the cart the horse will take fright. What I thought was, could we take up this fellow on a pretext?"

Madame Delavigne frowned.

"I don't like that, Castang. A mandate as you know must specify the charge." The Code of Criminal Procedure is fussy about warrants, as they are called in England. The police, even officers, cannot arrest persons unless taken *flagrante delicto*. The judge of instruction, on the other hand, has four different kinds of warrant, in ascending order of severity. It is all very formal and legalistic and concerned about the rights of the citizenry. As also happens with the Bill of Rights, the citizen gets arrested just the same because the police have a catch-all, the *garde-à-vue* which provides that a person may be held on suspicion for twenty-four hours, after which he must either be released or presented to the magistrate and charged, exactly like Habeas Corpus. Instructing judges vary widely in the latitude they allow the police in these matters, and Colette Delavigne was sticky about form.

"Something," said Castang, keeping his eye on her, "more or less fabricated that needn't concern these others. Suspicion of handling contraband or something." It can be so difficult, indeed, to secure adequate grounds for arrest that the police are suspected now and then of planting evidence. It has been known . . .

"And have the tribunal throw the case out on grounds of malpractice," on a rising note. Castang, who had been cherishing his role as Inspector Robillard of the Customs Fraud Squad, sighed and resigned himself.

"Why not go down and make a search?" A slight hint of

hypocrisy about this. A PJ officer – not a simple agent – is entitled to search without a mandate from the magistrate. "You might turn up the gun."

"Some hope! The gun's the first thing any murderer, however psycho, knows how to get rid of."

"Then if your eyewitnesses fail you I don't see much for it. If you've really got hold of the right one, you'll have to hope the one or the other will get rattled." He sighed again, and left.

"Don't see much for it," said Richard in the same tone. "Pull a gag like this, your witnesses fail you, you've nothing but to turn him loose: you've tipped your hand and for nothing. Clap the lot then under a twenty-four hour surveillance on the hope someone's nerve will go and he'll do something silly. Not an exciting prospect.

"You've no motive, Castang; these people are catspaws. There are arguments for picking up this librarian individual, and even better ones for leaving him; his mind's expanded that far there's nothing left of it. Thierry you can't very well touch: too far dug in.

"Furthermore there's a second assassination."

"Didier. I don't see how it can tie in, or how one can make anything of it at all. I haven't thought of it."

"I on the other hand have thought of it a good deal."

"We can't even be sure it's a homicide, except on very slender grounds of an expert opinion. There's no connection with any of these people unless you count the family tie. Or with Maresq, who is I'm convinced the moving spirit behind all this, though why or how the Lord alone may know."

"Maresq," said Richard, testing it. "Somewhere at the back of my mind, if I could just get hold of it, is the suspicion I've heard this name before. Now if I could recall in what context . . ."

"A link," said Castang slowly, "with Thierry. A link, which it seems reasonable to question Monsieur Jouve about, with both Marcel's son and his son-in-law. I've been wondering increasingly whether Noelle's peculiar behaviour may not have something to do with this. That

193

effing shrink won't let me anywhere near her, but it's only a question of time. Somewhere there's a fact staring me in the face, if I knew where to look for it."

Richard was staring at his blotting-pad, as though a carrier pigeon had just alighted there.

"Questioning Bertrand," went on Castang remorselessly, "isn't going to get me anywhere. He knows Monsieur Maresq. Why yes, they occasionally play bridge together. They may have some present or projected business connection. Then what? It's evidence of nothing at all. All these people have only to keep silence, and wait for us to get tired. We'll never get a shred of legal proof."

Richard's hand and wrist, which had been flexing and stretching like a serpent uncoiling from a nice sleep in the sun, was reaching slowly out towards the telephone.

"Would it be possible," asked Castang, "to throw a horrible scare into Thierry by suggesting we know why his mother attempted suicide? Mm, he's a cool card. And if it backfires – again, we've nothing."

Richard wasn't listening: he had picked his phone up.

"Massip . . . Massip, you recall we went through Didier Marcel's files, in an effort to discover anything questionable. It seems to me we made a record . . . Do you still have that paper anywhere round the office? Bring it up here would you." There was a satisfied look on his face, as though the snake had just swallowed the pigeon and was now digesting peacefully. Massip, whose office was always tidy and who never lost pieces of paper, entered with a few carbon flimsies stapled together.

"The originals must be in Fausta's file. It's not of any use – only a list of his house-dealing activities."

"Who was it made this?" asked Richard taking it. "Maryvonne was it?"

"No no; some clerical boy downstairs."

"As you say, house deals – nothing interesting there. Builders, and building promoters – ditto. Agency stuff, split-commission deals, all very normal. Rents collected for property owners. I knew I'd seen this before. Run of the mill stuff, as you say, Massip, it went into Fausta's file and the other copy, since Didier's death has an interroga-

194

tion mark hanging over it, to the examining magistrate. And somewhere along the way, I cast a perfunctory eye upon this mess of boring paper. Just shows you how easy it is to miss things, Castang – there's your link; letter M. The thing's in alphabetical order."

"Maresq, Jacques. Delestang et Cie. Rue des Ecuries no. 26. Where is that?"

"Big, old houses. Side street somewhere off the Boulevard Wilson." This in turn stirred something small which writhed an instant at the back of Castang's mind, but he could not tell what it was.

"Thanks, Massip, that's what I wanted. All right, Castang, there's now a link with both sons, and the daughter through her husband. As for the mother, the judge will give me an order for interrogation, and I should be able to overcome the reluctance of the shrinks. Now tell me again about this nonsense last night. Maryvonne typed it up but I haven't read it yet; I've been busy."

"Simply an oddity. The daughter – Magali – drove up into the hills and there had a meeting, I don't know could you call it in any way surreptitious, with Didier's ex-wife, who used to be a friend of hers so it arouses no particular interest, and with this woman who was Didier's secretary, and more or less his mistress. I took it to be irrelevant – some family matter connected with the estate, or the goodwill of the business or something: after all he was her brother, and Bertrand has been busy clearing up that office."

"Hence, possibly, a meeting with Monsieur Maresq. Whose rent Didier collected, for a property of Delestang's in the Rue des Ecuries."

"Yes, that's all quite plausible and very likely the explanation. If it wasn't that Maresq seems more of a family friend than that, huh? Can I use your phone? – I've just thought of something . . . Where's Lucciani? Not in yet? All right. Has Fausta got that report Lucciani did about the partouze?"

"Fausta," said Richard, "somewhere near the top of that voluminous dossier of yours is an extravagant piece of journalism concerning young Master Lucciani's adven-

195

tures at a sex party: somewhat embarrassed as I recall, at the thought of you, or possibly me, reading it."

"Should have been typed with a red ribbon – I'll dig it out."

"What's this then?" asked Richard.

"I'm not sure till I look," said Castang. "But as the instructor says pompously 'one can never pay too much attention to the most trivial of reports on seemingly unconnected circumstances'. You just gave a convincing demonstration and this might be another."

"Here we are," said Fausta.

"Reporting verbally to me the boy said something about a street off the Boulevard Wilson. And here we are, too. Number twenty-six Rue des Ecuries."

"Which as we learn is an investment property belonging to Delestang et Cie, wine merchants and shippers. This," said Richard, "becomes interesting."

"Lallemand, and Lucciani's other little drunken pals, got this address from somebody called Jackie. And the house is owned by Monsieur Jacques Maresq. Who doesn't know his tenants since Didier Marcel collected rents for him. Or does he? Shall we ask him?"

"Whom we might ask, I think, is Didier's secretary. See if Liliane's in yet, will you?"

"Aren't you going to ask the judge for a mandate first?" asked Castang, grinning now, no longer worrying about when he was going to get home and see Vera.

29. Verification of Identity

Police catch-alls contain several clichés of a disturbance-of-the-peace kind. Hold somebody for questioning, and a lawyer may turn up and say Look, what is it exactly you're questioning him about, and on what grounds. A variety of trivial misdemeanours, called in France contraventions, possibly punishable by the speed-tribunal with a fine of a hundred francs, provide the answer.

Thus, if you happen to be one of a dozen people picked up by the cops after a street demonstration got a bit riotous, the police, instead of charging you with an incitement to violence, will be likely, in France, to clap you for a longish moment in the waiting-room, idea of cooling your heels a little, for Verification of Identity.

Various intimidatory techniques can be added to this *ad hoc*. Harrowing you by being far too busy even to notice your existence. Bellowing at you that you're in deep deep Trouble and are going to be very very Sorry. Freezing silence while a lot of extremely important things get written on a paper, or while other important papers get read at great length, with occasional ominous glances in your direction; the implication being that this is your secret life, of which nothing is hidden from them.

With a little experience you realize that all this means nothing, and that they will do nothing. They just want to be nasty, a little.

With a person they really think might be a witness to something they are not going to waste time.

Castang was present at the beginning of the job; a temperature several degrees below zero and Richard looking at the woman as though she were something the cat turned up its nose at. A slow level voice; a deadly politeness.

"I am Divisional Commissaire Richard of the Police Judiciaire. You have been brought here on strong presumptions that you have wilfully concealed information relevant to a judicial inquiry, that you have obstructed police officers by withholding co-operation, that you have deliberately sought to mislead. These are delicts punishable by prison sentences.

"It is my duty to tell you that I have the power to hold you here, until the examining magistrate decides whether releasing you would be prejudicial to public interest, on the grounds that you hold communication with persons concerned in assassination.

"It is further my duty," gimleting, "to warn you that while you are not upon oath, and will not be charged with

197

perjury since the law provides that both silence and lying form part of systems of defence, you had better take refuge in neither. We have more than enough independent information to check all you say. You had better grasp how serious this is."

The woman stuck to stout denial, but inroads had been made upon her.

"Take her," said Richard in a patient tone of one who has heard all this too often, "to Commissaire Lasserre."

Since Lasserre left the door open, since he knew well how to be vary greasy affability with loud bullying, scraps of the resultant interrogation floated through to Castang and Liliane, supplying him with paper next door.

"You describe yourself as a house agent. Perhaps I should describe you more accurately as a Girl Agent. Tell me," at his chilly greasiest, "why I should not treat you like a common prostitute?

"A lawyer? You'll find yourself with a lawyer, my child, quicker than you bargained for. And you'll wish you Never Laid Eyes upon him.

"I have here a statement by a police officer concerning these activities in this flat in the Rue des Ecuries. You are going to tell me that you were unaware of them? That your employer Didier Marcel was unaware of them? That you don't know this 'Jackie'? Let me tell you that I Don't Believe you. You are known and you have been observed to have been in contact with these men. Against whom, I may tell you, very grave presumptions rest.

"Now we come to this meeting at the Hotel du Cerf. Don't bother to deny it. You see that we know all about it. Now I want the subject of this conversation, without omission and without evasion.

"Castang! " in a sudden fearful bellow.

"Sir," he said, appearing in the doorway.

"Take what people you need, and pull this rabble in."

"Sir! " resisting the impulse to jump smartly to attention and stamp his boots. He went down the passage to Richard, who had paid a silent, sinister visit to the scene of activities.

"She knows this Lallemand – she's been of course in

198

these partouzes herself. Lasserre will turn her over to Liliane; we'll rest her awhile and then we'll try a confrontation. We'll see too whether your eyewitnesses can identify him. Tell him you want him as a witness. Leave the other, the Bouvet, for the moment, until we want him."

Castang went back, found Maryvonne, and said, "Come on."

The little airfield was a peaceful place. In late afternoon sunlight the mechanics were tinkering with the usual little Pipers and Cessnas to a background of pop from a transistor standing casually on a wing, distorted by the metal walls of the hangar. It was too windy for jumping: the 'Pilatus' with its odd high square wing and its long turbo-engined nose stood sleeping and there was no overalled group with packs on. In the parachute hangar the careful, expert work of folding and repacking was going on placidly, to a quieter version of the pop accompaniment down the road. Lallemand, in his tracksuit, looked up with his cheery grin.

"Hello Monsieur Robillard, still enquiring into crime?"

"I'd have thought you were a bit vulnerable, here."

"I'll say. We've over three hundred packs, and they're worth ten thousand each. But a couple of us sleep close by, and we've dogs of course."

"I'd like a little word, and in private would be best."

"You want to go over the club, for a quick one? Nearly knocking-off time anyhow."

"These quarters of yours are closer by."

"Sure. We have this shack out the back. Lead the way, shall I?" A kind of prefab barrack, one storey, with half a dozen rooms, and a military type messhall; kennels at one end. Rumpled bed, chair and table, wardrobe and drawers, posters and caricatures. Guitar in one corner, fishing-rod and a hunting rifle in the other.

"Patrol a bit, nights. Wouldn't do to have any kites or anything outside. Vandals!"

"Monsieur Lallemand, I've come to ask you whether you'd mind coming down town with us, for it may be some

199

hours, to see whether you can help in an investigation we're conducting."

"I've already told you – we see to it we've no trouble with thieving and no stolen stuff gets passed on round here. And contraband I know nothing about. We care about physical fitness, and we don't use any drugs."

"Nonetheless you've no objection to coming, I'd hope?"

"Well it's a bit heavy, like, a bit thick, coming it like this."

"A duty of the citizen, right, to co-operate with law-enforcement officers."

"Well, I suppose, if you're making such a thing of it. Take long?"

"Shouldn't suppose so. This your gear, in here? Mind my taking a look?"

"Hey, that's personal."

"I am a PJ officer, Monsieur Lallemand, and I have the right as well as the duty to make searches and seizures on suspected premises, in the presence of the owner and with respect for his private property."

"What's this suspected?" on an angry high note. Castang was rummaging along the hangar rail for things green or brown. You mean I'm suspected?"

"Just look through the drawers, Maryvonne. Not unless you deserve to be: you tell me," lightly. "Those suitcases under the bed, mind opening them for me?"

"What you taking out that gear for?"

"I'll tell you, perfectly frankly; let's keep calm. Nothing to get excited for. We've a couple of fellows down town, we think might recognize people seen at the scene of a crime. To test their credibility and the accuracy of their observations, we often like to have three or four different types, looking more or less the same, wearing the same sort of clothes. These'll do. Your height and build will fit in roughly. Okay? Nothing to worry about, you see."

"You mean you want me to change into those things," said Lallemand in a more normal voice, sitting down on the bed.

"That's the general idea. Needn't fuss you, need it?"

"Then why's she looking in those drawers?" leaning

back with an elaborately casual air of sprawl, elbow on the pillow. "For a tie or something?" sarcastic.

"You might just get up till I can see in those cases. And reach down the box there, on top of the locker."

"Look for yourself: I don't see why I should help you," reaching over for a paperback book by the bedhead. "Go ahead and amuse yourself: I'll read while I'm waiting, if you don't mind that." As Castang made a half turn towards the wardrobe, dumping the clothes on the bed, Lallemand slid his hand under the bolster.

"Don't do that, friend," said Castang quietly; he had been waiting a minute or more with his thumb tucked in his belt. "Just look at the young lady and you'll see you're bracketed. Even if that thing is cocked" showing the gun in his right hand and pinning the wrist with his left. "Loosen your arms." Half lying, the man could not do much, but his left arm was ready for a punch and Castang was too close; he poked a muscle-packed rib with the pistol barrel. "Spare me any judo stuff," dryly. Maryvonne, standing quite still with her gun braced against a hip, gave a slight cough.

"Stand. Arms limp. Turn your back to me. Arms behind you. It's lined up on the centre of your back, Lallemand. Stay that way. You have resisted arrest, and you're armed with a prohibited weapon, I'm putting handcuffs on you. In the car, Maryvonne. Legs apart. Further. Flat on your feet, and wide apart: keep your arms behind you. Cuff him, Maryvonne. Now you can turn round, and don't be funny. We'll take a look. Well – I hadn't hoped for this." An old US army forty-five. "A blast, that," talking too much, aware he was still highly strung up. "I'd never thought you'd keep that. In fact I was categoric you hadn't. Read you wrong, I realize. You valued it too much. Weapons are very important to you. And when the revolution comes you'll know how to use them. Front line activist, what, us real freedom fighters. Take the clothes, Maryvonne, I don't know if they're right but we maybe won't need them."

"'S not my gun," said the man sullenly.

"It never is," cheerfully. "You borrowed it, or you

found it in the bushes. A man in a bar sold it you last week; wartime souvenir. You get in the front, busterboy. You drive, Maryvonne." He was talking too much but yes, his nerves were a scrap more fluttered than he would care to admit to himself. The heaviness in the butt told him the gun was loaded, and it wasn't the sort of antique cannon you cared to have pointing at you. He had a memory of what it had done to Etienne.

Richard poked at it in a disbelieving way.

"You got tied to it and blown from its mouth, in the time of the Indian Mutiny. It's an unexpected stroke of luck."

"He wanted to take a clap at me with it, which would have been another."

"Carrying it, was he?"

"Under his pillow. When I started looking at his clothes he felt the jaws tightening. One doesn't much like these types that want to be heroes. Think – cocked and the safety off: he'd have tried, I think, if it hadn't been for Maryvonne."

"Anybody left in I.J. this time of the evening? Doesn't matter. We'll have it test-fired timorrow and the cartridge marks compared. Leave this fellow in the cell: I've no time for him now. The girlfriend gave at the seams finally and told us a lot; not about this naturally, she'd no knowledge of that. But Maresq – he's quite a case. You'd better phone your house: you'll be out late. And now you've been seen escorting the handcuffed prisoner, etcetera, you'd be well advised to go pick up that Bouvet, before the light fades, because some wiseacre out there may phone up to say his pal's down the hole." Castang's face showed disbelief.

"I'm not talking about accomplices," said Richard. "I'm thinking of that helpful little man you meet on the road, who flicks his headlights to tell you there's a radar speed-control up ahead. Solidarity, my boy, against bastardly fuzz."

"And Thierry?"

"Liliane's gone after Thierry," calmly. "Let's just hope

Thérèse doesn't have a gun and decide to shoot it out defending him."

"What d'you make of the motive in all this?"

"What motive?" said Richard coolly. "Motives are old-fashioned things. That's where both you and DST went wrong, looking for motives. I should have thought it clear that you can get people to do anything, including murder and suicide, with a phony religious stimulus. You need a guru, and we've found the guru."

"You mean Maresq?"

"None other. I don't think he designed any assassination: that was going too far altogether and probably took him by surprise. But with the eye to profit of his kind, I'd guess he saw the blackmail possibilities. No time for that now; go find that librarian fellow with the expanded mind."

30. A Fly in the Eye

"Who's got Bouvet under observation?"

"Orthez," said the switchboard.

"Raise him on the blower for me."

"Here you are – you're through on the link."

"Castang – whereabouts are you, old son? I'm coming to pick you up: we're going to pinch this phenomenon."

"He left work a bit early. Mostly he walks home, and goes through the park. Pick you up at his home?"

"No; by the park – I want to see whether he knows anything. Might have got tipped off. I'll be at the corner of the boulevard by that big flowerbed, the one that's a clock. Waste no time or you'll miss him."

"No need to bust yourself; he stopped for a drink. Bit agitated but he's often like that: you know, talks to himself. There he goes – over the far side; see?" said Orthez.

"We'll leave the cars here."

Nobody would ever see the librarian as anything but a pathetic type, watching him. A Walter Mitty; the passion for souped-up cars and four-wheel-drift told one all. Not that he was particularly weedy or given to twitches, being indeed a colourless person with dusty hair, neither tall nor short, looking simply what he was; a junior functionary in one of the dustier of state or municipal backwaters; the Ethnographic Museum or, as here, the Bibliothèque Nationale. He was dressed conventionally, and taking a breath of fresh air and hygienic exercise on his way home. Lots like this can be seen jogging on the perimeter paths of any park. Perhaps, following him on foot at the same pace, as Castang was, one might find something odd in his walk, a queer way of balancing his shoulders, of tossing his head. He walked in a rapid broken rhythm, stopping to stare about him, at trees, or ducks or whatever.

"You think he's on to us?"

"He's always like this," said Orthez indifferently. "Might be on to me or Davignon: we've had to get too close this last time or two."

"We'll separate. He can't be on to me; he's never seen me. I'll get a bit closer and see what he does. You skirt off towards the middle."

Bouvet turned once, and stared at him, but showed no sign of suspicion. Even if he has been tipped off, and four or five people saw us walking Lallemand back to the car, a phonecall says 'Cops picked Jojo up' not 'a cop with a bluish jacket and dark trousers pinched Jojo'.

The Municipal Gardens are long and narrow, with a central path featuring Floral Display, grass, and paths near the edges lined with speckled laurels and conifers and such-like economical, pollution-resistant cover. The path is sandy, mixed with pine-needles, pleasant to walk upon. Castang got to within ten metres, but Bouvet was in no way disquieted. I'll walk him home, thought Castang, pinch him there, send Orthez back for the car. No, that's too far. The Gardens stretch out to near-suburb, where two main roads diverge and lead to middling-near suburb. Near the end there is a public lavatory in a chaste grove of yew trees; that'll do nicely. Helpful towards this project,

Bouvet turned into the lavatory. A very nice one, with elegant yellow tiling, kept extremely smart by a zealous Dame Pipi, who had now gone home. The gates here were closed at sunset, to discourage delinquency. Castang followed into the lavatory – deserted save for his chap buttoning his trousers. Nice and discreet: he felt he'd had enough publicity.

"Monsieur Bouvet?" The man finished tidying – please adjust your dress, as the neat notice has it – and turned to face him with a puzzled look, taking hold of his jacket lapels.

"Yes?" in a normally startled voice.

"I am a police officer. I have to ask you to accompany me to the commissariat, for verification of identity."

"Oh," he said. He stood, doing nothing, just looking startled.

"There's nothing to fear. Walk back, shall we? I've a car at the top end." This wasn't a violent man.

Imprudence? Guard a bit down, after the peaceful stroll? Simple stupidity? Or reaction, from the tension and watchfulness of the moment with Lallemand.

As the man walked quietly towards Castang he drew some sort of flexible club from his inner pocket, and as Castang sidestepped he swished with it, left-handed, in a quick backhand flip. An instinctive jerk of the head, backwards, in tune with the sidestep. Ward with your left hand, as your right goes back in a gesture practised already today, to the belt holster back of the right hip.

But all this too little and too late. Enough to make it what is politely named a Glancing Blow. Wouldn't like to have one that did more than glance: take my whole flaming head off instead of getting a black eye that can go in the Guinness Book of Records.

More eyesocket than eye – for which thanks – and it was not a cutting blow – more thanks and believe me, Sincere.

Castang went down on one knee, blind in his left eye bar catherine wheels, roman candles, a lot of things all wrong against this egg-yolk-yellow background. Come to that, the right eye felt like a strenuously shaken kaleidoscope. Lot of good a gun would do him : fill a few yew trees with copper-jacketed lead. He lurched out holding his eye. Fellow was running there like the March Hare, and so were the yew trees and so was Orthez and as the kaleidoscope changed they all came together in an untidy collision, but who hit what, in what order, he felt unable to say.

"Corblimey." Better not say that either: He nearly did.

"Come on jocko, upsydaisy," said Orthez' voice. Speaking to him? He approached with measured steps, something between a rumba and a slow waltz. In this part of the world was a cast-iron drinking fountain. Push very hard you get a trickle. Push very hard indeed, as he was doing, and you get it in the eye, which for once is exactly what we want.

"You sit here," said Orthez sensibly, putting him on a bench. "And jocko here I cuff to the bench, like this. And I go get the car. Right? You okay?"

"I'm okay." The yew trees had stopped being orange and vermilion like canna lilies, and started being yew trees again.

"Naughty, naughty, naughty," said Orthez, exactly the way one would to a dog that pissed in the corner. He was holding a thirty centimetre length of heavy-duty electricity cable. Creamy shiny skin: complicated core. Not altogether unlike a stick of Brighton Rock. Among my souvenirs. A cigarette that bears a lipstick's traces, an airline ticket to romantic places; these Foolish Things remind me of you.

"Raw beef steak," said Richard, sounding unfairly entertained. "Make that two raw steaks, one tartare, with olives, and capers, and gherkins, for ol' Moshe FitzCastang here." He had a black patch, supplied by Maryvonne from the Aid Box, following ice cubes and a stiff whisky from the other aidbox. "You want to go home?"

"No no, my wife would have a fit. And I'm quite eager to learn what happens next."

206

31. The Evenings of the Police Judiciaire

What happened next was that they all went to eat. Even the police has to eat. The tenacious legend that it subsists entirely on the beer and ham sandwiches sent in by the 'Brasserie Dauphine' is untrue. Since that dreadful ham sandwich is a reality, all too often, it is avoided where possible and especially by Commissaire Richard, who detests it. When all the boots are on overtime – a lot of which is not paid – they try to make up a bit of the leeway on expenses, and shovel down the grub. This is tolerated by Richard, whose troops fight poorly on an empty stomach, and 'given a certain measure of tolerance' by the Comptroller, who yields grudgingly, and chips assiduously at the drinks bill.

It is psychologically important too. If the boots, much of whose work is of the most leaden monotony anyhow, are kept late, especially scrabbling at paper by artificial light, then freighted heavily with bread and beer, the most ludicrous mistakes get made.

The Code of Criminal Procedure is pedantic, and remarkably punctilious, about the rights of detainees. The intervals at which they must be rested (the transcripts of all interrogations must state the hour and minute of beginning and ending or suspension) and fed are carefully laid down. It says nothing about when the boots get a break. Much police brutality is attributable to bad digestions.

The answer in general is the neighbourhood pub. It is convenient, and a place of relaxation in a way no canteen can be. It is quite cheap, and though not comfortable it's not like the office. One is known there, and little whims and preferences catered for. One is anyhow not Robbed. The menu, and the cooking, are far too well known and much criticized, but are more artisanal, and less industrial,

207

than canteen food. Not so much of the canned sausage and dehydrated-rehydrated mashed potato, both of which have made inroads into French grub. Briefly, however primitive, it is a place of rest and refreshment for boots. Richard, whose digestion is delicate and gets little meals cooked him by Fausta on camping-gas, rarely appears there, save on these occasions, showing solidarity with the boots.

The pub puts up with all this. The police are not particularly good customers; they are indeed rather bad and the landlord complains that he makes no profit at all, what with all the topping up of glasses, and squabbling with the Comptroller over grubby chits signed with illegible scrawls, and people who will go and make phonecalls while eating, and expect their food to be hotted up for them; and getting one's bills paid two months late, and never any tips. But he tolerates, and is even sycophantic, because it is a good thing to keep in with the police, because they turn a blind eye to little lapses in legality, and because boots in general are a bit subhuman but occasionally pleasant. He says he never makes a penny but this is a flagrant lie.

The pub has a tiled floor, varnished wooden tables, bottom-polished benches, and if you want to eat, paper tablecloths, knives which don't cut, and forks which bend under pressure. There is never enough bread. There are two waitresses, known respectively as Nixon and Carter because of pretended facial resemblances. The place is fairly clean, but never smells clean because the landlord hates fresh air and pretends there is a draught. This does not bother the boots, who get too much fresh air and are used to smells, much worse ones.

Richard (Lasserre was still conducting interrogations) hustled in with Castang, Orthez and Maryvonne. Liliane, who had 'lost Thierry', was God knew where: Davignon and Lucciani were keeping an eye on Magali and Bertrand, and probably eating too, and most other people had gone home.

"What's to eat?"

"Thon Bordedlaise. Delicious." Tuna in red wine sauce; yes, that is good but . . .

"The fish always stinks here. What else is there?"

"Some navarin of lamb over from lunch – that's very good."

"All bones, and too many carrots."

The voice sank conspiratorially.

"Pheasant."

"Young pheasant?" suspiciously.

"Well no, rather old pheasant. Braised. En chartreuse. With cabbage – but special. Not dear."

"You mean poached."

"Shush, we won't say anything about that."

"All right, pheasant, but I won't drink white wine; that stuff gives me the bellyache." Castang, who wasn't going to eat tartar steak here – it would be horse – said "Two."

"Three."

"Four." If one got pheasant at this price of course it was poached. In fact even old, with onions, cabbage, a bit of bacon, glass of bellyache wine, pheasant – that overrated bird – eats well all times of the year.

"And soup to start? And two jugs of the special beaujolais."

Richard filled his mouth with bread and mumbled, "Caught the judge before she went home." Judges of instruction generally do work late; it is a chronic complaint in legal circles. Tribunals are up to all hours.

"She give you a mandate?"

"Yes. Since we have the gun. Said blandly it was what she had expected. Need it." They were proposing to enter a dwelling-house in the hours of darkness, and even a Divisional Commissaire needs authority for this.

"Bloody lucky it's tonight."

"Yes, the moment Maresq smells a rat he'll wrap up and be untouchable. As soon as that Chantal gave away that the party is tonight it was try and get a wedge in, straight off."

"Unless Thierry tips him off."

"I don't think Thierry would do any such thing. If you were Thierry, don't you think you'd be happy to see him fall in the shit?"

"I don't pretend to understand Thierry."

209

"The others, sure, stout denial is their system of defence. They've never heard of Maresq, except oh, is that the billiards wizard? Incriminating him would do them no good. Lasserre got nothing out of the paratrooper. Normal – Lasserre is just like any sergeant-major every soldier has ever suffered from. The other one, who clonked you, is just going to go on acting dimwitted. Said he thought you were a mugger. I left, at that point. They always call this vegetable soup, and it's always beans. Now Thierry – he's part of the family. He's implicated fatally. He must know that, sly little bugger. But he held no gun, he committed no assassination – not Etienne anyhow. Parricide, just think. If he can pin responsibility on the guru, he has a chance of not much more than a concealment charge; conspiracy maybe."

"Psycho case anyhow."

"They all are, aren't they? Save Maresq, who probably is, but he'll find it less easy to plead. Incitement and instigation."

"I still don't see clearly how . . .?"

"Pass the salt. I'm not going to discuss this over a meal. But how many phony religions are there in California?"

"Aren't there around three hundred, registered for the tax dodge?"

"And how many dotty sects of ten persons or so who don't qualify?"

"God knows."

"And how many in France, would you estimate?"

"Maybe sixty?"

"Hm, I'd call that conservative."

"I don't manage to read Maresq as a guru."

"I don't suppose he is, in any accepted sense of the word," said Richard coolly. "This soup's not all that bad; any more in your pot there, Maryvonne? He hasn't organized a sect for financial purposes, has he? Got plenty of money. Nor for religious worship, with initiations and rites and stuff. Just in the sense of power over people. I'm not making any diagnosis, till I know him, and then as little as I can help . . . You know, there's a case in history that has always interested me. Galigai."

"Who's that?"

"The Marechale d'Ancre. Acquired, along with her husband, Concini, immense power, wealth and prestige during the regency of Marie de Medicis, who was not too bright in the head, and the minority of Louis Treize, who at no time was conspicuous for decision. Getting rid of the husband was fairly simple. Louis finally got fed up with being bossed around, all the nobility loathed this jumped-up Italian bastard and a chap called Vitry, captain of the guard or such, finally shoved a sword through him, shouted Long Live the King, and everyone cheered. You think he got pegged for murder? He got made a duke, and a Marshal of France, vide the unlamented Concini.

"But," slurping his soup, "the woman was the interesting one. She had the husband under her thumb, but more to the point she had the queen mesmerised. For years the imbecile Medicis woman did whatever she was told.

"Right, Concini dead, they felt bold enough to arrest the frau. Typically medieval; unable to explain her dominance they charged her with witchcraft.

"What was the secret – they asked, meaning how did you enlist the Power of Satan – of your influence over the queen?

"What could poor old Galigai say? No secret, no influence, no sinister machination.

"But there Was an influence! No more, gentlemen – can you see them all there – than the power of a strong mind over a weak one.

"I've an idea that's all there is here. Now shut up, and bring me this pheasant, so-called, and let me study it closely. Another jug, Gribouille."

They got back to relieve Lasserre, and Liliane, who returned cross.

"Thierry is nowhere to be found."

"Done a bunk."

"Yes, out the back, while Davignon was sleeping in front."

"Well," said Richard, "not a tragedy. He's no transport then, I take it."

211

'No. I've checked all the family places, the pub and so on – nobody's seen him there and would be surprised if they did, so the odds are pretty much against that. His friends, as far as we know them . . I've got the railway police looking out. The airport I suppose – he may have more money than we think; little cash reserve somewhere. Paris perhaps: mostly that's where they think of once they're on the run. But if he hitched a ride . . ."

"Not worth blocking the roads for," thought Richard aloud. "Make the usual telex signal, since there's a mandate, but it'll do tomorrow."

"He might be headed out to the hills?" suggested Castang.

"I'd be delighted if he is: have him bottled out there with no great pains. I left the gendarmerie instructions not to hold up any people heading into the village, but to stop anybody coming out, on the usual breath-test formula."

"He might not go out there with the idea of tipping Maresq off."

"Wreak a bit of personal vengeance, you mean? On the ground that if the cops were interested in Lallemand and the other, it could only be because Maresq had alerted them? An attractive scenario, but if I may say so, Castang, made up on the spur of the moment by your over-active imagination. Getting all the characters handily together like that is a thriller-writer's device. It's too tidy. Too melodramatic. Reality has looser ends, and more of them. Things as they stand . . . Catch some supper, Liliane: these brave people," looking at his watch, "will be making a move soon. It's a good hour's drive out there."

"What exactly did you get out of that female?" asked Castang. They were waiting for a signal from Davignon and had nothing to do but smoke. Richard seemed very sure of his ground.

"She told some very gaudy lies," sounding as though he had had lots of entertainment, while Castang was getting hit on the head in public lavatories. The piece of thick cable, unusually simple and competent form of blackjack, lay on his table as 'material evidence': been a stroke of luck, he said cheerfully, like the gun. Castang, who had been on the sticky end twice now, felt less cheerful even though his cheekbone had been pronounced uncracked and an 'anti-inflammation' pill had got prescribed by the police doctor who'd been called in to look at the catch: they always are nowadays, and as much to fend off any eventual defence tales about police brutality as for any other reason. Though Lallemand had been what written reports call 'over-excited'; not to say hysterical. He'd had some sedatives: being blackjacked by Lasserre was not among them, though people 'resisting arrest' have been known to acquire black eyes 'while being physically restrained' say the reports virtuously. To Castang's credit, he very rarely beat up anyone even when he'd had a few knocks himself. To Richard's credit, he kept his regiment tightly in control, and that included Cantoni's bangbang brigade, a set of toughs with much contempt for 'intellectual cops', which thought Castang a right milk-pudding. Nor was Richard the kind of commissaire who turns a deaf ear and blandly pretends he had no idea what was going on. He did not dodge his own responsibilities. A reason as strong as any other for the loyalty of his subordinates.

"Lots of lies," Richard repeated, playing with the supple club and narrowly avoiding a blackened fingernail on his own account, "but that kind of half-educated, pretend-sophisticated, chairborne clever woman is handicapped in her lying. Can't lie the way a gipsy does. Once they start talking you get at the truth. Muddled, and full of holes. And of course Maresq was too clever to let her know much.

"What's clear is this. Friend Didier, and there are a lot of question-marks still around that sly little operator, was fond of girls, and indulged happily in parties with other people's wives. Not really blackmail, but the definition that limits the word to a formal demand for money, backed by menaces, is very inadequate. He had some notion of municipal politics. Etienne played this game too, and we may guess it was his undoing. Collect, and file, every little scrap of information about anything: you never know when it might come in handy. To serve as leverage it must be discreditable. When it isn't, technically, can it be made to

213

look discreditable? In certain circumstances? – good, wait for those circumstances to arise.

"Didier used this woman, in lots of ways, as a go-between. Sooner or later her path crossed Maresq's: whether his tastes already lay in that direction we don't know yet. Put it that Maresq, much richer, much brighter, moving in much wider and more genuinely sophisticated circles, found these fish small, but useful. Whether he had singled out Etienne as a target, because of some real or imagined grudge, remains to be seen. There's no trace of him in any of Etienne's business affairs, which as you know we combed pretty thoroughly, looking for something of just this sort.

"Didier came within his orbit. So did Thierry. The others coincidentally. He had a plane, and may have seen or known something of Lallemand. That advanced-driving place, possibly, though Orthez doesn't think so, was a contact with Thierry. Later, no doubt, that billiards-playing café served as a place to meet, study, and instruct these disciples. The crank-religion soft spot, in your librarian type, which naturally fascinated a person like Thierry, of weak character, indolent ways, and an inflated notion of his own brilliance, would be another handy tool.

"Where the responsibility lies I leave to the judge: why should I let it bother me? Lallemand, once he gets the re-tractations and counter-retractations sorted out, sees a lawyer, begins to piece a system of defence together, will throw all the blame on Maresq. Who on his side will do just the same. I leave all that to a tribunal, but where do we come in?

"What do we have on Maresq? Nothing at all. He can laugh it all off. Sure he is remotely acquainted with these little people, but I ask you, Monsieur the President, do they look like friends of mine? And so forth. He'll have alibis for all the essential period covering Etienne's death. Did he kill Didier, who must have found something out and threatened to blow the whistle on him? Maybe he did, and maybe we'll never get to prove it.

"What we can feel certain of is that he decided to tighten his grip. He had Thierry in his pocket. Didier – but

Didier's death, even if he was not the author, lessens that hold. The woman Chantal – but she's small fry. If though he can get a good grip on the family, there's pickings there and money to be made. We may guess he tried to use what he knew on Noelle. She reacts violently, but not as he had expected. He shifts his ground a bit. Try to get Bertrand, or Magali, or both, into a corner. The one is vulnerable – big companies don't like executives that are linked to a scandal as smelly as this one is likely to be, in a town this size. The other – who knows? She might have strayed into some stupidity of this sort, in a moment when she'd drunk too much – it doesn't matter."

"She has still a strong family feeling."

"Look mate, what matters to us is to get this grip established that Maresq wanted, from spite, revenge or what have you. If he can use the leverage he's got to rope them into his wife-swapping games, then the more lock on them all round.

"Simply, we've had again a stroke of luck. That trip of Magali's out to the hotel was to get this set up. A party tonight – a small select party. The other woman, this Sabine –"

"Salome."

"That's right. Either in the act before or roped in too – she was friends with Magali before, you said. Makes no odds: it's the time factor, where we're concerned."

"If Maresq finds out we've got Lallemand he'd smell a rat, you mean."

"Draw in his horns and lie low, and abolish all the evidence. There may be some we don't know of. We haven't got Thierry yet. He may have news for us. But if he's cool enough to keep his trap shut . . ."

"Isn't this Maresq taking a big unnecessary risk, inviting people out to his house?"

"Risk on what? No criminal offence in the code. Where's any proof? Where's any real link? Don't you see, Magali, and Bertrand, will never say a word of what they know or guess of all this. From simple self-protection. Noelle will never say a word either. What, Thierry – involved in the killing of his own father even when not the

actual author – that really is traumatic; would be to anyone. No, he's safe there. Unless we can catch them *in
flagrante* – that'll lever their jaws open.

"Look at it from his viewpoint. Get Magali out to his
house for a purpose like this – likely the idea is to take a
few compromising pictures as an extra insurance – and she
won't broadcast any guesses, let alone hints, less still
knowledge. And incidentally – I haven't seen her –
wouldn't she be a pretty juicy catch?"

"Yes, she's extremely pretty."

"And wife, huh, of this highly regarded and successful
young executive. A plum, make no doubt of it. But if we
are any later than tonight – that arrest of yours was inevi-
table. It was not foreseen, but it could not be put off. How
many people saw it? Bound to be in the press echoes, tomorrow. You with your douane fraud-squad!"

"Seemed likeliest on the whole. The Bouvet and quite
possibly the Thierry are on the mind-expanding kick, and
a lot of that stuff could come in by private planes," said
Castang defensively.

"I'm not criticizing you, my boy. I never expected you
to find the gun; neither did you. Neither surely did
Maresq: he must have felt sure it was ditched long ago.
There was no other sound evidence against Lallemand.
But if it leaked out – there'd be no party tonight."

"You feel sure it hasn't?"

"I got a tap put on Maresq's phone," said Richard
simply. "Not that he'd say anything, ever, on a phone!
But I'd guess there'd be a code word, perhaps any call,
just to say wrong number, from the likes of Chantal . . ."

At this moment Richard's own phone went; the intercom from the switchboard.

"They're on their way," he said, putting it down.

216

32. The Nights of the Police Judiciaire

They were in no very great hurry, because they felt sure of their ground and because, as Lasserre said vulgarly (cross at being left at home and missing, he said, 'all the fun') one had to wait for the party to warm up enough for people to feel comfortable, and 'get into something loose'.

Castang wasn't sure it would be fun. There was a nasty kind of excitement about it, and something mean. Like picking a dead man's pocket. Vera said, when asked, that the nastiest thing she could think of – leaving aside, please, special circumstances like tortures in cellars or setting dogs on people in concentration camps (Irma Grese was a fresh, pretty young blonde, described by Mr Pierrepoint-the-hangman, a simple man, and highly self-respecting, as 'an extremely bonny lassie') – was perhaps bystanders, hurrying in their cars in morbid excitement to view the scene, looting the mutilated, burned, dishonoured bodies of aircrash victims. Castang had never been present at this sort of scene, though a cop in his thirties has already seen much human behaviour, and he didn't want to be. But yes, he agreed, if he saw that – it would bring out the worst in him too.

Richard, whose imagination was both less exuberant and better disciplined, for one doesn't become a divisional commissaire upon a talent for feeling queasy about what one has to do, didn't think about whether it would be fun or not. Obtaining convictions is the tribunal's affair, and the Procureur's aim: the job of the P.J. is to secure evidence.

They took as few cars as possible. Orthez, driving Richard's big Citroën, with Castang and Maryvonne in the back. Davignon driving the other PJ car, with Lucciani (battle-hardened, and exposed to jokes) and Liliane: the six that had been on the business from the start.

There was silence in the Citroën on the way up. Orthez

217

drove quietly once they were on the hill road, which was bumpy and narrow, and full of blind bends. Cops are as prudent as any bourgeois, over nine-tenths of the time.

The main road runs up the valley, branches off into the hills with little distinction between the wealthy, wine-growing villages with good soil and southerly slopes (only an expert, such as Monsieur Maresq, can tell at a glance whether it will be good, or merely drinkable) and the less fortunate areas of scattered forest and upland grazing. Not one of the more picturesque parts of France, but pretty enough. It was a still, clear night: they were telling one another that the weather was going to turn good at last, that they were due for it, etc. There was some discussion about holidays. The strong winds and heavy rains of recent weeks, the volatile shifts of temperature, with occasional ground frosts, had caught the grapes as they were 'setting' and made the farmers gloomy. A rotten spring, printemps pourri. Did this mean a good summer, or a bad one? Everybody had a different opinon on the subject. But for the most part nobody spoke.

Getting towards the village the leading car slowed, looking for the gendarmerie, in ambush hereabouts. Two or three cars coming down had flicked their lights: the boys in blue are around with their balloons. Richard stopped, and borrowed a chap to show him the lie of the house. Half a dozen bourgeois cars had gone up the hill, but nobody who looked like Thierry.

The house lay in the village, but the streets turned confusingly upon one another. Only just 'off the road': it lay upon the crest of the ridge, with the land falling away steeply behind the house. From the terrace the owner would look down upon his vines, and get a pretty sunset, too. In front were armorial gateposts, but no pompous avenue or grand approach. a simple cobbled courtyard with stable buildings on either side. The 'château' as usual in French villages was pretty but unpretentious and as much farm as manor, built in bits and pieces in a jumble of styles, most pleasing, one or two elegant. Numerous cars were parked: there looked to be twelve to twenty guests. They left theirs outside.

Everything was quiet. No light showed but a hospitable lamp over what looked to be the main entrance.

"Mm," said Richard, and took Castang on a tour round the corner, where there was a bit of lawn and flowerbeds, a sundial and a horrid little octagonal summerhouse where nobody would want to sit. At the back it was better: a paved terrace with wide shallow steps led down to a formal balustrade with urns: beyond were the vines. The garden facade had the high, beautifully proportioned windows of the early eighteenth century, glimmering in the starlight. Those on the lower level, down to the ground and opening onto the terrace, were curtained but not shuttered – heavy velvet curtains. Wisps of light showed here and there: a ghost of music filtered. "Good," said Richard. The other corner, masked by shrubberies of flowering bushes, was reached by a winding gravelled path leading round to outhouses and a kitchen entrance; and so round to the front again where boots were waiting for an instruction, beyond the fringe of light.

"No problem. A certain tact. Orthez, you and Lucciani round the back; there's a terrace with French windows. Polite but firm, nobody is to leave that way. You have no power to prevent people leaving but they will please do so by the normal way. You, my lad," to the gendarme, "the same outside the kitchen. Liliane, you and Davignon here, rather stiff and formal; names and addresses please, identities verified on grounds of possible association with, blah-blah. Anybody who high-hats, face them down. Anybody – being frightened, they're likely to – gets stroppy, don't argue. Refusal to co-operate noted, they will hear from the examining magistrate. Keep in mind: they won't be happy.

"Castang, you and Maryvonne come with me, you'll take the women, my girl. Simply, get dressed and leave quietly: repress any incipient hysteria: the party's over, behave in orderly fashion. No show of threat but any of the studs get bullish, Castang, use your judgment. General Dayan – is he one? – quelling discontent in the ranks." Castang did look sinister in the shadows with his black patch. "Okay? – dolce vita, here we come."

His ring was not answered for some time. The door was opened on a chain by an old woman in slippers, who stood peering suspiciously at the business-suited Richard. He bowed politely, and said nothing.

"Are you invited? Everybody came a long time ago."

"Yes, I am a little late, I'm afraid." But he has a reassuring country-clubby look, Monsieur Richard. Rather English. The others had withdrawn discreetly from the sightline. She gave him a very careful looking-over.

"Well; I s'pose . . . I didn't know there was anybody to come," undoing the chain. "Hey – who're you?" seeing the other two.

"A business call. Fetch your master, will you?"

"Can't do that. Got to go to the office, tomorrow: too late now."

'It won't wait, I'm afraid."

"No no, he's engaged I say, y'll have to leave, go on, please."

"No question of that," sharp and hard. They walked her back: she retreated across the wide shallow hall, arms spread, defending tenaciously.

"Can't come in here: 's private. I tell you I'll yell."

This was getting ridiculous.

"Do not yell," said Richard curtly. "We are police officers. You need not be frightened. Fetch Monsieur Maresq." But the old lady clung paralysed to the door handle.

"I can't, I tell you."

She knew; that much was obvious. And was terrified, which was making her more obstinate still. Richard hesitated: he did not want to use force on an old peasant woman. The whole tactic was to avoid a scuffle. Without even noticing she had pressed the doorhandle down. The door did not give: undoubtedly the key was turned.

Richard raised his hand for the knock of authority, but something had been noticed. There was no high noise level within: the door was solid, three-inch oak, fitting tightly, but one could hear the music. That worked both ways. The old woman's voice was a high squeaky soprano; Richard's, when raised, became sharp. Something of the altercation had filtered. The music seemed to die, or was lowered, and then was turned up again, higher. There was a short pause.

Then the door was opened abruptly, a crack, and an angry face appeared.

"What's going on, out here?"

"Business with you, Monsieur Maresq." Richard's voice was conversational.

He saw at once who they were: that was plain. He did not lose his head. The old woman was tiny and his face loomed over hers: her body blocked the aperture. He did not lose countenance either. He put an arm out, pushed her out of the way and said, "Off with you." He slipped out, closed the door behind him, crossed his arms and stood there frowning. He was not a big man. He was wearing an Oriental sort of djellaba, and bare feet thrust into mules. In this absurd costume he looked bigger than he was, and not ridiculous. Castang felt a certain admiration. He braced himself against the door, thrust his jaw out, and said "Well?" with aggressive concentration.

"Commissaire Richard, Police Judiciaire. These are two of my officers. I have come to take you with me, Monsieur Maresq. There are questions for you to answer."

"How dare you force your way in here! This is a private dwelling house. And, moreover, in the night hours. You will leave immediately. And complaint will be made against you, for abusive procedure. You are breaking and entering – bullying my staff. You'll get an official reprimand, I can promise you that, at the very least."

"We won't talk about reprimands. I hold a mandate from the Judge of Instruction."

"Judge of Instruction! What Judge, of what instruction? I'll tell him a few home truths, too."

"That," calmly, "in charge of the judicial enquiry into the death of Etienne Marcel." Maresq held his ground, tenaciously.

"That must simply be some absurd and only too characteristic aberration. I shall sue for wrongful arrest, and ask the court for civil damages."

"Don't compel me to use force," said Richard, bored with this.

Maresq looked at him as though sizing him up.

"You talk about force," he said more quietly. "You come

here in the middle of the night, while I am entertaining guests, and you talk about force. If that's the way you go on I suppose I can't resist you. You'll answer for it though. And you will permit me to tell my guests that I am victimized by this – gestapo inquisition. You will please wait."

"No. You will please come to your room, and put some clothes on. My officers will do all the explaining that's necessary, to your guests."

With Castang and Richard on either side of him, sidling him, he could not stand ground without losing more face. He opened his mouth to give a bellow but nothing came out. What was he to bellow? 'The fuzz is here'. 'Sauve qui peut.' 'Mayday'. Anything would be too little and too late and too ludicrous. It wasn't Mayday, it was already maynight. Castang took hold of the handle and he and Maryvonne walked in.

He had occupied himself on the way up with sardonic suggestions about pictures shown him at one time or another by Vera. Turkish Bath, by Ingres. Sack of Sardanopolis (he was sure he'd got that wrong) by Delacroix. Rape of Sabine Women, by – conceivably – Rubens? Déjeuner sur l'herbe, with gentlemen in frock coats, with side-whiskers, such as had greatly shocked the Academy. Around 1880 would that have been? And not Rubens surely – David, more like.

None of these classical, romantic, or impressionist visions met his critical, ho, baudelairean eye. Nor, really, was there an orgy. All that palaver outside the door and both nymphs and satyrs had taken fright. Lasserre would be disappointed. Ladies floundering, gentlemen getting tangled in their trousers, all much delayed by frantic hurry: it doesn't look erotic or even porny, but does look ridiculous. Well, the whole proceeding had been ridiculous up to now: might as well go on being so.

Japanese! He had seen art from that country with this cruel attention to humiliating detail. The ungainliness of the women, looking like either sows or camels. Men jumping out of bed with nightcaps still on and putting one foot in the chamber-pot. All the beautiful people changed into lumpish creatures, the sharpest light on knock knees and hammer toes. The beautiful blonde who a minute before had been the

Venus of Urbino, smiling inscrutably into a little looking-glass, gets someone's elbow in her eye, backs doubled in anguish and gets the spout of a boiling kettle wedged in her rectum. The judge, frantically getting his robe on back to front, treads upon the dog's tail and gets his ass grabbed. Coarse English caricatures too of the Regency time – Gill-ray was the name. Eminent Cabinet Ministers playing Titty-titty-Bumbum. The black humour, finally, of today's draw-ings – a young American Miss, hands clasped in ecstasy, beams at her birthday cake. Instead of candles, arranged in a neat ring are twelve sanitary tampons. The Hollywood athlete, whose penis has turned inexplicably into a tennis racket and has no balls left. The girl eyes it suspiciously and says 'Double Fault'.

Castang, stolid in his boots, wading through all this débris, now sadly detumescent.

The air was foul. The heating had been on, of course, and the windows shut. Cigar smoke, and pot, and perfume. A buffet supper had been lined up on the tables against the wall, giving a sickening smell of food and drink. Since some-one had tried opening the French windows the candles had guttered and some had blown out, adding another horrible stink. Entwined in it all was the shrill reek of changing-rooms; sweat and excitement, anticipation and fear. On court had been a lot of losers, and no winners.

There was plenty of food left, looking expensive, appetis-ing, aphrodisiac. Not even Lucciani, who never stopped eat-ing, would stretch his hand out to that. Kojak might . . .

The big drawing-room had been stripped for action: the kind of metaphor Kojak would use. Empire decorations and furniture. In old mother Delestang's day that awful colour called 'gris Trianon', he had been told. Brought back by Maresq to white and gold, and flashes of bright colour – the silk cushion, there, was peacock blue. A very nice room, for card parties, music parties, tea parties. Lucie will play us some Chopin. No, no, let's have Offenbach. To make more space, the piano had been wheeled through the folding doors into the library next door.

One man Maryvonne told after – had been getting his shoe on, and found himself standing on someone's earring that had been knocked off a table in the hustle.

The Police Judiciaire, a lugubrious party, gathered in the drawing room. Orthez, whose digestion was of the strongest, poured himself a glass of wine. It was time to go when Lucciani started looking at the food.

"I say – crawfish tails!"

"Come on," said Richard briefly. Even his features were looking sunken. Anything to get away from this scene of post-coital gloom.

The old peasant woman would have a lot of cleaning up, next day; was all anybody said in the car. But that would have been the case in any event. The Police Judiciaire had wiped its boots politely before entering, had broken no furniture, upset no glasses, had not wiped its fingers on the curtains, or even dropped ash upon the floor.

33. No Discharge in the War

Vera was awake, and reading. The tiny one was asleep, but would shortly wake, and demand food. No, she was not tired, or sleepy. She slept, still, during the day; huge self-indulgent siestas.

Nonsense, he said. You need the sleep; you haven't yet got your full strength back. Yes I have, she said; I want to start living and going out, and working too.

Well, we'll be having some fine weather now. And days off, again. This nonsense is as good as cleared up. Our end anyhow; the legal end isn't; won't ever be, quite likely.

I'm glad to hear that; you're looking awfully tired.

Yes; well, more depressed than tired. And wound up too tight to sleep. Hideous evening: no, I'm not going to tell you about it. It wasn't at all interesting. Just squalid. Hungry?

No, not for me. I'd get fat as an old cow again, and I don't want that.

Castang made cocoa, buttered bread, found peanut butter

(an acquired taste, neither French nor Czech, but now a great standby).

He enjoyed this simple meal greatly. Funny, after being nauseated by the crawfish tails. There'd been fresh asparagus too, which they could no longer afford more than once in the season – treat for Vera's birthday: she was of course a Bull. All that delicious stuff, and it turned your gut over.

"Are we completely crackers? I mean, everything we do is dotty. And so medieval." Castang, mouth full.

"I know, yes. I'm reading where someone says, I'm reading philosophy at the university, and an old man says approvingly Good, that's a noble subject, and a bystander thinks laughing what a very out-of-date attitude; nobody now thinks 'noble' a word to use at all – let alone about philosophy. Well, it Is a noble subject, even if no one thinks so but us."

"Or marriage. Does anybody but us still believe in fidelity? In total, unquestioning, utter trust, the one in the other. You pretend sometimes you think I've my hand up all sorts of unlikely skirts, because I'm a cop. But you don't really think that."

"No. And no, we're not behind the times. We're in front of them. Always have been; always will be. Means, of course, we'll never have any money. Or be thought of but as dull, worthy, square people, and sniggered at. Never be a Success."

"Right. Richard was here when you were in the clinic. A bit pissed – never seen him like that. Said what are you doing in this stinking job – why don't you fuck off out of it? Can't, of course. Wife, baby. Crippled wife, tiny baby. Awful drag. And without them, I'd just be another cynical cop, and crooked on that account."

'You are not crooked. And neither is Richard.'

"Oh, yes he is, and me. We are bent because the government bends us. It is crooked: they all are. A marxist intellectual has described it in unreadable jargon. Everything they say and do is meaningless, deliberately: no cause and effect, no responsibilities can be ascribed or attributed. Nothing to catch hold of. You can't revolt against it or even criticize it. A huge jellyfish, of which I am part. All that crap about

225

1984 – we're all brainwashed now. Have been for a generation. The young see through it, but even as they do, in their
plastic years they are caught, anaesthetized and deadened by
it."

"You've changed your mind then? What about the promotion? Being a commissaire somewhere totally insignifi-
cant, but we could have a house, and a garden. I'm ready,
you know, to take it if you will."

"No. I'll hold on, as long as Richard does. Anyhow. No,
it's not just schools for Lydia, or provincial boredom for
you, or whatever. This city – it's where I belong. My boots –
I'll stay in them.'

Boots . . . moving up and down again. No discharge in the
war.

No. Staying in the same place. Going backwards, often
as not. Handing people over to justice – God, the Assize
Court itself hasn't a clue how to judge things now. Looks
for a hint to the government. Doesn't get any. In the name
of executive power not interfering with the judiciary, what a
joke.

"The city's finished too, you know," said Vera abruptly.
"It's all irreversible now. No amount of little trees or pedestrian precincts can save it."

"You certainly won't be popular, girl, talking like that.
Heretics don't get burned any more, or put in camps. They're
just disregarded."

"Oh yes, I know. Silly woman. Hysteria, something wrong
with her womb. Doesn't believe in Growth or the Gross
National Product. Cassandra was as well a very tiresome girl
and a great bore, and came to a bad end. But even a city this
size; I'm not talking about Los Angeles. Can't you feel the
asphyxiation? Double the number of green spaces. Double
the number of cops. Where, how, and who pays? It's too
fragile, too rigid, and too complex. And too flabby to resist
the smallest infection."

"You mean – if Electricité de France sneezes, the whole
town catches cold."

"I think it would be simpler still. If you were an anarchist
and you had a bomb, where would you put it? In a power
station?"

"No. In the sewers."

"The days are gone when James Bond and Batman could save us from the diabolic plot. The destruction is in us. We aren't just biting our own tails now – we are devouring ourselves."

"So if it's crumbling, and the crumble accelerates daily, what will be left?"

"You, and me, and the tiny one in a bundle."

"Not six just men in the whole city of Sodom – in an ark? Where will the ark float to?"

"You're laughing at me. I'll tell you when the time comes."

"No, I'm not. Not America of course, and not a comet. The comet would be full of technicians . . . Perhaps just high ground. After all."

"Perhaps."

"Leave it to the women," muttered Castang.

"No. A woman is nothing without a man. Go to sleep. You have to work, tomorrow."

"Oh yes. And how."

He had a confused memory of waking for a moment before falling asleep again. A lamp over which Vera had thrown a dressing-gown, so as not to jar his eyes. The baby making grunting noises, doing hard physical labour. Vera singing, very softly.

That child would grow up understanding Schubert, anyhow.

34. A Bright Clear Day in Early Summer

The local paper did not have much to say, but what it said was to the point, for once.

'Inspectors of the PJ yesterday effected the arrest of two individuals as a result of the continuing inquiries into the assassination of Etienne Marcel, concerning which the authorities have been stubbornly silent. Commissaire Richard was not last night available for comment. It was given to

227

understand, however, that further arrests were likely to follow and despite the guarded language used it seems clear that the PJ is at last confident that this tangled affair, the motives of which contain still baffling elements, will at last shortly be concluded.

'The two men concerned were named as . . .'

Richard sat in his office with a face of disgusted disbelief, like the Pope being told that all the cardinals were in KGB pay. To one side sat Maryvonne, studious, head bowed over a dictation pad, stenographing. On the 'sellette' or stool to repentance where the 'alleged' get sat was a person Castang had difficulty in recognizing. An elderly version, for they are intent and reliant upon looking youthful and at forty it's tough sledding, of what Vera called Overfed-youngmen in Check Waistcoats.

It is a common type. Their suits, and their shirts, are always half a size too small. Their collars too tight and the points too long: there is too much flowing tie, and far too many cufflinks. They are bacon-heavy with good living: there is always a touch of jowl, thirty once passed, on the shiny skin of the overshaved jaw. They are assiduous buyers of toiletries and perfumeries. Their hair is shaggy, and youthfully disordered. On the beach, above the little bikinislip, there is more than a suggestion of sow around that hairy navel. They are all weighed down with credit cards and girls' telephone-numbers. Their cars are rather too expensive for their jobs. They can be divided, as the man in *Oliver Twist* said, between mealy-boy and beef-faced-boy. They are wise in the ways of this world, and they know of no other.

Maresq was not ordinarily in the least like this. Years of sophisticated and genuine expertise, of self-assurance and certainly, till very recently, of self-command, for old mother Delestang had had a gimlet eye, had put restraint upon him. No grossness or vulgarity had been apparent. Shrewd, concentrated, brainy – if narrow – he had been ruthless in pursuit of his objectives, had reached them, been thrown off his poise, possibly, by the discovery he wanted more. Jurists, and psychiatrists, and even journalists would rest an elbow on the table and stay with pencil poised while he talked and talked and talked.

But the shock of last night had cracked the plaster, and a night in a detention cell had flaked it: it had looked good, but been thin, a bit cheap. And now Richard scratching, peeling, levering. The flakes were getting bigger. The alloy underneath was pinchbeck stuff. Wrong metaphor (Castang was doing nothing, sitting; listening to the interrogation). A building. No good stone. Brick, and poor quality: once exposed to this sulphuric-acid-laden PJ air it crumbles, at the corners first; faster . . . And under the plaster, a smell, smell of damp and decay. The name of this smell is prevarication.

"Castang, there's no need for you to sit listening to these elucubrations. Your face betrays you: yes, they're cheap. You go and see Madame Jouve, and then all this voluble stuff, which is giving Maryvonne here the cramps, will be seen in its true proportions. See to this chap, Maryvonne, will you? I'm beginning to feel enervated by him." Summer is i'cumin in, said Richard's face, and yes, there were two rosebuds in a glass on his table. We've Found Rosebud.

Magali, in a thin pants-suit of a lavender shade that would have suited her ordinarily but today looked awful, looked awful too: her complexion was like candlegrease.

"I was expecting you. Come in."

"The house is empty?"

"The children are at school. Bertrand's gone to work. Waiting for the axe to fall."

"And yourself?"

"Come to gloat?"

"Come to verify."

"You saw me naked last night. Want me to drop my pants for you?" An odd echo of Clothilde. Whom everyone had forgotten.

"You needn't, you know, put on any further acts."

"My mother tried to kill herself."

"It's understandable. Thierry is her favourite: she admits as much."

"And I'm my favourite, huh?" She caught sight of herself in a glass. "Jesus. Mourning becomes Electra."

"Attitudinizing."

"That little redhead bitch of yours – looking at me, knowingly."

"She's young, inexperienced, and was much embarrassed. Seeing a lot of naked people was no thrill to us. There was no record made, no pictures taken. But we found – and confiscated – a camera."

"Ah."

"He had it hidden. Since reading spy stories they all know how. He wanted to make quite sure, you see."

He felt sorry for her: she was so limp. But he had come to wring her dry.

"When did you first know?"

"Telephone calls."

"You could recognize the voice – now?"

"The voice – a sort of whisper. One couldn't – can't – be sure."

He'd been careful, the pig.

"Saying – that Thierry was involved? In the killing of your father? Or could be made to look it?" It is that word parricide. Like incest. A crime within a family triples the horror.

"That Thierry had killed Didier . . ."

"Ah." So that was it . . .

"That it could be proved."

"Did you ask him what his proofs were?"

"Didier always had a shower after work. It was a habit of his. Everyone knew about it. Something Thierry used that would give him away."

"Did you warn Thierry – or try to?"

"Bertrand said," she whispered, "that that would make me guilty too. I didn't dare."

"When did Bertrand know?"

"I thought, only after I told him. Last night – he'd known all along. He's been afraid to tell me." Oh yes, clever. Sly. And nasty-minded.

"And then you were invited to the party?"

"What else could I do?" in a whisper.

"You knew before about those parties, didn't you?"

"Salome had been – with Didier." She was fidgeting with a cigarette between her hands. "How – how much of this is

230

going to come out?" It broke limply into two halves, the sound only just audible. Castang was content to take it as symbolic.

It was essential to find Thierry, now. And as essential to find the proof of which Magali spoke. If it still existed. And if Thierry is still alive.

Simon Tappertit . . . And the power of a strong character over a weak one. Vera, and Richard, had both been right.

The easy life. Indulged by both the women, defended and even protected against the angry, helpless bitterness and disappointment of the father.

Textbook cases. With hindsight so easy to perceive. Castang had half seen : laziness and stupidity had prevented him seeing the rest.

He started making excuses for himself. He'd been thinking, worrying about Vera; he was in no way to blame. Richard had only half seen too; Richard whose experience was so much vaster.

Look, Richard never saw Thierry : you did. And you're behaving like Thierry.

They can always find excuses : they cannot perceive their own feebleness without self-pity. The feebleness is fundamental, the vulnerability cumulative, self destructive. They seek the protection of persons with strong character, whom they resent, and attack. They invent systems and dramas to cover up. They are great ones for 'sensitivity', reproaching others for their 'lack'. Likewise generosity.

They feel pain, humiliation; are given to bullying, and to violence. They are 'Likeable' but not trustworthy. Incapable of action, they are despised : they take refuge in interminable argument and protest, chicane, perpetual wails and appeals for understanding.

They are always beaten in battle, and negotiation, because they always do the wrong thing at the wrong time. They never have any money : they are plucked, of course. They grow fatalistic about it, while never ceasing to resent it. A leitmotiv : 'I am always generous and trust people, and they take advantage.'

They are to be pitied : they always arrange to come out losers. Everything rankles with them : they mutter, they nurse grudges – and forget them again – till – when?

They have often much charm, which they use to catch people whom they then despise for being caught. They themselves are easily caught by people of charm . . . The naïveté, of expecting charm to substitute for reliability.

Rogues they always will be. Slip easily into petty crime. Will they commit major crimes? If a suitable – and easy – occasion presents itself, quite likely. Selfishness and vanity are the springs of all criminal behaviour.

Crashing platitude: right mate; that's why there's a lot of crime about. Their cowardice will put a brake on them, and their conceit of themselves.

King Charles the First's royalty, his noble air, his great physical courage – took everyone in for a long time.

A poor excuse, Monsieur Castang, a poor excuse.

Thérèse was as tart as usual, though more taciturn. She said she supposed she couldn't stop him going upstairs and snuffling about. He asked politely after Noelle. Mending, she admitted. She went every afternoon.

She knows, of course: they both know.

In Thierry's room there was nothing interesting. Well, he had never supposed there would be. A pleasant, comfortable room up there 'sous les toits' for sitting and dreaming. Books about astrology and occultism – that of course was what he went to the library for, how he had come to meet the Bouvet. He'd had a pathetic faith in becoming an expert on lamas in Tibet, monks on Mount Athos, Chinese sages. Myths of course, and nordic runes. The I Ching: to be sure. A dreamy romanticism: in far-off places there will be wonderful things. One must undergo purification, first. Maresq, with his tales of the West Coast and Big Sur and Carmel, of tea ceremonies in Japanese gardens, of sailing in the Caribbean, of the Search for Power – oh yes, an attractive guru. Have a look my boy, roping in girls is dead easy. They come crowding. Sex is a Way towards Domination. Sailing in the Caribbean . . .!

He pottered round there on the top floor, not very happy. If there was anything hidden, Thierry would hide it – in Thérèse's room, in the old people's quarters? Hardly; questions might be asked. What was this door here, next to the bathroom?

An attic. The usual junk, but neat and tidy. Broken furniture and oddments: clothes in plastic sacks, linen put away in lavender and camphor: piles of suitcases, hats, a wardrobe with remnants of furnishing materials, wallpaper.

Likely, more than likely; but he felt small enthusiasm for searching all this, especially not knowing what he was looking for. It would take a whole PJ squad to do a thorough job.

But what could it be? Didier was about to take a shower, without bothering locking the door. Unsuspecting. His own brother pottering about, saying perhaps 'I'll just have a bit of a shave' – it might irritate but wouldn't bother him. 'Please yourself; have a drink; I'll be ready in ten minutes.' What had happened to Didier? He'd been tapped on the nut, shoved under the running water, the electric fan pushed over. One, two, three. All that is wanted is something that will serve for the tap on the nut.

Maryvonne, and the IJ squad, had made a very thorough job of Didier's flat, looking for 'blunt instruments'. Almost anything will do, but Professor Deutz, pointing to photographs, slides and stuff, extravasated subcutaneous technical arguments, said 'something wooden or metallic no doubt, but covered with a substance like leather, something softer and more elastic . . .' A piece of fabric, a pullover? It had been a puzzle, and provisionally abandoned.

The light, from a dusty overhead bulb, was not good. Some bags here in the corner. Tent; sleeping-bag; air-mattress: well yes, Thierry – there was no other likely candidate – had or had had the camping craze. A box with the usual gas-cylinder gadgets, spare valves and cartridges. He rummaged half-heartedly. Another bag aroused curiosity: the sort of tightfitting one-piece suit, neoprene or whatever, carefully packed with talcum-powder. Not diving, or was it? – canoeing, kayaking. Well yes, Thierry shooting the rapids, river-of-no-return act, that was quite in character. Of no interest. A smaller sack, heavier; he jingled it in his hand, guessing – sure, tent-pegs and metal pickets, spare cordage for anchoring – what was this bigger, heavier thing; a torch or lamp? – no. Castang's hand dived in after fumbling some time with the drawstring.

He held in his hand a little mallet with a hard rubber head, sold to drive tent-pegs in hard ground. He stayed there squatting on his heels, holding it on his palm. The contour was very slightly convex. Not so much rounded, or even bevelled, as smoothed.

Castang had an idiotic vision of an IJ technician solemnly and earnestly tapping another IJ man on the nut, numerous times from every possible angle, and then taking the head to Professor Deutz to be photographed. The head in a neat bag, with a drawstring.

Some cops had always little envelopes and plastic sachets in their pockets, for putting Evidence in. Castang didn't. The rubber was smooth. The head had perhaps been wet. It was possible, it might be that a hair or a fragment of skin (dandruff or something?) had adhered. Regretfully he left his treasure behind. Send a technician . . . But he had a small sense of certainty, a tiny glow of triumph. It was the sort of over-ingenious device criminals did think of.

Didier had been all for the game of acquiring little lever-ages over people. To him, a natural extension of house-agency business. Didier, likewise, had a private life based on hedonism. Business is business, however petty, mean, or boring: one must do what one could to make after-hours lots of fun. Little dives and cosy restaurants, small delicious meals, slightly exotic drinks (saké, tequila with salt, bacardi with fresh limes). Lots and lots of girls. Married women are not just safer and more fun; they cause fewer problems. Girls are for boys.

Didier and Maresq had a small business connection, and Chantal was useful to both. Which first got into the wife-swapping ring, and introduced the other to this game (every little bit of leverage is a material advantage) was of small consequence.

But Maresq had more grandiose notions. A type like Didier was plastic but uninteresting; an imbecile like Bouvet, stuffing himself in his library with power fantasies and taking it out on old souped-up cars, of no interest at all. A type like Lallemand, eternal malcontent, bristling with grudges like a hedgehog and intoxicating himself with the rare air of Free Fall – interesting, but explosive, and likely to backfire (he did!). But put them together . . . This was not a gang to be used for banal hold-ups or robberies: that would be boring and they would do it badly. But an assassination, that would really be a high.

Why Etienne Marcel? A set of motives so muddled – he wished Colette Delavigne luck with that part of the instruction. To the one an oppressive and resented family tyrant. To another a symbol of capitalist hegemony. To a third, perhaps, a detested form of bureaucratic authority. To the guru? – who knows. Perhaps, buried in the past somewhere, an old resentment over a project blocked, a bit of easy money diverted into another channel. A rival, even? Did by any chance Clothilde know Maresq, even indirectly?

In fact the more he thought the more he thought about Clothilde.

He used the telephone, and waited till the IJ came for the rubber hammer.

He felt he'd been tapped a bit himself with a rubber hammer.

Richard had turned the different interrogations over to Lasserre. He had sent Liliane and Lucciani up to Maresq's house, to see if anything interesting came to light in his papers or possessions. Maryvonne had been sent to have a soothing (on the whole) tactful talk with Bertrand. He himself, very soothing, had gained access to Noelle, or would that afternoon. Davignon and Orthez had been put on a 'pending' that a judge of instruction was complaining about: no work been done for too long. The Mayor had to be seen. Something had to be told the press. Briefly, Richard was busy, and what was it now?

About Magali he was calm. He'd have a nice talk himself with Miss Magali. She held an important key, and would turn it. One had to put her, that what's-her-name – Salome – and the woman Chantal together in Colette Delavigne's cabinet, with perhaps an assurance about discretion, and it would all come tumbling out. Bertrand, if promised some sort of immunity, would unscrew his mouth about Maresq's proposals: come in with us, bring your charming wife: we'll

235

have a few more, and I can promise you – you'd be surprised. Any time you want to change your job, I can guarantee you . . . Since there was another civic councillor in the Partouze circle the Mayor would Not be anxious for publicity. It'll be tricky, though.

Thierry – that, Castang, was just fucking crass of you (Richard was tired or he would not be saying fuck). If you'd been a bit less casual a lot of trouble might have been saved.

It didn't do to make excuses. He produced evidence in a hurry of industry, zeal, intelligent deduction; an IJ man with a rubber hammer. This got the champing jaws quietened down a bit: not that Richard would ever be impressed (short of hitting him on the head with it) but judges love things like this. Material Exhibits, on dramatic tables in courtrooms, that they can have borne solemnly across to look at, and play with. Hand it to the Jury, please – held at arm's length by the usher, like a long-dead mackerel. Professor Deutz agreed that it fitted, said Castang virtuously.

He went home for lunch, and was taken aback to find Vera had been out, for the first time, with the object in a pram; secondhand pram, but given a new coat of stove enamel. He scolded: wasn't this too premature? No no, only up and down the street, and just as far as the Dirty-shop to buy greens, and those alsatian noodles called spätzle, and look, one of his favourite meals. Little medallions cut from a filet mignon of pork, flavoured and cooked in the pan; piccata alla marsala – should be veal really, but it's far too dear. And going out had done her good: just look at the weather, warm and mild like Mummy-milk.

Vera was not all that good a cook: secretly, Castang believed he himself was better. Just lack of practice, he said, when he turned out something horrible. But it was very nice, as well as piggy-chauvinist, to stretch one's legs out under one's own table, and stuff away lordly at dinner cooked by one's wife.

"Tell me," once it was stowed away where it belonged, "your Tappertit figure; would he go kill himself, if the game was up?"

"I don't think so, no. Surely not – far too conceited. He'd try to find a hole where he could hide. Rest up out of sight,

236

don't you know, convinced that things would blow over in a little while. Once he recovered his protective good opinion of himself and his doings. He'd find someone, be sure, to cosset him and be kind to him – they always do.' He nodded; he saw it that way too. Thierry would have slipped off to Paris, to some friendly pad, and would reappear jaunty in a few days, with a polished tale about his knowing nothing about any of this. Or well, yes, he'd known. But he'd kept quiet, you see, Inspector, out of loyalty to his friends.

Half-truths, arranged and repeated in his own mind until they became true: once they sounded convincing enough to him they had to be true.

He had bicycled. He picked up the car at the office. Remember to get the technical squad to take out that damn transmitter, or he'd have Cantoni's people asking to borrow it. Pinching it, likely as not.

There was a bolthole that had to be stopped. An unlikely one, but – could one ever be sure? And he was day-dreaming perhaps, but it would be nice to acquire a bit of prestige. He had not distinguished himself throughout this affair. Even finding Noelle the gendarmerie had done for him.

The village square was nice: the usual expanse of beaten earth, with a double row of plane trees, where the market stalls got set up; given over on other days to boule players: among the old, at least, this was still boule-lyonnaise country, rather than boring pétanque. It was extremely conventional, he thought parking the car, and noticing Clothilde's battered poison-green Alfa down the road; he hadn't wasted his trip. You'd find the same in most villages. But at least they haven't tarted anything up. Since all these village houses were bought up by townspeople . . . well, you could say little about the houses. Country people had money too, and as bad taste or worse. You saw stone walls two centuries old, covered in plastic tiles imitating travertine.

But townspeople would go filling their gardens with horrible things bought from suburban garden-centres: stuff with golden or silver foliage, ough, trained to weep instead of growing upright: proud examples of the hybridist's art. Nice and small. Sterile things. Trees? – pederast treelets.

He looked with approval at the scarred knobbly planes, only now getting into their full long-distance stride.

Warm! He would have liked to take his jacket off, but you couldn't leave a gun-belt, with a nine-millimetre Smith and Wesson, in a parked car! Not even in the village square you can't.

Toc – toc. A long wait. Clothilde's day for washing her hair? Scurrying sounds from within, indicative of hasty tidying.

She was in trousers, which suited her. In riding breeches she would look better still. The big horsewoman's hand went to her hair and pushed at it, while she looked at him ruffled yet resigned, as though it wasn't worth the trouble to get cross.

"The bad penny once more."

"Or, Alice is At It Again."

"Still determined that I can't be left in peace to rebuild myself?"

"I'll promise that this will be the last."

"Mm." Put your faith in a cop's word . . .

"Well, aren't you going to ask me in?"

"Can I refuse? It's like pulling at a half-healed scar. If the choice is between that and attracting the attention of all the neighbours – the lesser of two evils. Come on in then . . this room needs airing," opening the front windows, "I try not to, during the day, because of all the dust from outside." The room had a smell of stale cigarette smoke, but why make a fuss? Empty the ashtrays, by all means: she'd been smoking a lot. Or had a visitor over lunch.

"By yourself?"

"Of course I'm by myself. The housekeeping has to be done, you know. Can't always be sitting the elegant hostess with fresh flowers and the table just waxed."

"I thought it might be one of your days at the shop."

"Not always. A woman likes to potter in her own interior. A quiet day to do her nails. Anything wrong with that? Shall we come to the purpose of the visit?"

"Read the paper?"

"I never read papers; they're full of lies." One could agree with that! "I glance at it from time to time – skipping."

238

'You'd have seen a report, brief, that we've made some arrests in the matter of Etienne Marcel. Superficial, of course. There'll be a press release this evening in all likelihood."

"And this would interest me? I'm afraid you're mistaken. Etienne alive . . . But Etienne dead – I can't feel vengeful, or even really curious. Some people who got twisted, distorted out of their true balance."

"How can you know that?"

"How could it be anything else? You yourself said as much."

"It was always the probability. Degrees of responsibility are not my job, I probably added. Everybody can claim attenuating circumstances, and everyone does. Once we pinch them. My job is answerability. The rest is for judges. We've two, three people who have to answer for what they did, plotted, combined, or even just imagined."

"Well congratulations."

"One is missing."

"Oh? Bad luck."

"Etienne's own younger son. Thierry."

"I thought for a moment it was going to be me."

"Pretty bad, isn't it? Parricide, you know."

"I'm afraid I don't know. It's outside my experience."

"We don't in fact suppose it is, technically, parricide. Likely, to a person like that, the idea in abstract might seem rather fine. A blow for freedom. Even a dotty notion of gallantry. When it came to the point, probably he shuffled and backed out."

"Mm."

"We think, in fact, that the real moving spirit was elsewhere. We've got him too. A person whose unpleasant speciality was to see how far he could influence weak-minded, silly, fanatical or otherwise-stunted personalities. Vicious. He'll try to pin the blame on the others. We've two of those – the actual authors, it's as good as certain, of the assassination. Friends of Thierry's."

"Oh?"

"Thierry himself got wind, probably, of what was going on. Smelt something, had it confirmed by a phone call. Best

239

thing he could think of was to bunk. Paris or somewhere. Question of a few days, before we pick him up. Foolish of him."

"Really?"

"The instructing judge will charge him, of course, with the conspiracy. And this instruction will tag along, six months or so. The Prosecutor would then likely plead incitement or inducement – but with some good lawyers – there'd be a stubborn defence. Cases like that, naturally they try to shift the blame to other shoulders. You don't seem much interested."

"I told you, I'm not."

"The judge hasn't summoned you yet, as a witness? She will."

"I'll tell her what I've told you. I'm in no way concerned."

"You'll have a hard time convincing her of that."

"Why?"

"Because it sounds so phony."

"Neither you nor your equally odious boss, Monsieur Richard, were able to scratch up anything showing that I'm in any way involved, Mr What's-your-name."

"Things are different now."

"In what way, may I ask?"

"I tell you a story that concerns you, Madame Chose, in the most intimate areas of your life and feelings. You pretend indifference. In reality, I think, you'd heard it all before."

"What justification can you possibly have for saying a thing like that? You play throughout with my emotions in the most ignoble way."

"Your remarks have a fabricated, pre-rehearsed sound. Your lack of interest, in case I popped in, seemed to you then the most plausible front you could put forward."

"Then? When the hell is then? I hear all this stuff – invented for all I know this minute to put a squeeze on me – thirty seconds ago."

"You'll forgive my saying I think you're a liar."

"How dare you!"

"My experience of liars is comprehensive. Is he here?"

"Who?"

240

"He didn't know, of course, we could guess he knew you, or even knew of you. He snuffled out, of course, everything he could concerning his father's life. Made it his business."

"God – you are a filthy thing."

"Yes, it's a dirty trade, thinking evil of people. People have to clean the sewers too. Wear protective clothes, high boots, take a shower when they get home. Gravediggers have to examine people too from time to time. Do it before light. There's a smell, sometimes. All these people have to pick their boots up, go on putting one foot in front of another. However little they like it. Pathologists have to look at pus, and piss, and shit. Lab attendants take slides from a vagina, a rectum. They like that?

"I'm a PJ officer, I've search powers. I don't specially want to go in your bedroom. I daresay he appealed to your warmheartedness which is real. Maternal instincts, and a lot more. I don't have to know. The judge will want to. I want him to come out, or you to fetch him out. If he goes over the garden wall at the back it's useless: he's bottled, and I've two cars full of cops here in ten minutes."

She looked at him a long moment, making her mind up, and got slowly to her feet.

"I don't believe in a word you've told me. In any of it."

"You don't have to. As the man says, just stand and deliver." Castang hitched his open jacket back, put a deliberate hand behind his hip, and reached his gun out, put it on the table. She stared down at it.

"You don't need anything like that," with open contempt.

"Of course not. Tell him – if he has one, unlikely but possible – to give it to you." She turned and walked out of the room: he heard her go slowly up the old, creaky stairs. Oak. A nice feature to have in a cottage. But not if you have fugitives to shelter.

She called in a dead voice from the top of the stairs.

"You'd better come up."

Thierry was sitting on her bed, hands between his knees, round-shouldered and head sunken, staring out of the window at the little garden; there was a patch of grass with a table painted white and two wooden chairs.

A sunny wall. An espaliered peartree. A narrow parterre

241

either side. Dahlia bulbs, shooting up greenery.

Castang had always wanted a cottage garden. Things to make a bright warm mass of colour and happiness, all muddled together. Morning-glories and larkspurs and snapdragons and sweet-williams and love-in-a-mist. And nasturtiums all round. And if you had a wall, damn it, Huge Big sunflowers. AND HOLLYHOCKS.

35. Jacques Brel has Died

Colette Delavigne, the Judge of Instruction, after pulling so many faces – judges hate all those experts, and Maresq had already imported a talkative Paris lawyer, a red-hot, the PJ would have called him a shit-hot, on procedural points – was content . . .

She pulled that corniest of all instruction-gags, a Reconstruction. If they come off, lovely. The examining magistrate, ordering everyone around like a movie-director, saying more or less 'Places everyone. Quiet. Sound. Camera!' has a lovely time. And think of all the favourable publicity.

If they don't come off, in ploughed fields in a drizzle of a February day, oh well, there was only one wretched photographer from the local rag.

She chose the same time of day, to get the light right, had the whole Cours la Reine cleared of traffic. Cops with crowd barriers. Castang doing Etienne Marcel, collapsing riddled with lead. Orthez driving the getaway car, Lasserre with that clumsy great forty-five Army automatic. Richard, who loathed Alfred Hitchcock, stood there with the Mayor, but said they were strangers on a train, definitely. The eyewitnesses, much drilled, did several different takes. The lawyers were very obstreperous. The Paris lawyer kept saying No doubt, Madame, No doubt; I fail to see why it should interest me.

The employees of the Banque de France had crowded to their windows and so had everyone else. You'd think you were outside the Santé, at five in the morning, in the good old Public Execution days, with le père Deiber doing his stuff.

Riotous success all round.

For the PJ, finished, save for that excruciating chore of having to give evidence in front of the Assize Court, a job no cop enjoys.

A month, two, or three had passed. It had faded and grown dim. More – six, and the trial was slated for the next sessions. Castang came home, of a dreary November evening. Vera was sitting on the floor snuffling drearily, tear-sodden, blowing her nose on a ghastly dishcloth.

"What has happened?" Lydia, good as gold, was on her tummy on the floor some distance away, banging with both fists and quite plainly happy. "Please tell me."

"You haven't heard?"

"I've been in the country." Vera pointed wordlessly at the television set. Superimposed on a long, sad, horse face a reporter, overdressed as usual and with his national-mourning expression above his huge knitted tie, was saying, "Nothing, I believe, has so cut into us here," pointing at his well-filled waistcoat, "since Edith Piaf left us."

"Oh, God – no."

"Oh, God yes."

Vera cried buckets at the end of Verdi operas, and when she came out in a distraught daze, walked under trams. Castang the Boot, professionally insensitive, was not a weepie.

Now was different.

There are not enough poets. How many are good poets, and not just pop lyricists? How many go round the world? A Beatle once said 'We are more important than Jesus': he was mistaken, though forgivably.

Jacques had never thought of himself either in terms of importance or any resemblance to Jesus, but he was real, always.

No more would that voice say, with that dignity
          'It is late, Mister,
          And I must be going home.'

Jef, stop crying like that in front of everybody. Shift your
carcass, Jef. Mussels, Jef, and frites. And Moselle wine.
And at Andrée's, there are now girls. Come on Jef, it's
no longer the pavement – it's getting like a cinema, here,
with you crying.
It was only a false blonde, and three-quarters-whore at that.

> 'Fernand . . .
> Say he's dead.
> Say I'm alone behind.
> Say you're alone up front.
> Fernand I'll come to this whore of a cemetery
> And we'll drink silence
> To the health of that Constance
> Whose shadow meant as much to her as you did.'

And so much, so much.

The outrageous, glorious Jacky, selling boats full of
opium, whisky made in Clermont-Ferrand, real old queens
and false young virgins, and a bank on each finger, mate,
and a finger in every country.

You were the poet, boy. A poet is for the people. Or to
be polite, take Mr Eliot, stick him up his waste land. Real
poets sing. They go round the world on an enormous kite.
Shakespeare, tu connais? At the same time as they finish as
broken-down tango-singers. For old biddies. In the rain,
in Knocke-le-Zoute.

There are phony ones. The phony ones made more money.
But they're twisting slowly in the wind. While with what was
left of your lungs you – you were bawling out a bawdy
ditty.

> Hands, stop trembling.
> Remember them wet – you cried on them.
> Hands, do not open.
> Arms, do not stretch out.
> You my hands and arms keep still.
> You my girl Mathilde have come back.
> Spit right back into the sky.
> Mathilde has come back.

"I'm all right," said Vera, burying herself in the dishcloth.
"I'm all right, I'm all right, I'm all right I tell you," as he

got down on the floor and held her. "Mathilde has come back."

There we leave them : he undoing one boot, she struggling with the tight, wet lace of the other.